# SOMETHING *Old?*
# SOMETHING *New?*

By

## Marlee Rae

*Marlee Rae*

I dedicate this novel to You, the most important person in my life. I struggle daily to keep the good memories of you in my foreground and the pain of missing you in the background. Your memory inspired me to try something new by writing. I thank you for being my biggest motivator, cheerleader, and nurturer. But, I am most thankful for having you as my Mom. P.S. Don't close your eyes when you get to the good parts of the book, I'm grown:)

# Chapter 1 ~ Dawn

I was tired, my legs were burning, but I had to keep moving. I was two blocks away from home, and the sun was starting to show itself over the trees and houses in my subdivision. Although I was tired, I felt good because I'd been able to clear my mind and think of nothing for the most part. But, she was still present no matter how far and long I walked. It wasn't that I wanted to forget her, but I would like my heart to heal a little if possible. It had been seven months since I lost the most important person in my life, my Nurturer, my Rock, my Stability, half of my earthly makeup... My Momma. Oh no! Not again with the tears. I did well for the last forty-five minutes of what had become my morning ritual to clear my thoughts, but I didn't make it again today. I tried to cry and self-soothe when I was alone because I hated being such a burden on others. I never wanted anyone to feel sorry for me. I knew my family and friends didn't feel that way, but I did. So, I'd continue to do what I could to make myself feel better.

"Breathe in, breathe out." I looked down at my long legs taking shorter and shorter strides up the hill. I was wearing one of my walking uniforms as I called it, black bootcut yoga pants and a red V-neck tee with matching red sneakers. In my mind, the boot cut pants took the eye away from my large hips and thighs, while the V-neck tee made my breasts look less like a ski slope. I thought my size sixteen shape was okay, but I could stand to shed about thirty pounds if I was honest with myself. Maybe one day I'd get there if I could stay focused. My exercise had been consistent, but my eating had been like a raccoon's diet as of late, I ate everything. Oh well, I did what I could to survive. For now, I would concentrate on making it up the rest of this hill. I couldn't believe how much I was sweating; the front of my shirt was wet, and my hair was wet, except for my swinging ponytail. This was the best part of walking, no one knew if I was crying or sweating in the St. Louis summer heat. Right now, I was doing both.

I finally made it up the hill, my feet came to a complete stop. I bent over slightly with my palms against my lower thighs and took in a few breathers to normalize my heart rate. Now, this was the part of the morning walk I loved, all downhill during my cool down. I stretched and got back in stride. I took in the sights of the familiar homes and cars along the way. A few people were going to work, I did my customary wave and smiled as they drove by. I liked my neighborhood; it was quiet for the most part. The homes were single family brick front colonials in various sizes. Most of the streets were cul-de-sacs with center islands full of lush plants and bushes. In the middle of the subdivision, there was a large lake for fishing with a fountain in the center. My house backed up to the lake, and sometimes I would sit near the window to look out at the water as a stress reliever. It was my Mom's favorite thing to do when she came for a visit. "God, I miss her so much." Didn't take much for her to cross my mind but, I was smiling instead of crying. My emotions were completely out of control; I needed to pull myself together.

I had a lot to get done over the next few weeks. My grandmother needed to get moved into her new senior apartment. I had to find a new probate attorney to handle my Mom's estate. My current attorney wasn't doing a good job, and the emotional stress had taken a toll on me. The end of the fiscal year at work was approaching, and I had to catch up with so many of my cases. And to top it off, my Mom's house needed to be sorted and placed on the market to sell. That was the hard part, going to her house and she wasn't there. Most times I sat and cried when I was there; other times it was more nostalgic. My mind always went back to the first few days after we moved in; I was around ten years old. We were so excited to see rabbits in the yard. Coming from the city, we never saw rabbits outside, just squirrels.

Momma was so happy that she moved us to the suburbs, but it also weighed heavy on her. Although I was the youngest of the kids, I was most in tune with her. I knew she was happy, but I also knew the responsibility of her load. There were plenty of times I heard her crying or worrying about paying bills. I would go into her room and see the bills scattered across her bed. She would be lying face down as if she were sleeping. I'd gently rub the top of her head. Most times she would pretend she wasn't crying, but occasionally she would lie quietly and accept my attempt to comfort her. It was during those times I decided I would be her good kid and lessen her load.

"Hey, Dawn!" Someone yelled and interrupted my thoughts. I looked over and saw my neighborhood nemesis. Oh great! He walked towards me from across the street.

Calvin, a.k.a. The Complainer, was the kind of neighbor you loved, but also hated to see him coming. You loved him because he kept his lawn and home in tip-top shape, but he forced you to roll your eyes at him because he was never happy. It was such a shame too because he was easy on the eyes, single and had no children. He was clean shaven with dark caramel skin and short, curly black-gray hair. He favored a darker version of Rick Fox during his heyday. He was about forty-five years old and very tall. At five feet eight inches, it was a treat to look up at a man. However, this tall treat was a sour puss. I watched him as he strolled toward me looking like new money in his running gear. What a waste of good height.

"Good Morning Dawn, how are you? I hate to disturb you, but I have a question about the lake." He stood directly in front of me.

"Hello Calvin, what can I do for you?" I tried not to roll my eyes or lace my words with sarcasm.

"Well, I know we have a homeowners' association meeting coming up soon. I wanted to know what you and the other board members planned to do about the algae in the lake?"

"Calvin, I didn't see any algae in the lake, I'm not sure what you're talking about." Why was I the only board member that ran into him on a regular?

"It's not there now, but I saw some a few days ago. I think you all need to get a handle on it before it gets out of hand like it did a few years back." His hands gestured all over the place, like a choir conductor.

This dude was so ridiculous, I had to practice a few Zen mantras in my mind. I didn't want to ruin the rest of my day. "Do you have any suggestions?"

"Well not now, but you are a board member so you all should be doing something."

Okay, I was done here. "Calvin, I'll see you at the next meeting. Have a good day." I walked away smiling. I knew he was watching me; I refused to turn around and make eye contact. Now my cool down had turned into a brisk walk, just as I made it to the end of my driveway my phone rang. I was still wearing my headphones although I hadn't listened to any music. I couldn't get my phone situated in my carrying case to see who was calling so I decided to answer it blindly.

"Hello?"

"Dawn?" the female voice said.

"Yes?... Janae is that you?"

"Yeah girl, why do you sound so winded? I thought you would be finished with your morning walk by now."

"I'm done, I'm heading into the house now." I punched the code into my front door. "I ran into The Complainer again."

Janae laughed. "I swear that man needs a woman to put it on him, so he can start acting like a regular man."

I stopped and took my sneakers off at the door and proceeded to the kitchen to get some water. "Girl no one wants his negative butt."

Janae was quiet, I already knew what she was thinking. "He's not that bad, and he's cute," she whined.

I slammed my glass down. "Janae, I will never talk to you again if you try to date Calvin. Yes, he's cute, but he's annoying and complains way too much."

"Okay, okay, I won't talk to him... yet." She laughed again.

"Whatever, do what you do, I've already seen this movie, and I know how it ends. I'm telling you now, if he's sprung when you're done with him I'm not pretending like I don't know where you are," I said jokingly.

"I'm not that bad, am I? It's not like I love 'em and leave 'em," she said in her innocent tone.

"You're right, you don't, but you do love them and refuse to marry them." I couldn't with this woman this early. Janae Barnes was one of my best friends. She'd been my ride or die since freshman year of college. She was a beautiful woman, golden complexion, petite frame and long brown hair that she wore in all sort of styles. Her style was what we liked to call Urban Hippie, she wore anything from Chucks and cut off denim to spectator pumps and pantsuits. You never knew what she would wear, but you better believe she would be comfortable.

"I can't help I have some deep-rooted problem with marriage. I don't mind being monogamous, but the rest of it freaks me out."

"Janae, you know I get you, I think you haven't met the right person yet." I walked up the steps to my bedroom slowly and looked out the window at the lake. It was so serene that I barely heard Janae calling my name.

"Dawn you there?"

"I'm sorry, yes I'm here I was looking out at the water." My eyes were misty.

"Are you thinking about your Mother?" Janae asked quietly.

"Yep, looks like it's going to be one of those days again." I was sitting on the top stair staring at the water and holding the phone with my elbows on my thighs.

"Dawn, I'm so sorry. Is there anything I can do? You want me to call Dre, he's off today?"

"No, I'll be fine, I'm going to get showered, then start working."

"Okay, but I will give you a call later to check on you."

"Thanks, Janae, you're a good friend. I might let you date Calvin after all," I laughed.

Janae laughed. "Whatever, girl...Bye!"

I chuckled to myself and wiped my eyes. I never wanted to burden my friends. I always tried to lighten the mood, so they thought I was okay.

I went to the bathroom to shower and decided I would listen to some music to get me going. Hmmm, what should I listen to today? "Alexa play my playlist." After she rumbled off the title, the soulful trio came through my speakers singing about a girl being poison. Now that brought back good memories, exactly what I needed to get me through the rest of the day.

~~~~~~~~~~~~

What was going on? The doorbell was ringing, and my phone was vibrating. I was groggy. How long had I been asleep? I guess I should have answered the phone; it vibrated again. "Hello?"

"Come open the door."

"Dre?... Are you outside? What are you doing here?" I sat up and looked for my eyeglasses. I couldn't see a thing without them or my contact lenses.

"Come open the door, I've been calling you for the last two hours, and you didn't answer." He spoke slowly and sounded irritated.

"Really? I'm on my way down." I finally found my glasses, I walked past the mirror and glanced at my reflection. My hair was wrapped in a scarf, and I wore leggings with a long t-shirt that barely covered my behind. I didn't care, it was only Dre, and he'd seen me look much worse. Dre, a.k.a. Andre Brown was my absolute best male friend in the whole world. We had been friends since fourth grade, and we have seen each other go through some good times and some pretty bad times.

"Why are you still ringing the doorbell!" I shouted as I ran down the steps toward the door. Once I unlocked and opened the door, there he stood with an angry face and a bag. He brushed past me and headed to the kitchen. I closed the door and followed in his fragrant wake.

"How much cologne do you have on?" I asked once I got to the kitchen, my nose was wrinkled.

"About the same amount of sleep that you have in your eyes," he said without hesitation while unpacking the bag at the counter.

"Can you not insult me in my own house?" I rolled my eyes at him and walked off towards the steps.

"Where are you going?" he yelled as soon as I got halfway up the steps.

"I'm going to wash my face and brush my teeth, I'll be back!" I yelled.

As I went into the bathroom to get myself together, I already knew what this visit was about. Janae must have called him and mentioned my sadness from this morning. I was sad, but I worked about six hours straight then took a much-needed nap. I rarely slept much at night anymore. As I washed my face, I smiled to myself in the mirror. I could almost see my Mother looking back at me, we shared the same dark brown skin and bright wide eyes.

"What are you smiling at?" Dre was standing at the door of my bathroom staring at me in the mirror. He had a slight smile on his face, but his eyes were sad.

"Not you!" I chuckled and stuck my tongue out at him like we did in elementary school.

"Dawn come here." He had that sympathetic tone that I'd grown accustomed to hearing.

"Dre I'm good, just tell me you got something good in that bag downstairs, and I'll be happy." I tried to sound chipper. I made my regular alto voice sound an octave higher.

"You're not good, and you're not supposed to be good. Stop trying to act like you don't need us, we all care about you so let us do what friends do. Either come over here and let me hug you or I'm going to rub my cologne on your pillow." He walked towards my bed.

"That's cold." I quickly made my way over to his outstretched arms. Dre was about six feet tall with a medium build. He always made me feel safe and comfortable. He rocked me back and forth then kissed my cheek. He pulled back and looked at me.

"Better?" He smiled at me.

"I guess." I pulled away and shrugged my shoulders.

"Now see I know that's a lie because women will stand in line to get a touch from Dre. I've had a woman scale a wall to get next to me, Sweetheart." He popped his collar and headed for the stairs.

I could not control my laughter. I covered my mouth to stop myself, but it didn't work. "You're right Dre! Now I feel better."

Dre poked his head back in my bedroom. "You know it's true, I run the Lou!"

I threw one of my pillows at him, and he went down the steps laughing. Dre was extremely handsome, but his problem was that he knew it and thought he could have any woman he wanted. His medium brown skin was as smooth as a baby's, and he never had a pimple as long I'd known him, not even during puberty. He wore a standard close-cropped hairstyle and at forty-four had just started graying around his temples and goatee. I would have never told him it made him even more handsome because I wouldn't have heard the end of it. Luckily, we had been friends since we were kids or else I wouldn't be able to stand him. I shook my head at his antics and went downstairs to the kitchen. As soon as I rounded the corner, I saw the container and my eyes went wide.

"Is that wild berry lavender ice cream?" I nearly whispered.

"Yes ma'am!"

"But how? I thought it was a limited flavor." I stood there salivating at the mouth.

"Do you want a play by play on how I got it or are you going to come and eat some?" He went for spoons in the drawer.

I think I floated over to the container and snatched the spoon out of his hand. I sat at the island and started eating right away.

"Mmmmmmmm," I moaned.

"Really Dawn?" Dre chuckled. "It's not that good."

"I would beg to differ, but I can only focus on this ice cream right now." After I got my initial fix, I noticed him watching me with his eyebrows knitted together. "What's wrong?"

"Nothing, I'm worried about you. All you do is take your morning walk and then work for the most part. You don't go out much."

"My schedule is the same as it has always been since I started working from home almost ten years ago, nothing has changed. I get out when I want, but I'm fine... okay?" I gave him the biggest smile I could without choking on my ice cream.

Dre clapped his hands together and stood from his chair at my kitchen table. "Just what I wanted to hear because we are going to dinner. Run upstairs and get dressed."

Here we go, the whole *"get me out of the house campaign."*

"I'm not hungry right now, let me get a rain check." And right on cue, my stomach made the loudest noise. I couldn't even look at him, I got up and walked towards the steps with my head down. "Give me about twenty minutes and I'll be ready."

Dre said nothing, he stood there with a smirk on his face and watched me walk up the stairs. "And by the way, Janae and 'nem are meeting us, so hurry up!"

Of course, they were. I was sure Janae and Dre decided on dinner early this morning. And by Janae and 'nem I knew that was code for Tori and Robert. Tori was the third part of our female trio, and Robert was Dre's main sidekick. I loved my friends, I was looking forward to having dinner with them.

By the time I changed into an olive green maxi dress, pewter sandals and a hint of makeup I was almost ready. I went downstairs searching for my purse and heard Dre snoring from the sofa in my family room. I walked by him to get my purse from a chair, and slipped into the powder room off the kitchen I took my wrap scarf off and gently combed my freshly relaxed hair. My hair was a natural mix of black and gray, but I refused to succumb to the gray in my forties. So, every three weeks I was diligently perched in the salon chair getting my roots rinsed black. My hair was a little past my shoulders. I wished I had the guts to get it chopped off for once in my life, but I was a slave to simplicity and a quick ponytail. After a few swipes of the comb, I returned to the family room and tapped Dre on the shoulder. I stood with my arms folded across my chest and a serious side eye. He opened his eyes and looked around as if he had forgotten he was at my house.

"My bad, I had a long day," he said with a yawn and stretch.

"It's only seven-thirty, and you were off today." I walked towards the front door. "Do you want me to drive too?"

Dre finally met me at the door. "Nah, I got you, you can ride with me."

"Really?" I turned and looked at him with my eyes wide. "You don't have a lil' something lined up after dinner?"

"Of course, but she lives out this way. I can drop you off first." He shook his head at me.

Dre lived about ten minutes from me in the northern suburbs of St. Louis County. I assumed his "date" - and I used that term lightly - must have been his new neighbor that lived down the street. I didn't know why Dre insisted on messing around with a neighbor. He never committed, and this situation would most likely not end well. He never learned. As we walked out the door, I locked up, and he went to open the passenger side of his black Range Rover. He thought that truck made him look like a million bucks. It tickled me that he was so shallow when it came to material things and his looks. I finally made it to the passenger side and slid into the nice leather seats. It was neat, and it smelled good. Dre rounded the back of the truck and got in and situated before backing out of the driveway. Smooth jazz filled our surroundings; I relaxed immediately. He pulled off, and we were on our way to eat, which reminded me I had no idea where we were going; but, I didn't care. It would be a pleasant surprise; it was always good to hang out with my crew.

"You alright over there?" Dre picked up speed and merged onto Highway 367 not far from my subdivision.

"Yes, I'm fine, just a little hungry." I looked out the passenger window.

"If you're fine then why didn't I get reprimanded about chillin' with ol' girl down the street later?"

"Because you're grown, and you have never listened to me when it comes to your dating, correction... your sex life. You do what you want so there's no point in me saying anything."

"So, because I don't always take your advice you're not going to offer it again? Am I hearing you right?"

I finally looked at his side profile, he had a grin on his face. "Yes, that's what you're hearing."

"Won't He do it! I've been waiting for you to stop telling me how wrong I am since about the fifth grade." He did some elderly version of that Milly Rock dance. I couldn't help but laugh.

"You know I hate you right?" I laughed at him.

"No, you don't, you love me just like the rest of them do." He flashed that perfect set of white teeth.

"You're right, I do, which is why I want you to be careful messing around with that woman down the street. It could get messy, and we are too old for this sort of foolishness now." I tried not to sound too stern.

"I see that only lasted five minutes." He merged onto another highway. "But seriously Dawn, I know you are concerned, but I don't lie to anyone. I'm always upfront with them about my intentions, I'm not promising forever, but I do promise a good time." Now he was smiling and looking sly.

"Yeah, I know what you say, but it's not always that easy. It's rough out here for women and when they meet a good-looking guy, who's single and has his act together someone is going to want more." He was quiet, so I dove in deeper. "Most times a woman will go off your actions and may not always hear what you are saying. You wine and dine them and make them feel special, then when you're ready to move on, or you feel them getting clingy you close up shop and bounce..."

Dre shook his head. "It's my fault that a woman doesn't listen to what I say and chooses to get caught up? That's BS, and you know it!"

"It's not BS, and I'm not placing blame solely on you, but what I'm saying is that your actions conflict with your words. I've seen you on numerous occasions treating a woman like a Queen, calling all the time, sending flowers, the whole nine. Then you go dark after you win her over. It's like you enjoy the chase or the hunt, and as soon as you win, the game is over for you. It's not nice is all I'm saying." I dug through my purse looking for my phone, Dre's mind was working overtime on what I'd said.

"You..." He paused, "Okay look you might be a little right, and I do mean a little, so stop smiling."

I grinned from ear to ear. "You say I'm right? Hey, hey, hey..." I did a shoulder shimmy in time with the music.

"You know I can't stand you sometimes," Dre chuckled. "But on the real, I haven't found anyone that can keep my attention for a long period of time. I go in with my hands up because I don't want any problems if it doesn't work out."

"I get you, but all I'm saying is to be careful when you're dealing with matters of the heart because it doesn't feel good to the other person."

Dre looked at me with his eyebrows hiked up so far, they almost touched his hairline. "And how would you know? You've been committed to a total of one person, your story ain't much different from mine."

"Now you are trippin' I was MARRIED, that's the ultimate commitment!" I yelled playfully.

"Not if you're divorced." He glanced at me out of the corner of his eye.

"Really Dre?" My eyes were wide. "So, you're saying because I'm divorced, and you have never committed to anyone that we are the same?" I cocked my head to the side.

"You damn straight! You're only as good as your last game, and both of our last games are over," he said proudly.

He had me there, I didn't say a word. We were both in the same situation, no significant other. I guess it didn't matter that I had been married if the commitment was over.

Dre reached over the console and grabbed my hand. "You know I understand why your marriage ended and it wasn't all on you right?"

"I know, and it's been well over five years since it was final, but you know how hindsight works," I said softly.

Dre squeezed my hand and let it go gently. "You live and learn and know it wasn't meant to be if it ended. The perfect guy will come along, and it will be right next time. He might even be as good looking as me, who knows?" He ran his index finger and thumb over his goatee.

I laughed. "That's alright because some woman with one tooth wearing footies and house shoes is going to steal your heart and have your head spinning."

"You can kill that noise! If she does catch me, you best believe she gone be fine, stacked up and a chef in the kitchen and the sheets."

"Here you go," I chuckled. "Let me text Janae and Tori and let them know we are almost there, I assume we are going to the seafood place?"

"Yes ma'am, I figured you would be up for seafood since you damn near inhaled your plate and fork last time we were there."

I ignored his last dig and proceeded to group text my girls.

**Hey Ladies, Dre and I are almost there, where r u?**

**Janae: We are already seated and having drinks, hurry up.**

**Tori: Yeah hurry up, big head Robert is already here to...what do you want to drink?**

**Red sangria please and thanks.**

I peeped over at Dre. "They are getting me sangria, you want anything?"

"Naw, I'm good for now." He kept his eyes on the road.

"What? You don't want a drink?" I had an eyebrow raised.

"I'm carrying precious cargo remember?" He winked at me.

"Aww, you are too sweet to me sometimes." I gushed and batted my eyes at the same time.

Dre knitted his eyebrows together in confusion. "Oh, you thought I was talking about you? I was referring to me, myself and I."

I side eyed him as he pulled into a space and turned off the engine. "Jerk!"

"What?" Before he could get another word out, I was out of the truck and headed towards the restaurant entrance. "Dawn! Wait up!" he yelled over the hood of his truck. I kept moving and went inside looking for the rest of the crew.

I spotted Tori's curly blondish mass of hair as soon as I got to the hostess stand. Tori was more of Janae's friend when I first moved to the east coast, but we met and had been inseparable for the last seven years. Tori was a little petite thing with a sassy attitude. She was the opposite of Urban Hippie Janae. Tori sported the latest trends, and you rarely caught her in heels under three inches on her worst day. While Janae was more laid-back, Tori was a firecracker.

"Hey everybody!" I hugged Janae, Tori, and Robert. They sat at a round table with two empty spaces between Janae and Robert. I sat closest to Janae and left the remaining seat for Dre. Speaking of which, I felt him eyeing me as he hugged the girls and greeted Robert with their customary man hug.

"What's up good people?" Dre sat in his seat and reached for my hand under the table. He leaned in and whispered, "we good?"

I squeezed his hand and gave him a smirk. He smiled back, dropped my hand and proceeded to chop it up with Robert and Janae about work. The three of them worked for a major aerospace company in the area but were assigned to different divisions. Tori did contract IT work and owned a beauty salon. I worked from home for an intellectual property government agency based out of the Washington DC area, my former home. I missed it out there sometimes, but I loved my family more. Being home really helped me cope with losing my mother. I didn't think I would have survived if I wasn't here when she passed. Once again, I was slipping into darkness. If I didn't get into the conversation around me I'd be sad again.

"Yo Dawn!" Robert yelled over Dre.

"Huh? What?" I was slightly startled.

"We were trying to have a roundtable, but you're over there in your own world," Robert said. His arms folded across his chest.

Now, this was why I loved this big-headed guy. He always treated me the same and never felt sorry for me. I knew he cared, but he wasn't a coddler like Dre and my girls. Robert Young was a little over six feet tall with shoulder-length dreads, medium brown complexion, and a decent shape. He did have a slight gut from all that home cooking. Robert was the only one in the crew with a spouse. He'd been married for over twenty years to his college sweetheart, who was most likely away on business again. Robert's wife, Serena, was a fitness junky and she choreographed fitness routines for a living. "I'm sorry Rob, what's up?" I asked.

"Well, you know Lil' Robby is heading off to college. The wife and I are trying to decide what we should do with him gone... Now I'm trying to get the wife to go to a place that lovers go and do the things that lovers do, but she wants to open up a new studio."

I chuckled at his Kindred the Family Soul reference. "First of all, Lil' Robby is about six-four, I think you can drop that nickname. Second, you're talking to a table full of single, childless people that haven't gone through the empty nest syndrome."

Robert rubbed his clean-shaven face. "That's precisely why I asked this group, you all know what it's like to be free. Rena and I have been running around with Lil' Robby for the past eighteen years. We are counting the days down until that Joker is gone. I love him, but I don't want to see him again until Thanksgiving once we drop him off." We laughed and shook our heads.

Just as I was about to respond the waitress came to take our orders. She seemed a bit nervous, she was fidgeting with her pen and pad. "Hello, I see the rest of your party has arrived, are you ready to order now?" She was quiet and didn't make eye contact. Then I saw it, she was smitten with Dre, she kept taking glances in his directions. This girl looked to be around twenty-five and had the cutest shape and chocolate skin. Dre was looking at his menu and hadn't noticed her yet, but boy was he going to make a meal of this when he figured it out. Everyone else had already noticed her glancing at him, we eyed each other around the table. She took everyone's order then stopped in front of Dre. "Hi, have you decided, Sir? Do you have any questions about the menu?"

Dre looked up slowly and smiled. He realized she was gawking and he started in on her. "I'll have the crab stuffed shrimp entrée, Sweetheart." He pinned her with a stare, and she stood frozen. After about ten seconds she finally thanked us and walked away extremely fast.

Robert started in first. "Now man why are you teasing that pup?"

Dre put his hands up in defense. "Hey, I didn't say a word to her, but sometimes you gotta give the people what they want." Groans came from all around the table.

"Get the hell outta here!" Tori said across the table.

"I can't with him!" Janae groaned.

Dre chuckled. "Do y'all now get why it's so hard being this attractive? I have to fight off all ages, it's a hard-knock life." We all looked at him, and the table erupted in laughter.

~~~~~~~~~~~~

The morning after our impromptu dinner I went out for my morning walk. I didn't feel up to it, not to mention I needed to catch up with work. I peered down at my phone on my hip and realized it was 6:45 am, this was early for me, but I had a few phone calls to make regarding my Mom's estate. I was almost finished, but I had that dreadful hill. I turned up the music to keep me focused. I reached for the volume on my earbuds, and I heard Kendrick Lamar's "I" blasting in my ear. "Oh yeah, that will keep me going," I said aloud. I was in full stride pushing upwards. The sun peeked over the hill along with a large unfamiliar frame. Good Lord, he looked like he came out of the sun. I strained my eyes, but I was facing the sun, and I couldn't make out any features. When he was about five feet in front of me, I tugged my bud out of my ear and saw him in clear view. This stranger, this man, this mythical creature, had to be a figment of my imagination. He was beyond stunning. Okay, this was it! I needed counseling because he couldn't possibly be real.

"Hello!" he said.

OMG, even his voice was beautiful. It was a smooth baritone, deep, but not quite Barry White. Oh, wait he said hello, and I haven't responded. "Am I dreaming?" His eyebrows knitted. *Why did he look confused?*

"Well, I hope you aren't dreaming because that would mean we are both sleep right now." He chuckled and wiped sweat from his forehead.

My eyes went wide. *I said that out loud? Oh my goodness, what was wrong with me?* "Ummm, hello." He stood about a foot away from me. He had to be about six-four. His skin glistened like warm melted milk chocolate. He was so muscular, his thighs looked like they were carved out of ice. He was clean shaven with a fresh low haircut.

"Are you alright?" He moved a little closer.

*Pull it together girl!* "Yes, I'm fine, it's a little warm. I need some water is all."

"My name is Macon, I just moved here." He extended his hand.

I grabbed his large hand and shook it. He wasn't a stranger to hard work, evident from the roughness of his palm. "Nice to meet you Macon, I'm Dawn I'm one of the HOA board members, when did you move here?" I was sweating uncontrollably.

"Well actually, my parents live here. I'm here with them for a few weeks."

A few weeks? Nice way of saying I live with my Momma and Daddy. Should have known, why wouldn't this gorgeous man live with his Momma? Oh well...and just like that, another one bites the dust. I plastered on a fake smile. "Well nice meeting you, I better get going, see you around and welcome to the neighborhood." I walked away and waved at him.

# Chapter 2 ~ Macon

"Nice meeting you Dawn!" I yelled.

Why did she walk off so fast? I'd been trying to pinpoint this woman's walking schedule for the last two weeks. I finally caught up with her, and she runs off? Not about to happen! I jogged up the hill to catch up with her; she was in full stride.

"Excuse me, Dawn?" I tried to be cool, but this woman was not about to get away that easy. Not to mention she was even more beautiful up close.

"Oh hey." Was she irritated with me? Damn, what did I do that quickly?

"Do you usually come out to exercise every morning?" She stood with her hands at attention trying to block the sun, I moved to the side of her to block it for her.

"Thanks, yes I do come out most mornings if I'm feeling up to it but not at any particular time." She had the sweetest voice and the most beautiful set of plump lips. Everything about her was plump, and I did my best to keep my eyes on her face. I didn't want to come off like a pervert, but she was so curvy and soft looking.

"Well, I was wondering if you would mind if I meet you out here some mornings, makes it a lot more enjoyable if you have a partner?" I tried not to creep her out, but I thought she was going to scream by the look on her face. Her eyebrows were up, and she kept looking around.

"Well, maybe I'll see you around, because like I said I never walk at the same time, and besides you were jogging. I would slow you down with my walking." She fidgeted with her earring, probably trying to think of another out.

Think, think...what happened? She seemed cool initially, and then when I told her I just moved over here she wanted to get away. Why in the hell would she care that I moved here? ......hmmm... Oh damn! She thought I lived with my parents, as in permanent. I should have known better! I had three sisters. I'd heard them countless times saying they didn't want some man on his momma's nipple. And the first thing I said to the woman was that I moved in with my parents. "Okay Dawn, well maybe I'll catch you around. Like I said, I just retired from the Navy and moved home to St. Louis. Luckily my parents are here, so I opted to stay with them until my housing is set up in a couple of weeks. Nothing like Momma's cooking, right?" Silence, crickets, total knock-out, she stared... and not at me. I couldn't figure this woman out, that seemed to change her mood, but then it went south again, now she looked sad. Alright, I knew when I was defeated, for now.

"Well nice meeting you Macon, I better get going."

"Nice meeting you as well, Dawn." I watched her walk off. Why did she look sad after I mentioned 'Momma's cooking'? I couldn't figure her out, but at least I had her name. I could finally ask Mom about her.

I took off running towards the house and made it back in record time. I saw the garage lifting, it was time for Brock, my stepfather, to go to work. He'd been working at the same aerospace company since before he married my mom when I was sixteen. He was up in age now, and Moms had been after him to retire, I was sure he'd be making the announcement soon.

"What it do Brock?" I walked into the garage as the door stopped.

"Mac? You better announce yourself, Son, coming in here like that." He tried to give me a scowl, but it didn't last.

I chuckled, "and what are you gone do Old Timer?"

"I'll show you an Old Timer, Young Blood!" He shook his fist at me as he opened his truck door and put his bags inside.

We laughed a little bit and then I decided to do a little Dawn fishing. "Let me ask you something? Do you go to the HOA meetings around here?" Brock got in his truck and started the engine and let the window down. I stood on the step that led into the house waiting for his response.

"Nope, but your Momma does." He slowly backed his truck out of the garage then stopped. "So, if you want to know more about that little chocolate drop you checkin' for, your Momma can tell you." He tipped his ball cap and backed out the garage.

I stood there with my forehead wrinkled and my mouth open. How did he know? I hadn't said a word to anyone. And when did he get so hip? He'd been hanging out with the grandkids. I pushed off the wall and headed into the house in search of my Mother. "Momma!"

"What is it, Mac? I'm in the kitchen. You hungry?" She was standing at the kitchen sink when I came out of the mudroom from the garage. My mother was beautiful, and she always had been in my eyes.

"I'm always hungry, especially after I run." I leaned against the counter drinking water and eating a few grapes Mom most likely left on the counter after fixing Brock's lunch. "I guess you already know what I want to ask you?" Mom's back was to me while she prepped food on the counter across from me. She was giggling; her shoulders were slightly shaking. My mom stood about five feet nine with a medium build or a "brick house" as Brock called her. Those two acted like teenagers on any given day, and if my housing didn't come through soon, I was sure I'd walk in on something I couldn't undo in my mind.

"Her name is Dawn, and she moved here a couple of years ago from somewhere out on the east coast. She's not married, and she doesn't have any children. She is originally from St. Louis. She's one of the board members for the HOA, and in my opinion, she does a good job despite the trouble the neighbors give her." She looked over her shoulder with a slick grin.

"Is there anything you don't know, Woman?" I chuckled.

"Well, I don't know her blood type, but if you give me a day or two I can find out," she said sarcastically.

"How did you and Brock know about this anyway? I never said a word. I just think she's nice," I lied. I could not have my parents involved in something that didn't exist. They would never let me breathe if they thought she was right for me.

"Momma knows everything, Young Blood." She bent over laughing.

"Really Momma?" I couldn't keep from laughing along with her. This woman was my lifeline and had become quite the comedienne. "And how did you know I was talking to her anyway?"

"We saw you talking to her from the deck while we were finishing up our morning coffee. But I could see your body language from a mile away. Brock told me you would make a b-line around here to ask us if we knew her.... And I see my Baby was right."

I stood there shaking my head. Now that I thought about it, I did meet up with her one street over from their house, which would have given them a clear view since their house sat up high. Great!

"Did she shoot you down? I didn't see you exchange numbers or anything." Mom put an omelet and toast on a plate for me, and I went to the sink to wash my hands. I was way too hungry to get dressed for work before eating. "Sit down Baby so that you can eat."

"I'm sweaty, I'll stand plus I'm running a little late. But I would like to know why you think I didn't get her number?" Mom handed me my plate as I finished drying my hands.

"Because I didn't see either one of you touch those phones you young people can't live without." She had a hand on her hip.

"Okay, you got me. She seemed cool but then sort of froze up." I looked at her and waited for her to give me something.

"Well, I do know she recently lost her mother, poor child. Lord knows I know her pain all too well. I don't know if I would have survived if I didn't have you all and your father, Lord rest his soul." Mom had a distant look in her eyes. I knew she was thinking about my grandmother that passed when I was about seven and my Dad; we lost him when I was thirteen. I needed to get it together before I got wet in the eyes too. But now this made sense, I was out there trying to rap to Dawn, but I pulled a scab. Damn!

"Momma, you alright?" She was quiet, I went over and gave her a quick peck on the cheek, but she waved me off.

"Boy you sweaty, gone somewhere!" She laughed, but I knew we had opened a can of worms. As much as my mother loved Brock, she still loved my father as well. It had been about twenty-four years since he passed, and anytime his name was mentioned you could see the pain she carried. I guess Brock was cool with it because I saw the same hurt in his eyes when my step brothers mentioned their mom. Yep, those two were definitely brought together by God.

I cleaned my plate off and went to the sink to wash it, but Momma reached around me and snatched it. "Go get yourself ready for work, I'll clean up."

"Thanks, Momma." I turned and headed out the kitchen, but when I got to the door, I turned back. "What did you mean when you said the neighbors give Dawn trouble?"

Momma stopped washing dishes and turned to me. "That Calvin next door is always trying to get people to go against her. That boy, I tell you, complains about everything. Every meeting he's asking a million questions and challenging everything. He's sweet as pie, but he seems miserable. I thought maybe he liked her at first." *What the hell?* I met ol' boy a few times, and he was not her type. And even if he was, not on my watch. Okay now I was trippin'. But for real, Ms. Dawn and I were going to get to know each other. All those curves, mmm-hmm. She'd been chosen, and she didn't even know it.

My Mother's talking interrupted me. "... and I've seen him talking to her, he's nice, but he picks at her in the meetings, it's the oddest thing. Well, not really because he is odd. I think he needs a woman. I tried to introduce him to your cousin, Letta, but he ran her off after the first meeting." Momma was still rambling, and I was barely listening. I needed to get dressed for work and head out of here.

"So, Momma, when is the next HOA meeting?"

Momma stopped talking and gave me a side eye. "It's in two weeks, who wants to know?"

I put my palms up in defense. "I was just asking, I might go with you if I don't see Dawn again before then." I left the kitchen. I heard her chuckling as I went up the stairs.

~~~~~~~~~~~~~

The next morning, I'd been out jogging for over an hour and had not seen Dawn. My real estate agent called last night to let me know my new place was ready. I was moving out in a week, and I didn't want to come over here to do my morning jogs, but I would. I didn't know why I was so pressed, but something about her had me wanting to know more about her. I knew she lost her mom, so this may not have been the time but only time would tell. I was doing my final lap around the subdivision when I saw her. I had to push hard to catch her before she turned a corner. She was walking down the hill instead of up the hill like last time; I assumed she was starting her walk. I put it in gear and took off to catch her. When I was about ten feet from her, I called her name; I didn't want to scare her. "Dawn!" She turned around with her hand to her chest and eyes wild. "I'm sorry, I was trying not to scare you, but it looks like I did anyway." I smiled at her; she was pretty. She wore some of those black exercise pants all the women wear and a blue shirt. Her clothes fit her very well. She was on the verge of sweating; her brown skin was beautiful. I wanted to touch her.

"Oh Hi! Yes, you did scare me, it's okay."

*Hell yeah*! She was smiling at me. Her big brown eyes were full of life, she looked happy. "Did you just start your walk?"

"Yes, I did, I wanted to get out earlier, but I overslept."

She seemed cool with me talking to her; I decided to take it further. I was sweating like I stole something so there was no way I could tell her I just came out. "Do you mind if I walk with you? I want to get a little more in today."

"Sure, that would be nice, I could use the company today." She was still smiling, she seemed a lot more relaxed than last time.

"Glad I can be of service, lead the way." I held my arm out for her to start. When she turned to walk, I saw the most glorious, voluptuous ass I'd seen in a while. I knew she had some junk back there, but her hip-to-thigh-to-ass ratio was perfect, just the way I liked it. I needed to focus before I got hard and embarrassed myself. We were walking side by side, I knew I needed to say something, but I was sort of at a loss for words at the moment. "So how long have you lived over here?"

She smiled at me. "A little over two years...now, I know you mentioned you lived with your parents, what's your last name?"

"Yes, I do live with them, but only for another week, my housing is ready now. Their last name is Brock...Dexter and Lila." I glanced down at her, she was about five eight, the top of her head was right at my chin. Perfect height for my six-foot-four frame. I wondered if she wore high heel shoes? Hmmmm, all that junk hiked up another four inches... *get your head in the game man, pay attention.*

"I know Mrs. Lila! She's very nice, she comes to all of the meetings. I don't think I've ever met your father. But wait, you said 'their' last name, is yours different?" She looked at me. Her eyes were so full and expressive. This was good, at least she wasn't bored yet.

"My last name is James. Brock is my stepfather."

"I see...well, it's nice to see you again Macon James, my name is Dawn Simms." She looked straight ahead concentrating on her walk but still engaged in the conversation.

"The pleasure is all mine, Ms. Simms... what time do you have to report to work today since you overslept?"

"I'm not reporting to work today, if that's alright with you, Drill Sergeant?" She gave me the sweetest side eye. I guess I did sound official.

"Drill sergeant? That would be Master Chief...I'm a Sailor, Sweetheart." I gave her a full smile, showed all my teeth.

Her eyebrows went up, and she held her chest. "Pardon me...didn't mean to ruffle your sailor suit Master Chief."

Oh okay, she had a sense of humor, I liked it. I laughed and rubbed the back of my neck. "You're teasing me, but you're out here doing a senior citizen stroll for exercise?"

Her mouth dropped open. "You got jokes? If I remember correctly, someone asked on more than one occasion to join my senior stroll." She was grinning.

"You got me, I'm joking. I like this slower pace; it's relaxing." There must have been a few bugs around because she swung her arm and brushed against my arm, she was soft. I knew it.

"You don't have to say that... I know you're a runner. I'm sure this senior stroll, as you call it, is killing you right now. I won't be offended if you want to run now."

"I already finished my run, and I would much rather walk with you anyway." I think she blushed. "But I do have to take off shortly because I do have to report to work, unlike someone else I know."

"Ha-ha, real funny. Well, I don't want to hold you up sooo," she sang.

"You're not getting rid of me that easy, I've been trying to stroll with you for two weeks now." *My bad that slipped!* I hope she didn't catch that because I sure didn't mean to say that out loud. Yep, she caught it; her eyebrows went up. Now I had to go in straight damage control mode, I didn't want to sound like a stalker.

"Two weeks? What are you a passive-aggressive stalker or something?" She was giggling, and I was slightly relieved.

"Ummm no, I am not a stalker," I chuckled. "But, I will cop to seeing a very attractive woman a little over two weeks ago walking through the neighborhood, and thinking that I would like to meet her one day." When in doubt I went with a compliment; it always helped. I peeped over at her and flashed a smile. She blushed again.

"Nice save Mr. James, I like your style."

"Just being honest."

"Is that right?"

"And since I'm being honest, I do have to get going, but I would like to know if I could have your phone number?" *Please say yes.*

"Okay," she said quickly.

I looked like the Cheshire cat I was smiling so hard. I reached for my phone on my armband. We both slowed down as we got to my street and I felt odd, like she walked me home. This felt weird. "Dawn are you finished walking?"

"Not quite, I have about thirty minutes left on my stroll."

This woman was sarcastic too, I liked it. We might get along very well. "I was going to offer to walk you home if you were done. But, since your crawl, I mean stroll isn't over I will leave you here....

after I get your number." She smiled hard at my humor. She had a beautiful smile. I tapped out a few screens and pulled up my contacts. I handed her my phone. "Do you mind? I want to make sure I have the correct number, I wouldn't want to passively aggressively stalk you again." She laughed and took my phone.

After she handed me the phone back, I shot her a test text message. I wanted her to have my number. "Okay, Ms. Dawn I hope you enjoy your day off."

"Why thank you Mr. Macon, I hope you enjoy the rest of your day as well."

I walked across the street, while she continued in the opposite direction. I watched her walk off for obvious reasons and then I called her name, "Dawn!"

She turned around facing me and walked backward, without missing a step. "Macon!" she yelled back.

This woman had me grinning from ear to ear. "Thanks for letting me join you this time!"

"You're quite welcome! Anytime!" she yelled.

"I hope you mean that!" I yelled playfully.

"And I hope you take me up on that!" she said with a smirk, then turned and strolled off.

I took off running towards the house, one because I was pressed for time and two because I felt good about finally getting Dawn's phone number.

# Chapter 3 ~ Dawn

After I finished my walk, I stood in my kitchen guzzling down water when my phone rang. I looked down at my carrying case and pulled my phone out to answer.

"Hey, Janae, what's up?"

"You take your walk? Did you see the fine jogger?"

"I sure did, and we talked."

"WHAT!? And you didn't say anything!?"

"I just got home, I'm still drinking my water."

"Girl whatever, hold on let me three-way in Tori." She had already put me on hold before I could protest. These two were going to make a big deal out of this no matter what I said. We all swapped men stories, I guess this would be another chapter in the dating chronicles.

"Do I have two callers?" Janae said.

"Yes!" Tori and I said in unison.

"Now let's hear the story, Dawn," Tori ordered.

After I gave them the story word for word they were both quiet for a few seconds and I was a little concerned. Usually, there would have been a few jokes or something by now, and the three of us would be cackling. Tori broke the silence. "You mean to tell me this guy has been watching you for two weeks and trying to meet you?"

"Not watching, more like looking for me, but you know my schedule is all over the place."

"Either way it's hot and I want you to sleep with him right away." Tori had a serious tone.

Janae and I laughed. "Tori, what kind of rationale are you using? Why does she need to sleep with him right away?"

"Because, if he's been waiting for two weeks he should have a lot of anxiety and testosterone built up, it will be primal."

I shook my head. She was out of her mind! I could not stop laughing at her. My phone buzzed, I had a text message. I pulled up the texting app. It was my Aunt sending my sister and I a daily text letting us know she was thinking about us. She started sending them right after my mom passed. I think it was her way of caring for us in my mother's absence. It was very sweet and something I looked forward to receiving. Wait! I had a text from a rogue number. Who was this? I could still hear Tori and Janae planning out my next move with Macon as I read the text.

**757-722-9086: I'm looking forward to our next senior stroll.**

"Excuse me you two, Macon sent me a text."

"WHAT?!"

"What does it say?"

After I read the message, I said, "Alright Ladies, I gotta go shower and start my day." I needed to get off the phone before they had time to give me instructions on texting him.

"That's cool, but don't you mess this up for us. Neither of us is seeing anyone special. We are counting on you to make this one work," Janae warned.

"I know that's right!" Tori yelled.

After hanging up, I added Macon to my contacts and replied to his text.

**I might have to renege on that open invitation.**

I figured he would get a kick out of that response so I...Oh, he responded already.

**Macon: I thought u wanted me to have a good day.**

**Are you NOT having a good day?**

**Macon: I was until u reneged on my stroll invite.**

**Well I don't want to be responsible for the Chief having a bad day at work so your invitation is back intact.**

**Macon: Care for an evening stroll? It would really help my day. You're greedy:) ... but I think I can accommodate.**

**Macon: You are doing a great service for your country. I'll call u when I'm off at 6.**

**I do what I can for the people... ttyl.**

I was grinning from ear to ear. He had a great sense of humor. I sure hoped he didn't turn out to be crazy. I was on my way upstairs to shower when my phone rang again. It was Dre. "Hey, Dre, what's up? You're not at work today?"

"Yeah, I'm at work. I bumped into Janae. She was going on and on about some jogging dude that you've been talking too. Who is he and why don't I know about him?"

"Janae has a big mouth, it's nothing. I have only seen him twice, but we did exchange numbers today."

"Okay, she was acting like dude had spent the night and was posted up or something."

"You know she likes to run everyone down the aisle except herself."

"Tell me about it. But ummm, who is this dude? How did you meet him?" He had on his serious voice. I'm sure he was probably biting the end of a pen with his feet kicked up on his office desk.

"We met yesterday while I was out walking. His parents live in the sub..." Dre interrupted immediately.

"Wait a minute! Dude out pickin' up women and he lives with his Momma and Daddy? Dawn this is not you at all baby, what's going on?" He was sincere.

"Now I see why we have been friends for so long, we think alike. I did the same thing to him when he first told me," I chuckled. "I barely gave him a chance to explain before I politely walked off."

"Yeah okay, but I still ain't heard why he's over there."

"Relax Dre, yes he lives with his parents, but it's temporary. He retired from the Navy, and he is staying with them until his housing is ready. He's only been here a few weeks."

"Okay, that's cool, so you feelin' him or what?"

"So far, he seems cool, but I don't know much about him."

"Good, I hope he's cool, I want you to date." He was distracted, he pecked at his computer keyboard. "Alright I gotta get back to it but I'll swing by on the way home from work, text me if you need me to pick up anything."

He was so nonchalant about it. It was sad he didn't ask if I was going to be home or busy. I guess it had been a while since I dated, it was expected that I would be here. But maybe that would all change if Macon was cool and I could get my emotions together.

"I have plans with Macon, we are going for a walk after he gets off work." I was blushing like a school girl.

"Aaaah okay, ol' boy moves fast. His name is Macon? As in Macon, Georgia?"

"Yes, and I like his name." *Here we go with the jokes.*

"He sounds cornbread fed to me."

"He's eating something but it ain't cornbread...mmmm-hmmm." I was talking in my sultry voice.

"Alright, I gotta go now. But for real, have fun and go easy on Big Country." His serious tone was back.

"What is that supposed to mean?" I stood with my hand on my hip waiting for him to explain.

"Dawn you know exactly what it means because we've had this conversation a million times. You hard on a brotha. All I'm saying is to take it easy on dude and chill."

"I'm not the same, but okay I will do as you say. I'll talk to you later," I snapped.

"Are we good?" Anytime he asked that question I knew he was making sure I wasn't mad at him. When we were kids, he could never handle me being mad at him. And over thirty plus years later, he functioned the same way.

"Yes, we are good, go work. We can talk later. And do not call him Big Country," I laughed.

Dre laughed too. "We'll see about that. Bye."

After we hung up, I thought about what he said about me being hard on men. I would have never admitted it in the past, but he was right; I was a rough ride when it came to dating. I was raised not to take anything from a man. My mother made sure we went to school and got a good education. She always told her girls that you could never depend on a man, and to make our own way in the world. In hindsight, I knew she wanted us to be financially independent, but for me, it translated to emotional independence as well. It was challenging for me to completely trust a man with my heart and emotions for fear of him using it to his advantage.

I did fall in love and get married in my early thirties, but I didn't truly invest my heart the way it should have been in a marriage. Or I guess I should say I wasn't entirely vulnerable. But you live, and you learn. After losing my mom, I could say without a shadow of a doubt that I would never be the same person I was before she passed. My heart and my emotional defenses were utterly shredded in an instant. There was no time to prepare; no ready, set, go. She was talking and fine one day, and then gone the next day with no warning. It was as if my emotional state was in a head-on collision and I was left to figure out how to mend the pieces without instructions. My mom prepared me for just about everything in life, but she never prepared me for life after she left me. So here I was now, slowly picking up bits of my emotional being and trying to figure out how to mend the pieces; so the outcome would be a better *Me*.

Later in the day, I decided to work a few hours instead of taking the whole day off. I lost track of time and almost didn't hear my phone ringing from my bedroom. I left my office and went around the corner to my bedroom to answer it. I saw Macon's name flashing across the screen.

"Hello?" Oh my goodness, I sounded like Barry White.

"Dawn?" He sounded confused.

I cleared my throat. "Hey, Macon."

"I'm sorry, did I wake you?"

"No, I'm wide awake, I haven't been talking, I'm a little raspy." I was embarrassed, but oh well.

"Okay... are you up to going on our evening stroll?"

"Yes, I'm looking forward to it."

"So am I, I'm almost home. I'm going to change and grab some food... about forty-five minutes good for you?"

"Sure, where do you want me to meet you?" I was so rusty with all this, I felt like a teenager.

"Let's meet on the hill."

"Ok, see you shortly. Bye."

"Bye."

I dropped the phone and went back to my office to shut my computer down for the evening. I sat there for a few minutes thinking about getting to know a new person. Was I ready to talk to anyone? What if I cried? I'd been crying randomly for months. Okay, I wasn't about to play this "what if" game. I'd get dressed and go, I would be fine.

Forty-five minutes later, I was at the top of the hill walking down. Macon walked towards me. He was wearing a grey t-shirt with a blue Nike Swoosh across the chest and blue running shorts that stopped right above his knees. He also had on a fitted blue baseball hat. Who looked this good in gym clothes? As he moved closer, I noticed his chest slightly strained against the inside of his shirt. I tried not to make a complete fool of myself by smiling and showing all my teeth, but the man looked good. I was a little jealous of that perfect chocolate skin. What was that? Hmmmm...I thought I saw a tattoo on his upper left arm peeking out from under his shirt. When we were within earshot of each other, I decided to speak to cover up my excessive smiling. "Hey, Macon."

When he opened his arms to hug me, I was slightly thrown off. I tried to give him a church hug, but he pulled me in close and then released me quickly. "Hello again Dawn, how was your day?"

We faced each other smiling. "Very productive, and yours?"

He started walking down the hill; I joined him. "It was hectic. I've only been there a few days. I'm still getting acclimated."

We were walking at a comfortable pace. "Where do you work? If you don't mind me asking."

"Of course not; I work at the VA hospital in the city. I'm a therapist."

"That sounds interesting, will you be working with veterans?"

"Yes, I will be working with mostly veterans but also active duty as well." He seemed very relaxed talking about work, so I decided to ask more, I was interested.

"So how did you decide on that career path?" *Did I sound like a journalist?* "Am I being too nosy?"

He chuckled. "No, not at all, these are perfectly normal questions for two people just meeting. But I will say that my reasoning for going into the field isn't a happy story so is it okay if I tell you later?"

"Of course." Hmmm, now that was weird.

"Let me ask you a question, what is it that you do that has you out walking at fifteen different times of the day?"

I laughed at him and shook my head. "I work for the government as well, in Intellectual Property. I work from home, I can adjust my schedule. Hence the different walking times."

"Ahhhh, now it all makes sense. So, IP as in inventions?"

"Yep, you got it."

"Sounds interesting. What do you do for fun in St. Louis?"

"It depends. Since I was born and raised here, I spend a lot of time with my family and friends. Other than that, it's more sporadic. I don't do any one thing in particular. I guess I can't ask you the same thing since you moved here a few weeks ago. But where did you move from and what do you like to do?"

"I was stationed in Norfolk, Virginia before coming home. I can't say I did much of anything adult wise for fun."

"Adult wise?" I was confused.

"My fun has been entertaining my children. I have two."

Thank you, Jesus! I hoped he had a reasonable number of children. We were heading towards the front of the subdivision. He was good company, I didn't mind the distance. "I see, how old are your kids?"

"Sixteen, I have twins." He started smiling, more like a proud smile.

"Biological or ghetto?" I asked with a side eye and smirk.

"Huh?" His eyebrows knitted together.

"One momma or two?" I clarified.

"How can you have twins with more....ah." He stopped walking and bent over laughing, I laughed too. "I never thought of it that way, but I guess it's a valid question. But to answer your question I have biological twins."

After we sobered from laughing, I continued. "I think I have a ghetto twin, a boy."

His eyes went wide. "My bad, Dawn I'm sorry I wasn't laughing at the situation, it was..."

I waved my hand and cut him off. "No, no, no...it's fine, please don't apologize."

"Okay...so wait, you said you think?" His eyebrows were knitted in confusion again.

"Yes, I said I think because I've never met him, and I was only told that we are close in age. My mom told me about him when I was around fourteen, but she never met him either, so that's why I say I'm not sure. I was into boys by then, and she didn't want me to end up dating him, so she told me everything she knew."

"Damn, for real? Where does he live? Have you ever tried to find him?" He drew his eyebrows together.

"As far as I know, he has always lived right here in St. Louis, and no, I've never tried to find him because I don't know his name. Well, I have what I believe may be a nickname but no last name." I needed to change the subject; his brows furrowed, he looked concerned.

"I'm assuming the father you share is, ummm, where? No wait, listen I didn't mean to pry we can change the subject." He stopped walking and turned to face me with the sincerest look. He was so handsome I could barely look back at him.

"No Macon, you're fine. Besides, I brought it up anyway. It's not a big deal to me. I forget that it makes me seem weird to the average person who knows all of their siblings." I tried to reassure him.

"It's not weird, it's your life. I wasn't judging you at all. If anything, I was thinking that you genuinely look to be at peace and not mad at the world." He started walking again.

"Well thank you, I don't mind talking about it because you're right, it is my life. I believe we aren't put into our families by mistake. And to answer your question, the father we share is in St. Louis."

Macon's mouth dropped open. "Is he an addict or one of the other usual suspects?"

I chuckled. "Everyone always assumes he's an addict or in prison or something, but it's quite the contrary. He's married with a family and has worked his entire life. While I do recall him drinking cheap beer during the occasional childhood visit, he's not an addict of any sort."

"Hell, I feel like I'm at work right now and I should have a legal pad.... let's not talk about family stuff anymore, this is too heavy," Macon sighed.

"Oh my goodness, I feel so bad for ruining our stroll talk." I couldn't believe I told him that on our first outing, I was sure I wouldn't hear from him again. I always forgot what was normal to me was NOT normal for other people.

"No, you didn't ruin anything. I'm enjoying myself, but I don't want to make you feel a certain way. I have no problem listening to whatever you want to tell me." He was pleading his case, but I agreed with him. We should lighten the conversation up a bit.

"That's very sweet of you so why don't we put a pin in that topic and revisit it later. Soooo, you seemed to smile when you mentioned your kids, tell me about them, if you don't mind."

He smiled again. "Those two are my heart and soul. I can't imagine life without them. Chloe and Major live in Kansas City with my ex-wife. We divorced about five years ago, she remarried a few years back. It's one of the reasons I wanted to come back to Missouri. The plane tickets were killing me. Now I can hit the road and pick them up or meet them halfway in Columbia."

"That's good, how often do you see them?"

"It depends on what's going on. They are older now and involved in so many activities, they don't come to me as much. I usually go to KC. During the summer, they are with me most of the time. I always see them holidays. Their mom is from St. Louis, so we agreed to always meet here for holidays, so both sides see them. And I can see them."

"Sounds like your children are blessed with a good set of parents." I smiled at him.

"Oh yeah, we agreed that we were divorcing each other, not the kids. They have been fine, and her husband is cool. The kids like him, and he treats them well. I have no complaints... What's your rundown? You know I have two kids, and I was married once."

"No kids and divorced once. I've been divorced about five years too."

"Look at that, we have something in common." He smiled, and I smiled back at him. Even his teeth were perfect.

"I was born and raised here in St. Louis. About two years after college, I moved to the DC area for my current job. I started working from home about ten years ago and was finally given the green light to live outside the DC area, so I came back home a couple of years ago."

"What made you move back? You didn't like it out there?" He glanced at me.

"Oh no, I loved it out there, and I go back for work and to see my friends all the time. But really, I wanted to be closer to my family again. Not to mention the cost of living is so much cheaper here."

"How has the move been so far?"

"If I had to sum it up with one word I would say bittersweet." I was thinking about my Mom again. I felt sad.

"Hmmm, I won't ask you to explain that one." He smiled. "For now."

We talked so much we were almost back to the hill, but I didn't want it to be over. We were quiet for a moment, and then Macon broke the silence. "We are almost back to the meeting spot, but I would love to continue talking if you're up for it."

"Sure, we can sit on my deck if you don't mind."

"Sounds good to me. Or if you like we can go to my parents' deck, whatever makes you feel comfortable."

"I think my deck will work, I know your mom has binoculars." I couldn't help laughing out loud.

He closed his eyes slowly and looked down shaking his head. "My mother's nosiness knows no bounds. Can she see your deck from their house?"

I kept laughing. "No, she can't."

"Good, I was hoping you wouldn't choose her place because she would be in the window facetiming us to the fam."

"Oh wow, yeah I don't want to be in your family chat tonight."

He put his hand on his chest. "Confession time." I looked at him with my eyebrows up. "That's a thing I do with my kids, I give them the opportunity to come clean with the truth. The punishment is less severe if they fess up, but if I find out later... the hammer comes down."

"Well, let's hear your confession then."

"You're already part of the family chat."

I stopped walking and looked at him. "How is that possible?"

He put his palms up in defense. "Yesterday, when I stopped to talk to you, my parents were sitting on the deck having coffee, and they saw us."

I started walking again and grinned at his story. "But we didn't talk for long, and I'm pretty sure they couldn't hear us."

"I may have gone home and asked them separately if they knew you and gave it away." He had the nerve to flash that handsome smile at me.

"I see...so why confess? I would have never known?"

"Then you don't know my mother. Wait until she sees you again; she may show you a photo album of my baby pictures." We both laughed.

By the time we were in front of my house, we were still laughing at his mom. I led us around the side of the house to the back area. We climbed the stairs to the deck and sat in two wicker lounge chairs with large cushions. Macon was quiet, and he stared at the lake. I needed to go in the house for a moment. "Would you like some water or anything to drink?"

"Sure, water is fine."

I opened the back door that led into my kitchen. After I was inside, I fanned myself. I went into the house to have a moment away from him. He was so handsome, and he made me feel things I hadn't felt in a while. I slightly opened one of the blinds in the kitchen window. I could see his broad shoulders leaning over the railing. Was it possible to be this attracted to him so soon? Well, the body didn't lie. And right now, my body was talking loud and clear. I looked down, my breast were slightly swollen, and my nipples poked through my sports bra. Mr. James had definitely caused my current situation. I walked around for a minute to get myself together, then went to the refrigerator to get the bottled water. I went back outside, Macon stood with his forearms resting on the railing looking out at the lake. He must have heard me come out.

"I like the view of the lake from your deck, it's very relaxing," he said.

I went and stood next to him and handed him a bottle of water. "Thank you, I find it relaxing too."

"Thank you for the water."

"You're welcome."

"I knew there was a fountain in the lake, but I didn't realize a light was on it." He continued to look out at the water.

"Yes, there is, it comes on at dusk and goes off at midnight." I was enjoying myself, he was so easy to talk too.

"You know Dawn, you are easy to talk too." I almost choked on my water, but I caught myself.

"Thank you, I was thinking the same about you." I leaned over the railing and looked out at the water, watching daylight disappear.

"I hope I'm not keeping you from something... or someone?" He was looking at me. I saw him out of the corner of my eye, but I wouldn't dare look at him, we were way to close. Those eyes, full lips, and that smooth skin would've had me jumping him right on this deck.

"No to both." I didn't look at him.

"Good, can I take you out this weekend?"

"I would like that." I finally snuck a peek, and he was still looking at me. I walked away and sat back down in the chair. No way was I able to stand next him looking at me like that. He followed suit and sat in the chair next to me.

For the next three hours, we laughed and talked and had a great time. He kept yawning, and I made him go home. Once I was in the house prepping for bed my phone buzzed.

**Macon: Thank you for spending your evening with me, sleep well.**

**You're welcome, and I thank you too, I had a nice time.**

**Macon: Anytime**

**Macon: ... and my invitation will not be reneged.**

**LOL! Go to bed!**

**Macon: I would if my Mother didn't have me hemmed up in the kitchen asking me questions about you.**

**What!? Are you serious?**

**Macon: Yep, she and 2 of 3 sisters are on speaker and they are asking me questions.**

**You have 3 sisters? Where do you fall?**

**Macon: Last**

**You're the baby!?**

**Macon: I prefer last but not least.**

**Tomato-Tomata**

**Macon: Saved by Brock...I'm free at last.**

**Good night Mr. James**

**Macon: Sweet Dreams Ms. Simms.**

# Chapter 4 ~ Macon

The weekend had finally arrived, and I was still trying to figure out where to take Dawn on our first date. We talked and texted every day and were getting along great. She seemed like a genuine person, and that was very rare in this day and age. I heard sadness at times, but I hoped this date would make her feel better. I couldn't ask my parents or my sisters about a nice place to take her, so I decided my brother could help me. I was on the way home from work and stuck in Friday's traffic. I turned the music down and pulled up his number and used the truck system to call him. He answered right away.

"What's up with you baby bro'? Or should I say Romeo?" He laughed.

"Man, what are you on now?" Donald was the youngest of Brock's two boys and a bona fide clown.

"I heard you done pulled the chick in charge over there already." He was full of humor. I could tell he was smiling.

"Damn man, not you too? I see you on that family grapevine." I shook my head; my family was nothing but a gossip line.

"Nope, it swung my way. I stopped by the house a couple of days ago to holla' at Pops for a minute, and Lady B told me you went out walking with some HOA chick."

Donald and Brock's oldest son, Dale, referred to my Mom as Lady B. They were both away in college by the time Brock and Mom married, and they didn't want to call her by her first name. Somehow Lady B came into play. My mother loved it; she said it made her feel regal.

"Yeah okay, but since you mentioned it, Dawn is why I'm calling." I paused because I knew a few jokes were coming.

"Word? You need a few pointers on sealing the deal?" He was in his garage working on his bike. Metal tools were dropping on concrete.

"Naw fool, and if I did I wouldn't be asking your womanless..." He cut me off.

"Womanless? Man, you know how I gets down. I got 'em comin' and goin'."

I couldn't help but laugh at him. Donald dated, but was definitely not classified as a ladies' man. He could talk trash with the fellas, but he choked anytime a good-looking woman came around. His good looks were the only thing that kept him dating. "Yeah, I hear you Bro... but for real I know you like to treat the ladies to a good time so what's a good place to take her on a first date?"

Donald let out a long whistle. "It depends on what you trying to do. Besides I don't know her."

I see I should have figured this out on my own. "It's cool man, I'll come up with something. So, what's been up with you?"

"Same ol' thing, aye does your girl have any friends?"

"She's mentioned a few, but I haven't met them yet, but I'll let you know." I guess he wasn't seeing anyone at the moment because Donald was a one-woman type of man.

"Alright good lookin' out. I gotta run, but holla at me later."

"Yep." I ended the call and thought a little more about my date with Dawn. I was supposed to pick her up at 8:00 this evening and I had no idea where I planned to take her.

~~~~~~~~~~~~

It was 7:58 when I pulled into Dawn's driveway, and for some reason I was nervous. I reached for the flowers I bought earlier and got out of the truck. I told her to dress casual, I thought jeans and a button up shirt would be fine for me. I walked up to the door and rang the bell. I could hear her walking across the floor and unlocking the door. She peeped her head out and smiled and then reached to unlock the storm door.

"Hi Macon! Come on in, I'm ready."

I was speechless, this was the first time I saw her in clothes other than the walking gear. I didn't realize she had such long hair because it was usually in a ponytail or something. She had on a black skirt that fit like a glove and some type of flowy blue shirt. She had on a little makeup but all I paid attention to was her lips, they were bright red. "Hi Dawn, you look beautiful." I handed her the flowers. "These are for you." I had to relax.

She gave me the biggest smile. "Thank you so much, that was so sweet of you. I love flowers. I'll put them in water and then I'll be ready. Follow me."

She turned around, and I almost groaned out loud. This was going to be a long night if I had to watch all that ass and not touch it. Her skirt came right to her knee. She wore sandals with a small heel; she smelled good too. I followed her into her kitchen. Her house was nice, and the decorations weren't too feminine looking. It was nice with a comfortable feel. A few pieces of artwork on the wall caught my eye along with a few candid pictures in frames, but I wasn't close enough to make out any faces. She finished putting the flowers in water.

"These are so pretty, Macon."

I smiled. "Are you hungry? I thought we would have dinner and drinks. I remember you mentioning your love of wine and mixed drinks while we were on your deck."

"Sounds perfect, let me grab my purse." She headed out of the kitchen and stopped, I almost bumped into her. She reached out to hug me. "Thanks for the flowers again, it was very nice of you."

I pulled her close and held her around the waist; she fit perfectly. "You're welcome." I held her a little longer than I should have but I didn't care. I let her go, and she walked into another room to get her purse.

"I'm ready!" We went out the door, and I held the storm door while she locked up. I put my arm out for her to grab it and she smiled up at me. "Oh wow, aren't you chivalrous. I got flowers and now an arm escort?" she teased.

I chuckled a little. "I'm always a knight, Sweetheart." I winked at her, and she blushed.

After I helped her into my truck and got in, my phone rang through the speakers and announced the caller. I couldn't believe I forgot to disconnect the Bluetooth. "Call from The Girl," the speaker announced. Dawn smiled and gave me a side eye.

"It's my daughter, I need to take this." I tried to answer the call before it ended.

"No problem."

"Hey, Chlo!" I said to my Baby Girl.

"Hi Daddy, what are you doing?" I swear Chloe was clairvoyant.

"Not much Baby Girl, what's up?"

"Maj has a new girlfriend, and she's loose," she announced loudly.

Dawn giggled and covered her mouth, but I knew Chloe heard her. Before I spoke on the 'loose' girlfriend, I waited for her questions.

"Daddy who was that?" Her background went silent.

"It's my friend, Baby Girl." I shook my head.

"Oh... May I say hi to her?" I looked at Dawn with an eyebrow raised asking what she wanted to do. I was literally on the first date and my whole family knew her name now.

She smiled politely. "Hi Chloe, my name is Dawn. It's nice to meet you."

"Hi, Ms. Dawn, nice to meet you too."

I cut in before she decided to say anything else. "Alright Chlo, now I know we talked about you judging people."

"Yes, we did, Daddy, but I'm not judging her, I'm stating facts."

"You do not know for a fact that she is loose, so it's not good to say it, Baby Girl," I said sternly.

She blew out a breath. "It's a fact alright! And Maj..."

I cut her off. "Alright let's talk about this tomorrow, okay? I'm being rude to Ms. Dawn." I started my truck and backed out of the driveway.

"Okay Daddy, I'm sorry Ms. Dawn. I'll talk to you tomorrow."

"That's quite alright Chloe." Dawn was silently laughing.

"I love you, Baby Girl. Bye."

"I love you too Daddy. Bye, Ms. Dawn."

"Bye Chloe!"

As soon as the call ended, Dawn covered her face. "Macon I'm so sorry I didn't mean to laugh out loud, but she caught me off guard." Her eyes were wide, and she tried not to laugh.

"It's alright, Chloe has a way with words, and she's nosy as hell."

"I did notice how quiet she got when she heard me." Dawn was smiling again.

"Oh yeah, that will be the first ten minutes of our conversation tomorrow. She says she can feel a person's emotions or aura or some stuff she says. I can't quite remember her exact terminology, but she's sizing you up right now. She will tell me tomorrow."

Dawn looked over at me. "Has she ever been right about anyone?"

"Always, and it freaks me out most of the time, she's been doing it since she was a toddler." I thought about my Baby Girl and what she would have to say about Dawn.

"Well let me know what she says about me, I think it will be interesting to know what 'The Girl' has to say," she teased.

"I see you caught that." I smiled. "I call them 'The Girl' and 'The Boy' most of the time."

"I think it's cute." She gave the cutest smile.

I looked at her and shook my head. "I thought we would go to the West End for dinner at this vodka bar. I heard it has good food too."

"I know the place. I love it!" She clapped her hands together.

"Good to know." I was glad she liked the place. I didn't want to be too formal or too casual.

"The food is delicious and the drinks are good too."

"Good because I'm starving." We drove in silence with a little talking here and there. I decided to turn the music on to give us a little background noise. I had no idea why I was so nervous. I'd gone on plenty of dates, and I'd never been like this.

"Macon, I'm nervous." *Whoa, Chloe junior, was she reading my mind?* She blurted that one out.

I reached over the console and took her hand, it was cold. "I'm a little nervous too, so we're even."

"Are you?" She cocked her head to the side and stared at me "You seem fine. I guess it's been a while since I've had an official date."

Now I looked shocked. "You're beautiful, Dawn, and as far as I can tell you have a great personality. I find that hard to believe."

"You're sweet." She smiled. "But it's true. I've met people, but nothing has taken off."

I had to let her hand go so I could parallel park. "I can understand that. I've run into a few that I had to cut before the first date."

She giggled. "Oh wow, I passed the first test?"

"You passed a few tests." I winked at her and opened my door. "And do not touch your door until I come around and get you." I was serious about that chivalry thing. My father always told me the easiest way to win over a woman was too be honest and chivalrous. I didn't understand it before he passed, but as I got older and watched Brock with my mom and heard my sisters complain, I had no choice but to learn early.

She put her palms up. "Yes, Chief!"

I rounded the hood and opened her door. My truck was a little high, I held out my hand for her. I parked across the street from the restaurant, so I held her hand until we were on the sidewalk. I opened the door for her and went to the hostess stand. The place was cool and had a nice vibe; I saw all sorts of vodka at the bar. I told the hostess we were there for dinner and she led us to a larger, much quieter dinner area with small tables. When we arrived at the table I pulled Dawn's chair out and waited for her to be seated. She smiled up at me. "Thank you, Macon."

I sat in my chair. "You're welcome."

After we ordered our meals and got our drinks, we small talked for about twenty minutes. She seemed to relax a bit after she had a few sips of her Peachy Vodka drink. I sipped a Vodka Tonic and relaxed a bit myself. "Let's do this thing, give me your full timeline." She seemed eager.

"My timeline?"

"Yes, you know – your rundown as you call it."

The waitress arrived with our food before I could speak. I blessed the table, and she pulled a small bottle of what appeared to be sanitizer from her purse and reached towards me. I held my hand out, and she squirted some in my hand then some for herself. That was cute; I liked a woman that looked out for others. "Well, my rundown isn't too long. I was born and raised here in the Lou." I popped my collar, and she laughed. "I was in the ROTC program in high school and planned to go away to college but my then-girlfriend and current ex-wife, Mia, got pregnant senior year and changed all of that." She ate slowly and stared at me intensely. "We were young and had been together for three years, so I decided I would enlist in the Navy and we got married. I graduated early and went in at seventeen. My mother had to sign off, and boy was that a long conversation. Mia finished out her senior year and stayed with her parents while I was in basic training. After I got my orders, we moved to San Diego; unfortunately, we lost the baby."

"Oh no! I'm so sorry Macon, that must have been extremely difficult for both of you, especially being so young." She had her hand on her chest.

"It was a nightmare, but we survived it."

"I'm impressed that you guys were able to stay together and have a family later." She ate her fries slowly and stared at me, waiting for me to continue.

"Well, it wasn't that much later; the twins were cooking by the time I was twenty."

Dawn put a finger up. "I have a question...You said your kids are sixteen, right?"

"Yes, headed into their junior year of high school this fall."

She had a strange look on her face. "So that makes you what? Thirty-six?"

"Thirty-seven, I was twenty-one when they were born," I corrected.

"Oh my God, I'm robbing the cradle." Her mouth was wide open.

Okay now I knew black didn't crack but how old was she? I assumed she was a few years older than me, but maybe I was wrong. I didn't care how old she was, but apparently, she did. I smiled at her. "Alright Dawn, I know I'm not supposed to ask a lady her age, but I doubt if you're robbing the cradle."

"I'm forty-four," she said plainly.

"Okay well see, I was only off a few years. I gave you thirty-nine or forty, but honestly, it wasn't on my mind. You could have said fifty, and I wouldn't care."

"I was in the first grade when you were born!" She yelled playfully; her voice was higher than usual.

I popped a few sweet potato fries in my mouth and drained the last of my drink. "Hold up! So how old did YOU think I was?" She had the nerve to look sheepish. I knew I had a few grey hairs, and I thought I looked fairly youthful, but not now. I waited for her to answer.

"I don't know, I guess I assumed you were a couple of years younger or the same age as me." She shrugged her shoulders.

"You're trying to hurt somebody's feelings." My eyes were wide, and my forehead was wrinkled.

"No, No, No...." She laughed, her hands were gesturing, but I cut her off.

"Yes, Yes, Yes! You're telling me you thought I was five to seven years older than I am?" My mouth was open.

She was giggling. "See what had happened..."

"I'm waiting. I can't wait to hear this one." I propped my elbow up on the table and rested my cheek on my fist.

"Okay, so really you look good for your age but..." Her eyes were wide, she couldn't stop giggling.

I jerked my head up. "I look good for my age!? What? You are not helping the situation."

She tried to stop giggling but couldn't. "Okay, so what I'm saying is that you are mature? I," she stammered, "I don't know what I'm trying to say."

I leaned across the table, grabbed her hand and looked into her eyes. "What I hope you're saying is that my age only measures my time here on earth and not my life experience. And what I hope you are definitely saying is that insignificant number won't get in the way of what's going to happen between us."

Our eyes locked, and I refused to look away. I could look at her all day. Her hair was hanging on her shoulders, and a breeze from somewhere was blowing a few strands across her cheek. She cleared her throat and looked away and then slowly pulled her hand away. "Okay, but we just met this week."

"Dawn?" She looked at me. "Are you getting caught up in time again?"

She shook her head then gave me a small smile. Of course, the waitress chose that moment to check on us. "Can I get you anything else?" She gathered our plates.

"Dawn, would you like anything else?"

She seemed to be daydreaming, she didn't blink. "Oh, um no thank you."

"I'll take the check." After I settled the bill, I asked Dawn if she was ready to go and she nodded. *Was I losing her?* She seemed distant. I hoped she wasn't trippin' off this age thing because that was the one thing that couldn't be changed. I helped her out of her chair and led her out of the restaurant. Once we were outside, I looked down at her, and her mind still seemed preoccupied.

"Would you like to walk around for a while or are you ready to head back?" I asked quietly.

"Can I treat you to some ice cream?"

I wasn't expecting that one, but I rolled with it. "Okay, where would you like to go? I know there used to be one across the street back in the day."

She smiled. "That one is long gone, but there's an ice cream shop about a block down if you don't mind walking."

I hadn't walked around in the Central West End since I was in high school. It was a cool area in the city with little shops, restaurants, and large older homes. "Lead the way."

We walked side by side, and she finally broke the silence. "Macon, can I share something with you?"

"Of course, lay it on me." I tried to lighten the mood.

"I lost my mom about seven months ago." She was quiet and didn't look at me.

"I'm sorry, Dawn." I didn't know what else to say, I let her take the lead. I knew I didn't want to put on my work hat and turn into a therapist on a date.

"It's been extremely difficult for me. I'm still trying to pull myself together. If I seem distant at times, I wanted you to know the reason."

"Thank you for telling me. If there's anything I can do to help, let me know."

"I know you told me you were a therapist, what's your area?" She looked at me, her eyes were glossy.

"I do all sorts of therapy, but I mostly deal with grief and PTSD."

"Maybe you can tell me when my heart will heal." She had the saddest smile.

"I wish I could tell you that it does heal, but it doesn't. You have to learn to live life with a broken heart. It's like losing a body part, it won't ever come back, but you can learn to live without it."

"That's a perfect analogy. It applies to me one hundred percent. I guess you could say that I'm at the stage where you keep forgetting the body part is gone, but when you remember the pain starts all over."

This was what I studied in school, but I had no idea what to do right now. It was much different when you added that personal element to it and removed the legal pad. I stopped walking and touched her shoulder to stop her. I held out my arms and pulled her in for a hug. After a few seconds, I let her go and looked at her. "Better?"

"Yes." She giggled.

"What's so funny?" We started walking again.

"My best friend hugged me earlier this week because I was sad. He asked me the same thing. I feel pitiful sometimes."

"Don't feel that way, we all go through things in life. We need other people to help us through."

"I know you're right so please excuse my mood swings. I'm in and out." She finally gave me a real smile, teeth and all.

"I will if you excuse the way I'm about to handle this ice cream. Is this the line out the door?" I slowed down as we approached the small storefront.

"It sure is, and it's well worth the wait, prepare to be amazed." She wiggled her eyebrows.

After we waited in line for about fifteen minutes her mood was much better, she seemed to be back to herself. She chatted with the girl behind the counter about samples while I read the menu on the wall. They had some weird flavors, maybe I wasn't about to chow down. Dawn grabbed me by the hand and pulled me out of the line to a table.

"Sit please and close your eyes," she ordered.

I sat down, there was a cup in her hand with a few metal spoons sticking out. "Are you going to feed me?" I was smiling from ear to ear.

"Yes, I am; are you going to close your eyes?" Her lips were in the cutest pout.

"Isn't it a little soon for you to be blindfolding me and feeding me?" I closed my eyes.

She laughed. "You are not blindfolded and..." She paused. "Are you getting caught up in time Mr. James?"

I opened my eyes, she had a little clever smirk on her face for using my words on me. "Touché, Ms. Simms." I closed my eyes.

"Thank you, now this ice cream has intense flavor. I'm going to tell you the flavor as soon as I feed it to you."

"Okay, but why do I need to close my eyes?" What was she up to? Didn't matter, I was going to do whatever she asked.

"Because I only want you to focus on two of your senses; hearing and tasting. I don't want your vision to dictate your taste buds, it looks nothing like it tastes."

"I'm ready." My eyes were closed. I felt the heat from her hand getting close to my mouth. Maybe this wasn't a good idea.

"Creampuff!" she said and at the same time put the small spoon in my mouth. That was good! It tasted like a cream puff. I held onto the spoon with my teeth as she tried pulling it out of my mouth.

"Let go!" She laughed, and I let go of the spoon. "How was it?"

"I'll tell you after. Keep feeding me, Woman!"

"Open up... blueberry lemon." She slid another spoon into my mouth.

"Oh wow!"

"Here we go...wild berry lavender." What the...? Before I could say a word, she had the spoon in my mouth. That one was even better, I was surprised. She tried to pull the spoon from my mouth, but I held it with my teeth.

She laughed. "Let go of the spoon, you're such a savage."

I opened my eyes, she was right in front of me. "You. Have. No. Idea," I said slowly and winked at her. I heard her breath hitch after I closed my eyes.

"Alright last one...gooey butter!" My eyes flew open as I tasted the ice cream that was identical to my favorite cake.

"You know that's my favorite cake. My mom used to ship them to me wherever I lived."

Dawn gathered the spoons. "Really? I've been eating gooey butter cake for years and I learned to make them when I moved away. My mom used to walk me through the recipe over the phone."

"Good to know." I was impressed now, not only was this woman fine, but she knew how to make my favorite cake. "I liked all of the samples, but you know which one I want don't you?" She nodded. "And you were right, the flavors were much better with my eyes closed and you feeding me." I was smiling.

She laughed out loud. "Maybe I should have rethought that idea."

"Here you go again trying to renege on stuff. That is how I want to eat ice cream from here on out." I pointed at her, "with you feeding me."

We both laughed and then went to the counter and placed our orders. I got a bowl of the gooey butter ice cream, and she got a scoop of the lavender flavor on a cone. When we got to the register, Dawn handed the cashier her card. I leaned over the counter. "Excuse me?" I read her name tag, "Lucy?" She stopped and looked up at me. "I'm on a date with this beautiful young lady and because I asked her out, I don't want her paying for anything. If you don't mind can you give her the card back, please?"

Lucy smiled and handed Dawn her card, and I handed her mine. I didn't bother to look at Dawn until I paid. "You ready?"

She walked ahead of me out of the ice cream shop. Halfway down the block she turned to me and broke the silence. "Thank you for the ice cream. I didn't mind paying because it was my idea. And you paid for dinner."

I was inhaling my ice cream. "I know you didn't mind, but I did."

"Okay Chief," she laughed.

"Where to now?" I looked at my watch. "It's a little past 11:30."

She was licking her ice cream cone. What I wouldn't do to be that ice cream right now. "You're in charge remember? Isn't that what you told Lucy at the ice cream shop?"

"Yes, I guess you have a point but I'm all out of ideas.... Oh, you want to go dancing or something?"

Her eyes went wide. "You dance?"

I did a quick little two-step on the sidewalk and smiled at her. "I've been known to cut a rug or two on the dance floor...how about you?"

"I do okay. I won't win any contests, but I love to dance." She was smiling and still tormenting me with that ice cream cone.

"Well, stick with me, I'll have you winning contests all over."

"This I will have to see," she giggled.

"Don't worry, you will at some point. I guess I am a little tired, I've been up since 5:00 am." I finished off my ice cream.

"Okay let's go home."

We headed back to our area of town and talked until I pulled into her driveway. She seemed to have a second wind. I was exhausted, but I was enjoying her, and I wanted the night to last a little longer. "I have something I would like to give you; would you like to come in? Or I can run it back out? I know you had a long day." She unbuckled her seatbelt.

"I can come in." I got out and walked around to her door and helped her out. She led the way to her front door and let us both in. I followed her to the family room area, there was a wall of windows on the far wall with a perfect view of the lake. The fountain light was shining bright; I could look at this all day. She turned on a few dim lights and took her shoes off.

"Can I get you anything to drink?"

"I'll take some water, and do you mind if I use your restroom?"

She led the way to the restroom, which was right off the kitchen. When I came out, she was standing at the kitchen island packing up some containers. She looked up at me. "Hey."

"Hey yourself, what's all this?" She handed me a bottle of water and a bag with the containers.

"A few sweet treats I baked, including a few pieces of gooey butter cake."

My mouth opened. "Are you serious?"

She folded her arms across her chest proudly. "Yep!"

I opened the bag and saw pound cake and... "Are these tea cakes!?"

"What do you know about tea cakes?" Her eyebrows went up.

"I know I haven't had them since I was a kid, my grandmother used to make them." I opened the container and popped a whole tea cake in my mouth. "Mmm, damn this is good! You made these?"

She watched me stuff my face and shook her head. "Yes, I made them. They are my mom's recipe. My mom used to sell cakes after she retired, it was one of her favorite things to do. Now I bake when I miss her, it makes me feel close to her. Needless to say," she pointed to the bag, "I missed her this week."

"What do you do with all the food you bake?" I closed the container and drank some of the bottled water.

"I eat a little if I'm in the mood, but most of it goes to my family and friends."

"Can you add me to the list?" I moved closer to her and put the bag and bottle on her kitchen table.

"Of course." She smiled.

I leaned over and kissed her cheek. "Thank you." She blushed.

"Can we talk for a minute or do you want to get some rest?"

"Sure, but I thought you were sleepy." She walked towards her family room, and I followed.

"I was, but I think I'm on a sugar high from the ice cream and tea cakes."

She sat on the sofa, and I looked at her pictures on the mantle. "Do you mind?" She shook her head. "I see you like to travel, who are these people in the pictures with you?"

She came and stood next to me. "Yes, I love to travel, I usually go with my friends a few times a year. These are my friends, Janae..." She pointed out her friends in the different pictures. "Tori, Dre, Serena and Rob."

"This is nice, your collection is sort of self-explanatory."

"Anytime I travel I buy a picture frame with the name of the city or country on it, and I put a picture from the trip in it. It gives me daily memories."

"That's a good idea. I see you've been to some fun places. And I see you love the beach." I picked up a picture of her and a guy who seemed to have not missed any of the trips.

"That's Dre being silly." She laughed. "We have been friends since the fourth grade."

"That's a long time, he must be a cool dude."

"Oh yeah, Dre is my boy, he's seen me at my worst." She sat back down on the sofa, and I followed her.

"Tell me more about you. I know you like to travel and bake but what else do you like to do?" We were sitting with about a foot of space between us.

"I love to read. I sew, but not as much as I used to, and I picked up skiing a couple of years ago." She scrunched her nose up. "But I'm not that good."

"Oh yeah? I snowboard."

She sat up straight. "Really? Maybe you can help me with my skiing. There's a place here that has a small slope I've wanted to try."

"Sign me up, I'm there. Not sure how much help I'll be, but I'll be there to catch you when you fall." I gave her a sly smile.

"Thanks for the vote of confidence." She smiled.

"What else?" I was very interested in this woman. She was attractive with curves in all the right places. So much so that it had been a struggle to keep my hands to myself. I was a touchy-feely type dude, and this was like being on punishment. All this danglin' right in front of me and not being able to touch.

"Okay, well you know I have a possible ghetto twin brother, and I also have a sister on my father's side too. My Mom had three children; one boy and two girls."

"And where do you fall in your Mom's lineup?"

"Last but not least." She covered her face with her hands.

"So, you were messing with me because I'm the youngest, and now I find out you're the baby?" I pulled one of her hands away from her face. She was smiling so hard I could see all of those pretty white teeth.

"Yes, I'm the baby. My brother is eight years older than me, and my sister is six years older than me."

"Do they live here?"

"My sister, Summer, lives about ten minutes away from me. My brother lives in California."

"Oh yeah? What part? Remember I told you I was stationed in San Diego for a while?"

"I think he's in the San Bernardino area, but I don't know for sure. He's the family wild card."

"Wild card?" Hmmm. "How often does he visit?"

"He doesn't, last time we saw him I was in high school."

"For real?" Does this woman have any stable men in her life? Her father sounded like a joke, and the brother didn't seem much better. She did mention that friend from fourth grade.

"Macon?"

"Yeah? I'm sorry I must have zoned out." She gave me a suspicious eye. "What's up?"

"I know what you're most likely thinking."

"I doubt it, or you would probably ask me to leave." Her eyes grew wide. *Wait I'm not crazy.* "I'm joking Dawn...relax. Lila would kill me if she found out I did anything to upset her "HOA Girl" as she calls you."

She laughed. "I did not know that was my nickname." She pulled her legs up under her and turned to face me. "But really, I know I've mentioned a father and brother that no one in their right mind would ever trade me for, but those are the only two duds in the family." She stood and walked over to a bookcase next to the mantle to get a picture. She came back and leaned over so that I could see the picture. "Now this is the true fam right here." I looked at the picture and saw a large group of people sitting on a staircase. "We tried to sit according to age, with the youngest at the top."

"This is a nice picture, let me see if I can find you... I see you, how long ago was this taken?"

She had a longing look but still happy. "Exactly two months before my mom passed." She pointed to an older version of herself. "This is her." Her Mom was pretty, and she didn't look sick.

"What happened? If you don't mind me asking? She looks so healthy."

"She wasn't sick, she was at home one day and the next day she was gone. No warning, a heart attack. We had given her a seventieth birthday party the day before this photo. Most of the family was in town for the party, so we took this picture at my sister's house."

She pointed out cousins, a niece, and nephews in the picture and I tried to listen. But, I was thinking about how hard this must be for her, it was the same thing that happened to my father. "You know, Dawn, my father passed similarly. He was in a car accident, but it was the same thing. Here one day and gone the next. I was thirteen, but I remember it like it was yesterday. It was tough for me. I went through a lot of therapy, which is how I went into the field."

Her eyebrows shot up. "I'm sorry Macon, I guess you do know exactly how I feel. And I hope I'm not bringing up bad memories for you."

"No, not at all." I grabbed her hand. "You were saying what was on your mind, and I'm glad you feel comfortable enough to talk to me."

She looked down at the picture again with sad eyes and smiled. "You know, my mother was a great woman, she was the perfect nurturer, she gave us all the love she could. I'm thankful that I had her as my mother."

I squeezed her hand. "Thanks for telling me about her."

"You're very easy to talk too, it doesn't seem like we met this week."

I tapped her on the tip of her nose with my index finger. "That's because you and I don't measure time, remember?"

"Yes, I remember." She smiled.

We were silent for a while, I looked at my watch. It was after 1:00. I didn't want to leave, but I was exhausted. "Dawn, I have enjoyed talking to you tonight, but I have to get some rest."

She jumped up. "I completely lost track of time, let me get your bag of goodies."

I stood and stretched. "Yeah, I can't leave without that."

She walked to the kitchen and came back with my bag and handed it to me. I put the bag on a table and gently grabbed her hands and pulled her into a hug. I pulled back a bit so that I was looking down into her face when she looked up. She lifted up and gave me the gentlest peck on my lips. She stepped back and smiled at me. I shook my head. "Dawn?"

"Macon?" She was still looking up at me.

I moved closer and cradled her face with one hand and reached around her waist with the other. "You know I'm greedy," I gave her a peck on the lips, "and a savage." I pecked her lips again, but this time I stayed in place. She slowly put her arms around me with her hands landing on the back of my neck. I gently ran my tongue across the crease of her lips silently asking for her to open. The moment her lips parted my tongue was in her mouth looking to join with hers. She tasted sweet, and she was so damn warm. I deepened the kiss, but she slowed us down a bit to a nice rhythm. I felt her pull back; I put both of my hands in her hair and pulled her even closer. She moaned, and I almost lost it, so I ended the kiss. I watched her eyes slowly open. I kissed her forehead, then pulled her into a hug, she felt so good. I finally let her go, grabbed her hand and my bag of goodies, then walked to the door. "I would like to see you tomorrow if you're free."

We were at the door facing each other. "I think that can be arranged, what time did you have in mind?"

"Well I get my keys to my place tomorrow. I need to check it out and possibly clean it before the movers come on Monday. I'll do that around ten. Hopefully, it doesn't require too much." I was staring at her and trying not to kiss her again.

"Do you need some help?"

"You would help me clean?" She nodded. "I was going to get my mother or one of my sisters to go, but of course I would prefer if you were there." This woman turned me the hell on!

"Of course, I don't mind."

"I'll text you the address in the morning, it's not far from here."

"Okay. I guess I'll see you in the morning."

I gave her a quick kiss, and she opened the door. "Thanks again, I'll see you in the morning."

"You're welcome, see you in the morning. Bye-bye." I walked out the door and looked back at her, she gave me a little wave, and I smiled at her.

By the time I got home the house was dark and quiet. I went up the stairs to the guest room to shower. When I got out of the shower and was getting into bed, I heard a knock at the door. "Come in."

My mother poked her head in the room. "I see you're home."

"Yes, I am and why are you up so late?" I was getting myself situated in bed.

"I was thirsty."

*Wow, really Momma?* "Okay, see you in the morning."

"Did you have a nice time with my HOA Girl?"

"Yes." I had to cut her short or she would never leave.

"Did she have a nice time?"

"Come on, Momma." I laughed, she was nosey. "I'm tired, and yes Dawn had a nice time."

She smiled. "Okay, see you in the morning." She closed the door. I reached for my phone to send Dawn a text.

Sleep well and thank u 4 going out with me.

**Dawn: You're welcome and thank you too, see you in the morning.**

**Dawn?**

**Dawn: Macon?**

**u moaned.**

**Dawn: OMG! shut up! That slipped out because I'm tired.**

**Confession time?**

**Dawn: I'm pleading the fifth.**

**Can u do it again tomorrow? I want it 4 my ringtone.**

**Dawn: LOL! I can't stand you. Go to sleep.**

Going to sleep now so I can dream about that moan.
Dawn: Sweet dreams.

## Chapter 5 ~ Dawn

I was up extra early and had just returned from the store. I was still excited about my date with Macon last night. He was a little younger than me, but I didn't care. I was tired of always trying to box a guy into a category based on this and that. The new and improved me was going with the flow. I had a couple of hours before I had to meet him at his new place, so I decided I would call my sister. I scrolled through my recent calls and pressed her number. She answered immediately.

"Hey! I'm about to pass your subdivision, I'm coming over." She was loud.

"Okay?" This was odd, why was she out so early? "What's going on? Is something wrong?" I was worried.

"No." I was relieved. "I thought you would be sleeping. I wasn't going to bother you. Are you sleeping better at night now?"

"It depends, some nights I'm fine and then other nights I'm up." I was messing around in the refrigerator looking for food. I knew Summer would want a snack. Every time she came over, she would look around for food. I would offer her something, and she would turn her nose up, only to go back and eat it five minutes later saying how "kinda" good it was.

"Okay, I'm pulling up now, open the door." She hung up. I went and unlocked the door. I decided on a breakfast wrap with scrambled eggs, veggies, and turkey sausage. A few minutes later I heard the front door close.

"HEY! Where you at?" My sister always talked in stereo.

"I'm in the kitchen, Loud Mouth." I heard a couple of small sets of feet. I turned around and saw my sister's two grandkids coming towards me, one boy and one girl. Now those two brought this family joy in the wake of my mom's death. It was hard to believe I was a great aunt or "Level 2 Aunt", as I had dubbed it.

"Ti-Ti! I want the juice." They were now walking circles around my kitchen island and making all sorts of noise.

"Hey babies, come give Ti-Ti hugs." I reached for them and hugged them, kissing each on the forehead and cheek. I hugged my sister as well. "What are you doing out so early? I didn't know you had the kids today."

"I kept them last night, and I didn't want to wake them up so… PUT THAT DOWN!" I laughed to myself. My sister was funny, she could be in mid-sentence, and she'd break it off to yell at a kid in a minute. It was so weird to see her as a grandmother at fifty, but she loved it. She had three children of her own, but to see her with the grandbabies, as she called them, was beautiful. "What are you making?" She looked in my pantry.

"Breakfast wraps. Get the kids animal crackers while you're in there." I kept animal crackers or graham crackers for my babies. "You want a breakfast wrap?"

"Nah, I'm not hungry, we ate before we left the house." I side-eyed her. "But did you bake anything this week? I want something sweet; oh, and the hubby wants some too." She walked into the family room and turned to the cartoon channel for the kids. They were getting situated on my sofa with their animal crackers, preparing to drop crumbs all over the place as usual.

"I did bake some stuff, but I passed it out already. I'll make some for you guys next week." I was busy sautéing peppers and onions.

"Wait 'til I see Dre again, I know his greedy butt took the last of it. When is he going to get a woman, and stop eating up food over here?" She pulled out a bar stool at my island while I stood at the cooktop on the opposite side facing her. She scrolled through her phone; she was a social media junky in denial.

"Dre didn't have any this week." I added my turkey sausage to the skillet, but I didn't look at her.

"Oh really?" She looked up from her phone, but I refused to look at her. "Well, who did you give it to, Janae and Tori?"

"Nope." I turned my back to her and went to wash my hands in the sink. When I turned back, she had her phone down looking at me with a half-smile.

"Then who ate the sweet goods?" She leaned across the island.

"It might have been my date." I whistled and prepped the tortilla flours.

"Hot DAMN!" She jumped up and danced around. She watched too much *Good Times*. "Who is he? I can't believe you didn't tell me!"

"Relax, we just had our first date last night, it's still very new. Stop getting excited." I decided to shoot Macon a text to see if he wanted a breakfast wrap.

**Good morning! Did you eat breakfast? Would you like a breakfast wrap?**

"Whatever, you haven't dated in a while. We worry about you over here by yourself. Who are you texting while I'm talking?" She snatched a piece of sausage off the plate and popped it in her mouth.

"I'm texting Macon, that's his name. We are meeting at his new place in about an hour or so, and I am checking to see if he wants a wrap." I looked at her and smiled.

"Oh, you like him! Offering up food, I know you have a ..." My phone chirped, I had a new text. "Is that him? What did he say?"

"Would you calm down." I picked up my phone.

**Macon: Are u feeding it to me?**

I laughed out loud and typed out a response. Summer came over to look at the phone. She knew she couldn't see over my shoulder with that five-foot-two frame. I turned my back to her.

**Give a person an inch and they take a mile:)**

**Macon: My greediness was established on day one.**

**I guess you're right Mr. James aka The Greedy Savage.**

**Macon: LOL! I prefer Mr. James aka Moan Seeker.**

"What is he saying? This is way too much texting and giggling." Summer was back on her barstool eyeing me.

I was still on my phone. "Umm, okay give me a second."

**LOL! No wrap for you!**

**Macon: six days in and u holding out already?**

**What is this 'time' thing that you speak of?**

**Macon: u got me again on the time...lol... but seriously, I'm finishing up breakfast with Moms. Thank u, you're sweet.**

**See you shortly.**

Summer folded her arms across her chest. "Oh, sorry," I said and gave her a sincere smile. I tapped out a few more screens on my phone to get to Macon's social media page. We became friends a couple of days ago. He said he wasn't a daily user, but he mentioned needing to keep track of his kids and what they were doing. His profile picture was of him sitting on a rock near some water. He wore a t-shirt and shorts, and his legs hung off the side of the rock. His hands rested on his lap while he gazed at the water. He wasn't paying attention to the camera, it was very natural and beautiful. The caption read, "Look at my Dad! #Dab". I passed my phone to Summer and took a seat at the table to eat my wrap. I watched as she slowly looked at the picture then back at me.

She pointed to the screen. "This is him?" The kids ran into the kitchen; I'm sure they smelled the food. I cut off a couple of small pieces of my wrap to give to them.

"Yep!" She didn't say a word. "Fine ain't he?" I laughed and gave the kids some of my food.

"I mean, I have no words. He's ... where did you find him?" She leaned over the island and took the second wrap off the cooktop. I shook my head and laughed to myself.

"Outside." The kids moved over to her and asked for food from her plate. I knew they would want juice soon, so I got their little sippy cups from my cabinet.

"What do you mean outside?" I relayed the story to her while I poured the kids juice. She sat quietly taking in the whole story. "So, you're heading to meet him now? You're wearing that?"

I guess she didn't like my lounge pants with the New York boroughs written all over them. "No, I'm going to shower and throw on something because we will be cleaning." I started cleaning the kitchen, I checked my microwave clock for the time. I had an hour, but luckily his new place was less than five minutes away.

"I know, but don't go over there looking a mess, put on something cute." She wiped the kids off and gathered them to leave.

"I did tell you we met when I was out walking, right? My hair was a mess, and I was sweating like I was under suspicion. Trust me, anything from here on out is a come up."

"Yeah, that's true." I threw the dish towel at her, and she laughed. "Alright kids, let's go see Pa-Pa and let Ti-Ti get ready to go get you a new great uncle."

"Get out of here," I joked. "I'll call you tomorrow, we need to discuss Momma's estate, you know your brother is not cooperating."

Summer rolled her eyes and shook her head. "I can't stand him." Our wayward older brother was a major problem. But, he always did cause trouble, even as a child; I didn't know why either of us was surprised. I'd been stressing about it but there wasn't much I could do, nor was I emotionally ready to deal with it. Just another thing I needed to mend. I hugged Summer and the kids, helped her get them in their car seats and went into the house to get ready.

By the time I got out of the shower, my phone was ringing. It was Janae. "Hey Girl, I was..." She interrupted me.

"Hold that thought and let me pull Tori in." I reached for my body butter and put the girls on my Bluetooth.

"Do I have two callers?" Janae asked.

"Yes!" Tori and I said in unison.

"So how was the date? We were trying to let you sleep in," Janae said quickly.

"I've been up for a while, but Summer and the kids stopped by and they are just leaving." I was trying to find something comfortable but cute to wear.

"Ah, how are those cutie pies doing?" Tori chimed in.

"Adorable as ever, but listen I have to go, I'm meeting Macon shortly. I'm still getting dressed." I knew I sounded winded because I was going back and forth between my closet and my dresser drawers looking for a shirt. I decided on black capri leggings and a yellow shirt that was currently MIA.

"Well damn!" Tori said. "Can we get an update?"

"Leave her alone Tori." Janae sounded amused. "Girl you go and have a good time. We will catch up with you later, but I guess last night went well?" I giggled. "Uh oh," Janae said. "She's giggling, somebody is smitten."

"You damn right she's smitten, didn't you see his pictures?"

I showed the girls Macon's pictures from social media a couple of days ago. Correction, Janae's investigator behind looked him up as soon as I told her his name. It was what we did to watch each other's backs in this crazy world. I could not stop giggling, I found my shirt and decided to knock a few wrinkles out. "Yes, we had a great time last night, we had dinner and drinks in the west end, and then we came back here and talked...oh, and we had ice cream."

Janae started in first. "Tori, our girl has started speaking French overnight, do you hear all the 'we this,' 'we that'...oui-oui?" We all laughed.

"Whatever, Janae." I giggled and pulled my scarf off to comb my hair. "Alright I have to run, Macon is getting the keys to his new place. I'm meeting him there to help tidy up before his furniture is delivered."

Now it was Tori that chimed in. "Alright now, that's what I'm talking about! You go ahead and do your thing. We will catch up with you later."

"Alright ladies! Bye!" I ended the call, grabbed my purse and my cream and gold low top Chucks then headed for the stairs. I was okay on time. I had about fifteen minutes to spare.

After locking the house, I sat in my driveway waiting for my garage door to close before I backed out. As I took my foot off the brake, my phone rang. "You have got to be kidding me, if I had no plans no one would have called me today." I looked over at the phone, it was Dre. "Hey, Dre!" I waved to my neighbor out in her yard across the street.

"Hey Stranger, what's good?"

"Not much I just left the house, where are you headed?"

"I'm on my way to the folks' house. I was going to head your way and see if you wanted to ride to Soulard to get some fruit for Moms, you know she still on that smoothie kick." He hummed lightly to the music in the background. "But it sounds like you out already, where you headed? I can wait for you." I loved getting fresh fruit from the local farmers at Soulard, but not today.

"I'm meeting Macon, he got the keys to his new place. I'm going to help him get it ready before the movers bring his furniture." I was out of the subdivision and driving down the main thoroughfare.

"Alright Dawn, I see you." He laughed. "When do you plan on bringing Big Country around the group so we can iron him out?"

"Shut up Dre! We've only been out once, it's still early." I giggled, I knew Macon would have reminded me of not counting time if he heard me right now.

"It doesn't matter, bring ol' boy around, seems like you diggin' dude already." Dre sounded surprised.

The townhomes were on the left side, I slowed down and turned onto the side street. I could have walked, he lived so close. "I can't lie Dre, he's cool, he's funny. We talk until one or both of us is yawning. And, let me not mention the chemistry. I am really, really attracted to him and..." Dre interrupted me.

"Yeah, I get it, I don't need details," he sighed. "But I'm glad this is working out for you Baby, you deserve something positive after the year you've had."

I found his street. His truck sat in the driveway of a brick front, two-car garage end unit. There was another car parked next to his in the driveway, I pulled in behind Macon. I sat in the car gathering the basket of cleaning supplies I made for him from my early morning store run. I used a bucket instead of a basket, with my favorite cleaning supplies arranged with a fancy bow wrapped around the top. I was a nurturer, definitely got that trait from my momma. "Thank You Dre, I feel good about him. And I know we just met, but I don't have the cynical thoughts I usually have when I meet someone. Or maybe I'm too vulnerable right now, and I'm forcing happiness to replace the sadness, I don't know..." I was panicking. "Oh, my goodness Dre listen to me. I'm sitting in this man's driveway and I'm all up in arms!"

"Dawn, stop it!" He was so stern I jumped. "What the hell just happened here?"

"I don't know," I said quietly. "See this is why I don't need to date right now, I'm a mess."

"Listen, you have to stop and think about what your moms would say to you right now. And we both know she would tell you to stop whining and get in there to that man."

I smiled sadly. "You're right, she would." I took a deep breath and looked in the mirror. "Okay, let me get in here. Thanks for catching me before I derailed." I opened the door, Macon was looking out a window upstairs. I waved to him, he waved and disappeared. "Alright, he saw me, I think he's coming to the door."

"Alright go ahead, and call me later." I opened my mouth to speak, but Dre interrupted. "And Dawn?"

"Yeah?" I was out of the car and reaching in the back for my purse.

"I love you."

"I know Dre, and I love you too. Thanks again for always being there for me."

"Anytime Baby, now go have fun with Big Country," he said playfully and ended the call.

I walked up the walkway, and the door opened, Macon came out in a grey shirt, grey shorts, and sneakers. He was happy to see me; he had the biggest smile. I couldn't control the smile on my face. "Hey, let me take that for you, what is all of this?" He took the bucket from me and pulled me into a one arm hug.

"It's your housewarming basket! I wasn't sure what you needed, so I got the stuff I use on a regular." He looked down at me and then surprised me with a quick peck on the lips.

"Thank you, Dawn, that was very kind of you. I planned to run to the store once you were here and my agent left."

"Oh, is that who's car that is parked next to you? I wasn't sure, and I didn't want to block anyone." He grabbed my hand with his free hand and led us into the townhome. It was very nice and looked brand new.

"Yeah, my real estate agent is still here finishing up the paperwork for the final walk-thru, but she's leaving shortly." We were in the living room, it opened up to a dining room and large kitchen. The walls were painted a neutral color, and the floors were dark wood. "Did you have trouble finding it?"

"Oh no, I've seen these before but never been inside one. I like it." I was looking around when I heard a woman's voice coming from upstairs, I assumed it was the agent.

"Macon?" She sang his name. She came down the steps and stopped when she noticed me. "Oh hello, I'm LaTrice, Macon's real estate agent...you must be one of his older sisters." *No this heifer didn't.* "He has talked so much about his family, it's nice to meet you finally." She walked towards me with her hand out to shake it. "Which sister are you?"

I extended my hand to shake hers. "Hi Latrice, nice to meet you, I'm Dawn, I'm..." She cut me off. I looked at Macon, he shrugged but kept quiet.

"Well good meeting you Dawn, I know you're happy your baby brother is back home, aren't you?" She walked towards Macon, she was a little shorter than me and very thin. She was an attractive woman with medium brown skin and wavy natural shoulder length hair. She wore a pair of cool glasses with a multi-colored frame. She peered over the top of the glasses when she spoke. "Macon maybe we can do a celebratory lunch since we are finished with the walk-thru. Your sister is welcome to join us." She stood next to him touching his arm.

"Thank you for the offer for lunch, but we are going to get this place together." He walked into the kitchen and placed the bucket on the counter then looked through the supplies. I was still standing in the living room. "Dawn, could you come in the kitchen please?" I walked past LaTrice and into the kitchen. Macon didn't say a word, so I looked at the supplies with him. "LaTrice do you have the final paper for me to sign off on for the walk-thru? I don't want to keep you."

"Oh sure, let me grab a pen." She turned and went to her bag near the front door.

I looked up at Macon with my eyes wide. He shrugged his shoulders. I heard her coming back to the kitchen. "Here we are, sign this portion here that everything checks out."

Macon signed the paper. "Thanks again for helping me find this place LaTrice, I think we are going to like it here."

Macon extended his hand. She looked at him over her glasses and slowly took his hand. "Walk me to my car, Macon?" She asked suggestively, fake lashes fluttering.

"Come on Baby, let's see Latrice out." Macon grabbed my hand and pulled me in front of him.

I saw the look in her eyes when she realized I wasn't his sister and that he wasn't interested in her. "No need, I can find my way out." She walked out and didn't look back.

After LaTrice left, I turned to look at Macon. "What just happened?"

He shrugged his shoulders. "That Woman has been flirting with me since I moved here. We worked over the phone, and we didn't have any problems. She was professional. But, once I got here she put it in fifth gear, professionalism gone."

I smiled. "Aww, what's wrong with a woman taking the lead?"

"Nothing, if I want you taking the lead, but she wasn't taking the lead." He brushed a few strands of hair from my face and stood in front of me.

I scrunched my face up. "I'm not following."

He pointed at the door. "That woman there is a huntress, the same way I am a hunter, we don't mix." He leaned in closer. "Now you, on the other hand, were my prey and I hunted you down until I captured you." I stood there like a statue looking up at him. I was mesmerized. "Last night when you kissed me first..." he kissed my lips, "that was taking the lead...see the difference?" I couldn't say a word. I just stared at him.

"Dawn?" He squinted his eyes.

"Macon?" He smiled, and moved to kiss me but, the doorbell rang.

His head popped up. "If that's LaTrice, I'm going off." He quickly walked towards the door. "I don't like to be mean to women, but I will..." He looked out the peephole and turned to me with a lopsided grin. "It's my mother."

I smiled. "Uh-huh, that's what you get."

He gave me a side-eye and opened the door. "Hey Momma, come in." He moved to let her inside.

"Hey Baby, I can't stay but a minute, Brock is in the truck waiting on me, he wants to put some meat on the grill tomorrow and he wants to get to the store. You know how he is about marinating that meat and all that other stuff he does."

I walked towards the living room. "Hi Mrs. Lila, how are you?"

She smiled brightly. "Hi Dawn, I'm fine, how have you been?"

I walked over to hug her. She gave me a big hug. "I'm fine, I can't complain."

Mrs. Lila was a good looking older lady. She was a little taller than me with dark brown skin. She wore her hair in a short grey bob and she was in good shape for her age. Every time I saw her she had on jeans and some sort of shiny shirt and jazzy shoes. Today was no different.

"Has Macon been treating you right?" He looked at the ceiling and shook his head.

"Yes ma'am, he's been nothing but a gentleman." I smiled at Macon.

"I'm his Momma so I know he has a mouth on him, I've heard it." She cut her eyes over at him.

"Momma what are you talking about? And isn't Brock waiting?"

"You let me worry about Brock...anyway, Dawn, I had one of your tea cakes. They taste like the ones my mother used to make but I don't have her recipe, would you mind sharing yours?" Her smile faded.

I immediately recognized her sadness, she had lost her mother too. It was odd that I could see the loss in people now. I never saw it before. "Of course, I don't mind at all."

"Thank you!" She clapped her hands together. "I've been trying for years to recreate that recipe."

"No problem, I can give it to Macon later today."

"Or you could bring it to me and we could sit and talk." She grinned.

I laughed. "I think that's a good idea, I will come by one day next week."

Macon opened the door. "Well I'll go talk to Brock since no one is talking to me."

Mrs. Lila and I laughed. "Boy I'm leaving now, I came to see where it was, I can come back by myself now." She walked out the door and turned back. "Dawn come on out and meet Brock."

I peeped up at Macon and he extended his arm for me to walk outside ahead of him. When I reached the truck I heard sports radio, he let the window down. "Well, you must be Dawn, the woman responsible for making that good cake I had this morning." He smiled at me.

"Thank you for the compliment and nice meeting you Mr. Brock."

"Brock is fine, it's what the rest of them call me." Brock was a good looking older man. He was a lot lighter than Mrs. Lila with a bald head. He appeared to be slim and tall from what I could tell from his truck. He was clean shaven with kind eyes. His golden skin was sun kissed, but flawless. He had crow's feet on the end tips of his eyes when he smiled, but no other wrinkles. Mrs. Lila definitely had a nice catch, he was aging gracefully.

"Okay, Brock." I smiled at him.

"We better get going I have to get my meat together, Dawn you come by for some of my famous BBQ tomorrow. You eat pork, don't you?"

"I sure do." I laughed.

"Good, I like you already." He looked over my shoulder. "Macon, you bring her around tomorrow. And Lila, come get your fine self in this truck."

She giggled and moved fast to get to the truck. "Bye, you two."

After they left, Macon and I went in to start our cleaning. The place was so nice there wasn't much to do. I cleaned the kitchen while Macon handled the two bathrooms upstairs. When I finished I went upstairs and found him sprawled out on the floor in the master bedroom. I walked over to him and sat down. "I thought you were cleaning and you're up here taking a nap."

He opened his eyes. "I'm finished and I'm tired because someone kept me up last night."

"Wonder who that could have been?" I teased.

"Dawn, thank you for helping me." He sat up and moved closer to me. I sat with my legs stretched out in front of me and my hands behind me. He was sitting in the same position but facing me.

"You're welcome, I really didn't mind." I smiled at him. "Do you know how you're going to arrange your furniture?"

"I'll figure it out when it gets here, as long as I have somewhere to sleep I'll be fine. But I do need to get the kids' rooms together, they will be down next weekend."

"That's nice, and speaking of the kids, did you talk to Chloe this morning?" I was curious about her reading me.

"I did." He looked at me with a sly grin.

"Uh-oh, did she say I was loose or something?"

He laughed. "No, she didn't say that, and aren't you too old to be called loose?"

My eyes went wide. "I'm old now? What happened to all that 'we don't measure time' stuff?"

"No, that's not what I meant." He tried not to laugh. "I was trying to say..."

"I'm listening." I had my eyebrows stretched.

"Okay, I'm pleading the fifth." He finally stopped laughing and cleared his throat. "Chloe said she thinks you are okay and that you're pretty, but she will need to meet you to determine more."

I scrunched up my face. "How did she see me?"

"She stalked my social media page after she talked to you, you're the only Dawn on my friends' list; she kind of knew it was you."

I chuckled to myself, now this was funny, I was getting researched by a teen. "I see, like father like daughter? Except, she's all aggressive with her stalking "

"I guess so," he chuckled and stood from the floor. "I do need to figure out where the beds are going in the kids' room, can you assist?" He reached for my hand to help me up.

"Sure, let's do it." I rubbed my hands together excitedly. "Decorating is one of my hobbies. I wanted to be an interior decorator when I was growing up."

"Really? What stopped you?" We were walking down the hall to the two smaller bedrooms.

"I didn't know anyone that decorated for a living, and we didn't have all the decorating shows they have now. I really didn't know what to do, so I decided on computer science."

"But you don't do that either." We were in the larger of the two bedrooms. Macon opened the blinds to let in some light.

"Nope, I decided against that after my first programming class in high school. I'm a visual person so none of it made any sense to me."

Macon walked towards me. "Well, you're in luck because I don't have a designing bone in my body. If you're up for it you can tell me exactly what to do around here. Mia, my ex, is an interior decorator, I never had to deal with it until we were divorced."

"Really? Yes, I would love to decorate for you. But, I'm not a professional, I'm sure it won't look like Mia's work."

Macon smiled. "I'm sure it will look great. Besides I've seen your house and I like your style."

"Thank you." I had the biggest smile on my face. "Okay, so which room is for The Boy and which is for The Girl?" I teased.

"The larger room is for the boys, I have two twin beds for them." He was busy looking at the closet space and I froze. I knew he said he had twins and not triplets, why was there an extra kid?

"Boys?" I stared at him and he finally turned around looking at me with his brows knitted together.

"What do you mean?" Realization finally dawned on him. "Oh damn, I'm sorry I never told you about MJ."

I should have known! This dude was way too good to be true. He had a whole other kid. And the boy was a damn Junior? MJ? Really? I didn't even know why I was mad because the lies usually flowed better than the truth around these parts, so this nonsense was par for the course. Oh well, he could get his knees in the breeze because I didn't fool with liars and people who forgot they had kids! He was dead to me!

"Well I sort of have three kids instead of two kids on a regular, MJ is Mia's stepson and he's the same age as the twins." *Oh... Oops.* "Mia married Mike about three years ago. When we sat the kids down to explain the whole getting a new brother in the house deal, they were cool with it." He walked towards the door and gestured that I follow him. We went next door to the smaller third bedroom. "The first time I went to get the kids after they were all living together MJ came out with an overnight bag too. And of course, Chloe, the speaker for the trio, told the grown folks that since they were a family now that it only made sense that MJ go with us. And how do you say 'no' when you told them to treat each other like siblings?" He shrugged his shoulders. "But MJ is a cool lil' dude so I don't really mind. Mike and Mia also have a two-year old daughter together."

I was beyond ashamed, I had mentally funeralized this man and here he was taking care of his kids' stepbrother. "That is very nice of you, I don't know too many people that would take another kid on a regular basis."

"It's all good, besides Brock has two sons older than me and they were real cool with me as a kid. Hell, they taught me how to drive, so I'm good with the blended family thing."

"You have three sisters and two stepbrothers?"

"Yep!" Macon walked closer to me. "You get a good look at the layout?" I nodded. "I'm getting hungry, you want to go grab some lunch?"

"Sure." I smiled, and we headed for the stairs.

Over the next few days, Macon and I were busy getting his new place together. I was so excited about decorating that we ended up hanging out there most of the time. Janae and Tori decided our group needed to get together for happy hour on Friday and I invited Macon. I knew his kids were coming on Saturday and staying for the next six weeks. I wasn't sure how much time we would be spending together.

# Chapter 6 ~ Macon

"Hey." I was answering Dawn's call and trying to finish up some work at the office before the weekend started.

"How is your day going?" I knew she had gone to pack a few things at her Mother's house a couple of times this week. So, not only was she physically tired, she was emotionally drained.

"I've been busy most of the day, but I'll be leaving here shortly, are you sure I can't pick you up?" We were meeting her friends for an after-work happy hour on the south side of the city.

"No." She yawned. "Excuse me for yawning... you're already close to the happy hour spot so there's no need for you to drive all the way over here to pick me up."

"Dawn you sound exhausted and I don't mind." I was concerned.

"I know, and I appreciate it, but I think Dre went home after work, I'll catch a ride with him and I'll ride back with you. I can't wait for you to meet everyone."

"Okay, that's cool." I wasn't jealous, but I was feeling a certain type of way about this Dre dude, she talked about him a lot. "I'll see you soon."

"Okay, bye." We ended the call.

~~~~~~~~~~~~~

I took the elevator and went up to the rooftop bar area. Luckily it wasn't too hot, my dress pants and shirt were comfortable. I looked around until I saw Dawn walking towards a group of people at a table. Her hair was bouncing all over the place and she had on a gray dress with a bunch of different lengths at the bottom. I couldn't see her feet, but she had to be wearing heels because she appeared taller than usual. As I got closer she looked up. She smiled and walked towards me. When she was close enough to me I reached out to hug her. She definitely had heels on and I was happy, this was the first time I'd seen her wearing tall heels. "You look pretty."

"Thank you," she blushed. "You clean up pretty well yourself."

We stood there for a few seconds staring at each other. "Dawn?"

"Macon?" She smiled.

"Are you going to introduce me to your friends? They are watching us."

"Yes!" She grabbed my hand and led me over to their table. "Hey everybody this is Macon!" Everyone looked familiar from the photos around Dawn's house, but I couldn't match the names with the faces, except Dre. His eyes were narrowed, he was sizing me up, but he didn't say anything.

Dawn started the intros. "This is Janae, Tori, Rob, and Dre," she pointed at each one of them.

I shook hands beginning with the ladies. "Hello, nice to finally meet you all. Dawn talks about you guys a lot."

"Nice to meet you." I think that was Janae.

"Hi, nice to finally meet you as well." The lady with the bright hair spoke. I think that was Tori.

I shook the two dudes' hands, Rob had the dreads, and the other one I knew was Dre. "What's up man?" Rob shook my hand.

"Hey man, what's up?" Dre gave me a firm handshake.

I waited for Dawn to sit, I sat next to her. We were seated on two lounge sofas that curved into a circle with a round table in the middle. Janae, Tori, and Rob were sitting on one sofa. Dre, Dawn and I sat across from them on the other sofa. Dawn was seated between Dre and me, but she was closer to me with her purse next to Dre. The waiter came over to me. "Hello, can I get you anything to drink or an appetizer?"

"Sure...Dawn would you like anything?"

"We ordered our food and drinks. I ordered an appetizer for you already."

"I'll take a vodka tonic." The waiter took my order and walked away. "And thank you for ordering my food." I winked at her, and she smiled.

"Is this what we are going to watch all night? You two cheesing at each other?" Tori asked.

I shrugged my shoulders. "If it makes this lady right here smile then I guess so."

"My Man!" Rob reached over and gave me some dap. "See that's how you do it, you come hard right out the gate!"

Dre looked at him and said, "You've been married a whole lifetime, you don't know a thing about the ladies, other than the one you got!" I laughed, these two were characters.

"Alright, Alright, let's not start in front of company," Janae said.

The waiter showed up with the food and my drink a few minutes later. We all started talking and eating. Dawn and I were talking to each other, Dre leaned over towards us. "Macon what have you been gettin' into since you moved here?"

"Not much, I've been working and trying to get settled before my kids come down for the rest of the summer."

"That's what's up... but I see you've been keeping our girl busy; we haven't seen her much." He took a few sips from his drink.

Dawn looked at him. "Really Dre?" He shrugged and continued staring at me waiting for me to respond. I looked across at the others; they were all looking at me.

I finally decided I needed to ease their minds. These people were Dawn's friends, and I knew they were looking out for her making sure I was on the up and up. They had nothing to worry about because I didn't plan on going anywhere. We had great chemistry, and it was easy. And I knew if we had this much fun talking, the sex would be even better. She was sexy without trying, and I could not stop imagining her legs wrapped...

"Macon?" Dawn whispered, and everyone watched me.

I cleared my throat. "See what she does to me?" I brushed her hair away from her face and looked into her eyes. "But you're right Dre, I have been keeping Dawn to myself since we met, I enjoy being around her."

"I like him already!" Tori said.

"Oh yeah!" Janae cosigned.

"Didn't y'all meet like a week ago?" Dre mumbled. Dawn's head turned so fast in his direction I thought it would snap off.

Before Dawn could say anything to him, I grabbed her hand and answered. "You're right we did meet almost two weeks ago, but we don't get caught up in time, do we Baby?" I leaned over and kissed her cheek. She was smiling from ear to ear.

"That's right!" I saw her side eye Dre, and he shook his head.

After another round of drinks, the conversation seemed to be going well. I could tell this was a tight group and they were very protective of their own. I was having a good time, they were all funny and seemed to warm up to me. Everyone except Dre. He watched Dawn and me like a hawk, and I was starting to think he considered himself to be a little more than a longtime friend. I understood looking out for your girl, but he was taking it a little too serious. Dawn excused herself to go to the ladies' room with Janae. A minute or so later, Tori left the table to take a phone call, leaving me with the fellas. After a few moments of silence, Dre spoke up.

"Ay man, you seem like cool people." He reached over and gave me some dap. Rob nodded in agreement.

"Thanks, man." I waited to see where he was taking the conversation before I said anything more.

"Dawn has been through and is still going through a lot. I want to make sure you got her back. She doesn't need anybody playing around with her right now, so if you ain't for real, then brotha needs to move on." He leaned back and put one arm across the back of the sofa.

I had to make a quick decision; I decided to entertain this fool for Dawn's sake. I knew if I didn't, I wouldn't stand a chance with her. Yeah, we had this not counting time thing going on but, I knew for sure no matter how much time I didn't count, this dude had over thirty years of Dawn time under his belt. I leaned forward and put my glass on the table. "Listen, man I get where you are coming from, and I have no plans to play around with her. I know exactly what she's going through, I've been there, so I understand."

"That's good to know Man, good lookin' out," Rob said, but Dre shook his head no.

"No disrespect, but I thought your people lived in Dawn's subdivision?" Dre's forehead was wrinkled.

"My father is deceased; my mother and stepfather live there." My patience was wearing thin.

"See that's what I'm talking about, she doesn't have ANY parents left. She doesn't have a father, her moms did it all. So now..." Rob cut Dre off.

"Come on Dre, he knows what you're saying." Rob tried to smooth it over, but Dre kept going.

"Naw Rob. You saw her! She was messed up, and she's finally pulling herself together. She's even sleeping some nights. All I'm saying is that damn woman ain't the one to be played with so..." he paused. "Okay look, man, maybe I'm coming at you all wrong. All

I'm saying is she's not as strong as she looks, so please don't play with her." He looked at me then looked over at Rob. I could tell Rob didn't know what to say; he messed around with his phone. I picked up my drink and drained the glass. I wanted to be mad, but I couldn't. He was sincere as hell, and he put something on my mind. Was I ready to have her back the way she needed me too? Now, I was questioning it myself. Just as I opened my mouth to respond, I felt Dawn's hand on my shoulder. I stood to let her in. Janae and Tori were moving into their seats; it was quiet.

Janae looked at me then Dre and Rob. "Okay, what's going on? Macon what did Dre say?" Janae said, and side-eyed him.

Dre threw his hands up. "Why does it always have to be me?"

"Because it's always you," Tori said.

Dawn was burning a hole in the side of my face; I couldn't look at her. She nudged me. "Are you okay? You ready to go?"

I finally looked at her; her eyebrows knitted together. "I'm cool, we can stay as long as you want." I was trippin'. The conversation picked up again, we sat and talked for another thirty minutes. Dawn seemed to relax, so I was cool. I thought a little more about what Dre said, but I let it go. I was interested in this woman; I planned to see how far things would go between us no matter what he said. I got where he was coming from, but I wasn't concerned.

"Alright ladies and gentlemen, the wife is home, I'm heading out." Rob put a few bills on the table. He hugged Janae and Tori, gave Dre some dap then hugged Dawn. He dapped me up. "Alright Macon, good to finally meet you. I'm sure I'll see you soon." He leaned in and said, "Don't trip off Dre, he's lookin' out for Dawn." I nodded, and he left.

Janae and Tori gathered their purses and phones to leave, and Dawn yawned. I signaled for the waiter to bring the check. The waiter came right away. "Sir, the bill has been taken care of already."

I was confused; I looked at Dawn. "Thank you," she said to the waiter, and he walked away. "Macon, we took care of the bill when we went to the restroom."

"Thank you but...." She placed her index finger on my lips.

"You're welcome." She smiled and lifted an eyebrow. I wanted to pull her finger into my mouth. "I invited a handsome young man out, and I wanted to pay for his food." I kissed her on the cheek.

"I hope you paid for mine too!" Dre yelled as we all stood.

"Shut up! And yes, I paid for yours." Dawn laughed. We said our goodbyes and left.

Dawn and I rode in silence for most of the ride home. The radio was on, but it was low. I was still thinking about some of the things Dre said, and wondering if he was going to be a problem in the future. "What did Dre say to you?" I could feel her watching me.

"Not much, the usual man stuff." I didn't want to tell her what he said because I wasn't quite sure how she would react.

"Uh-huh, I bet." She laughed. "You know I've known him since we were kids and I know him very well. I want you to know that his thoughts and opinions belong to him, and not me." I didn't say anything, so she kept going. "Dre has been a great friend forever, but this year is the worst he's ever seen me, and I know it scared him."

Hmmm, now I was confused. "How so?"

"Dre was used to me being the strong one and not letting much get me down. But seeing me break down emotionally after my mom passed changed things for him. Now he looks at me like I'm fragile and I'll break at any moment. His mission is to protect me from anything or anyone that could break me again, and that means you in his eyes." She looked at me with a sad smile.

I grabbed her hand; we were sitting at a stop light not far from her home. "Dawn I like you, I want you to know I have no intentions of causing you any kind of pain."

"I really hope you change your mind about that in the near future."

"I..." Wait! What? I stared at her, and she laughed out loud. What was...OH! Damn! "Really Dawn?" I laughed too. "I'm over here puttin' my feelings all out on the table, and you crack a sex joke?"

She was laughing so hard. "I wish you could have seen your face!"

The light changed, I turned my attention back to the road. "I really can't believe you." I was still chuckling and shaking my head.

"I'm sorry, Macon." She grinned.

"No, you're not." I side eyed her playfully. This was one of the reasons I liked her. Yeah, she had a lot going on, but this woman knew how to laugh and have a good time. I enjoyed being around her and from what I could tell she enjoyed being around me.

"No, really I am sorry, I wanted to lighten the mood. I like you too Macon, and I want you to know that no matter what Dre says or thinks, this thing we got going on is between YOU." She pointed at me then herself, "and ME. I know Dre is concerned, and I understand it. But, I can't let my broken heart keep me from living, my mom wouldn't want that for me." She smiled at me.

"So, we got a thing going on?" I looked at her, and she blushed.

"Most definitely." She blew me a kiss.

"And Dawn?" I paused. "I can guarantee you it will be all pleasure and no pain." She stared at me with her mouth open.

~~~~~~~~~~~~

The next morning, I went to Columbia to meet Mia and Mike to pick up the kids. I was sleepy, I stayed at Dawn's talking and laughing until almost four in the morning. I wanted to call her before I left but she needed the rest, so I shot her a text letting her know I would see her later this evening. The more time I spent with her, the more I liked her. I hoped she felt the same way. I would have invited her to come to Columbia with me, but I didn't want to torture her with Chloe for the one-and-a-half-hour ride back. I also didn't know if she would be comfortable meeting the kids and Mia at the same time, and so soon. Last Sunday she came to my parents' house for Brock's BBQ. They loved her, well my mom already knew her; but, Brock was impressed with her cakes. She made a 7-Up cake for them and a gooey butter cake for me. Luckily, my sisters didn't stop by nor did Dale, my oldest brother. I wasn't ready to expose her to all that nonsense yet. I was sure my mother conveniently forgot to mention the BBQ to the family because she knew it would have been too much. But, somehow Donald happened to drop by and made a fool out of himself. I laughed thinking about it. That clown saw Dawn helping Mom in the kitchen and damn near tripped over his own feet trying to get in there. After I introduced them he said nothing; he watched her to the point that she eyed me. I explained later that he was shy and asked if she had any friends. She said she would think about it, but I knew that was code for "Hell NO!" My phone rang. I looked at the screen on the dashboard, speak of the devil.

"Wad up, D?" I greeted Donald.

"Not much man, where you been? I called you a few times this week."

"I know, I've been busy trying to get the house ready for the kids, that's where I am now, picking them up in Columbia." I already knew he wanted to know if Dawn said anything about her friends.

"Cool, so the young'uns comin' down to chill?" Donald loved my kids.

"Yeah, they will be down until school starts."

"That's what's up...but on the real, your girl is cool." *Here we go.* "Did she say anything about me?"

"Like what?" I decided to mess with him.

"You know how chicks are, they like to match make."

I tried not to laugh. "Nah playa, she didn't say anything."

"Oh." He sounded a little sad.

"But I did meet two of her female friends last night, they are cool people."

"Oh yeah? You think I might like one of them?"

"Yeah, probably her friend Tori, but I'm not sure of her situation." My call waiting buzzed. It was Dawn.

"Hook ya brotha up." Donald was excited.

"A'ight, let me see what I can do. This is Dawn calling now, I'll call you when I get back."

"Okay, tell her I said hi." I shook my head; now I had to figure out a way to get Dawn to introduce Donald to Tori.

"Yep!" I ended the call and answered Dawn's call. "Good morning, Sleeping Beauty." I was smiling already, and I hadn't even heard her voice.

"Well good morning to you to Handsome Sailor." I could tell she was smiling.

"How did you sleep?"

"I slept like a log. I'm kind of groggy. How far are you from Columbia?"

I pulled into the Columbia Mall parking lot and found a parking space. "I'm here, but they aren't here yet."

"Glad you made it safely." She paused for a second. "You said in your text that you wanted to see me this evening, but won't you be hanging with the kids?"

I knew where this was going; she thought we were going on pause because the kids would be there. "Dawn, I don't plan on not seeing you because my kids will be with me." She was quiet. "My kids aren't small anymore; I usually have to make an appointment to see them when they're in St. Louis. Between my nieces and nephews and the cousins they have on Mia's side they will use my place like a hotel."

"Okay, I was just checking, I understand if we did need to see each other less. You know I'm a big supporter of daddy time," she chuckled.

"I appreciate you saying that. I will probably have to make them hang with me at some point, which brings me to my next question. Would you like to meet them while they're here?" I wasn't sure how she felt about meeting them so soon, but I was cool with it.

"Umm, sure that would be fine with me." She hesitated.

"Dawn there's no pressure, either way is fine with me."

"No Macon, it's fine. I would love to meet your children. Besides, I'm sure Chloe already has my credit report and tax returns anyway." We both laughed.

"You're probably right, and she's not going to rest until she meets you in person. Before I forget, my brother, Donald, wants to know if you have any single friends, I was thinking maybe Tori." She was quiet, then she whistled. This woman was something else, I chuckled. "Dawn, did you hear me?"

"Was somebody talking to me?"

I couldn't help but laugh. "Come on, he's not that bad. He's shy around beautiful women, but he warms up and is cool."

"Are you serious? Tori would eat him up and spit him out. I don't think he could handle Tori nor do I think he would want too."

"Hold up, that's my brother you're talking about, and I know for a fact he could handle Tori. He's a good dude." We were still laughing.

"If you say so, but let me talk to her and see what she says, we may have to do a happy hour and invite him."

I saw Mia and Mike's truck turning into the parking lot. "Hey Baby, the kids are pulling up, I have to go but a happy hour would work."

"Okay, I'll see you this evening but text me to let me know you all made it safely."

"Will do, have a good afternoon and get some rest, you didn't sleep long."

"I wish I could sleep another couple of hours, but I'm going to Soulard with Dre to get fruit...You want anything for the kids?"

Does this cat hang with anybody else other than her?... Alright, Macon check yourself, this jealousy thing ain't you at all. I knew I was trippin' and I knew ol' boy was worried about her, so I needed to chill. "No thank you, Sweetheart, I'm going to the store when we get back."

"Macon, I don't mind, and the fruit is so much fresher and cheaper than the grocery store." She was very helpful.

Mike pulled up in front of me, and the kids got out and stretched. "You're right, I would appreciate it. They eat pretty much anything."

"Alright, I'm on it and be safe driving back."

"I will, bye."

"Bye-bye." She ended the call.

I watched Chloe do some type of yoga move that had her looking up at the sun. I shook my head and couldn't help smiling at my Baby Girl I jumped out of my truck, and Chloe ran over to me. "Hi, Daddy!" I hugged her tight.

"Hey, Baby Girl!" Chloe looked like me, same brown complexion and athletic build. She was about five-eight, the same height as her brother, Major. He hated that they were the same height, but I promised him he would get taller. Chloe was my little hippie; she had on a short blue sundress and blue Chucks. Her hair was always in a big puff ball at the top of her head. She loved anything natural or homemade. She wasn't into make-up or clothes or any of the other things most girls were into at sixteen. She ran to the back of their truck to get her bags.

"Hey Dad!" Major yelled from the back of their truck. He and MJ were pulling out their luggage.

"Hey Mac!" MJ yelled.

I went over to the driver's side of the truck to talk to Mike and Mia. "Hey boys, the back is open. And make sure you carry your sister's luggage." I heard them groaning.

"Hey Macon," Mike said. I shook his hand.

"What's up Mike?... Hey Mia." I leaned down to see her face. She was reaching in the back to adjust their sleeping two-year-old daughter's clothes.

She leaned over the console. "Hey, Casanova." She grinned.

I couldn't help but grin back at her. I guess Chloe told her about Dawn. Mia was an attractive woman with caramel skin and a puff ball on top of her head like Chloe's. But, Mia wasn't as tall, she was about five-two with a bold attitude. The kids moved over to my truck and started loading up. "I see your daughter can't keep her mouth shut." I chuckled, and Mike shook his head.

"You know Chlo can't hold water." Mia laughed then turned serious. "Or as she says, it stagnates her energy if she keeps secrets." Mia laughed again. "That's your nosy daughter....so you're dating somebody already? You ain't been there but a minute."

"You are worse than Chloe!" Mike said and put his head down. "I'm sorry Macon, you know how they are."

"Yeah, the apple didn't fall far from the tree."

"Or the root." Mia paused. "Because I know your momma has binoculars she uses in the neighborhood on a regular." We all laughed; she knew my mother.

"Alright, let me get back on the road. Be safe going back."

"You're not going to tell us about Dawn?" I knew she wouldn't let it go.

"Nope!" I walked off and waved to them.

"That's alright, Chloe will tell me all about her." I could hear her laughing as I got in my truck. They pulled off and blew the horn.

I got situated in the car and looked back at the boys, Chloe was in the front seat. "Alright is everyone ready?" I pulled off.

As soon as we got off the parking lot, Chloe started. "Daddy, where's Ms. Dawn? Are we going to meet her?"

"Who's Ms. Dawn?" Maj asked.

"Yeah, who is Ms. Dawn?" MJ asked.

I thought their headphones were on. I had to kill all of this. "Dawn is a friend, and yes you will most likely meet her." Chloe tried to say something, but I cut her off. "And there won't be any more questions about Dawn." The boys shrugged, but Chloe had a sly grin on her face.

# Chapter 7 ~ Dawn

I was checking my mailbox at the curb when Dre turned onto my street. I was slightly pissed at him; I knew I needed to talk to him before he said anything else to Macon. He stopped in front of my house and lowered the passenger window. "You ready?"

"Yes, let me grab my purse, I'll be right back." I turned to walk up the driveway.

"Dawn?" I looked over my shoulder. "What's wrong?"

Dre knew I was upset, it was written all over my face. "Give me a minute; I'll be right back."

I went into the house and grabbed my purse. By the time I came back outside, I saw him fidgeting as I walked towards his truck. I got in and put my seatbelt on, but I wouldn't look at him. I knew he was watching me.

"Hey." I finally looked at him. "I'm sorry okay? I'm worried about you, I don't want anyone messing around with you if they aren't serious."

"What are you talking about?" I crossed my arms over my chest and stared at him.

"You're mad because I said something to ol' boy, right?"

"Oh, so you did say something to him?" He turned his head. "Don't get quiet now, tell me what you said."

"See, that's exactly why I said something to him!" He had the nerve to raise his voice. I narrowed my eyes. "His weak butt went crying to you, and now you're all upset. If he can't handle a few words from a friend, then how is he supposed to be there for you? How old is he anyway? He looks like a big ass baby?" He backed out of the driveway.

I knew I needed to stay calm, but I wasn't having it with him today. "First of all." I hated doing a countdown. "Macon did not say a word to me about your little talk. I was at the bar paying the bill, and I saw YOU over there holding court. When I went back to the table, I knew exactly what was going on because all of you were quiet." He kept driving and wouldn't look at me. "Second, I know you are concerned about me, but I will not allow you to bully Macon."

"Bully? He's bigger than me!" His voice was high pitched.

"You know what I'm saying Dre. Macon has been nothing but nice to me and I think he was extra nice by tolerating that conversation of yours. That could have easily gone a different way if he were a lesser man. I'm sure he let it go because he knows how long you and I have been friends. And he's thirty-seven if you must know."

He scrunched his face as if he smelled something foul. "Thirty-seven? Since when did you start messing around on the playground?"

"He's thirty-seven, NOT twenty-seven! And what happened to you wanting me to date? I finally meet someone that I like, and you act a DAMN FOOL the first time I bring him around!!!" So much for staying calm. I was angry and for some reason, on the verge of tears. I crossed my arms over my chest and tapped my foot uncontrollably.

Dre pulled off the street and into the parking lot of a strip mall. He found a space and put the car in park then faced me. "You're right, I'm sorry, and it won't happen again." His voice was low.

"NO! That's what you should have said when I first got into the truck! You're only saying it now because you think I'm mad at you! You're not being fair to me, and it's RUDE AS HELL! I'm finally smiling and enjoying myself with someone, and you try to jack it up?" I threw my hands in the air. "Do you want me crying and sad all the time!?" I had no idea why I was so angry with him, but I could not control it. He stared at me. He didn't know what to do with me right now, and neither did I. I turned away from him and looked out the window. I rarely got upset to the point of yelling, but I guess this was what happened when your emotions were raw and exposed. We were both quiet for a minute.

He tried to speak, but my phone rang. I dug through my purse to find my phone; it was Macon. "Hey, are you back?" I tried to sound chipper.

"Yes, we just got to the house. I'm going to unload the kids' luggage, then go to my parents' house." Tears slipped from my eyes. I had no idea why I was crying, but when I heard Macon's voice, I wanted him to hug me. He continued talking. "Brock is on the grill again."

I found a tissue in my purse and wiped my eyes. I was mad at Dre, but I knew deep down the tears weren't because of him, it was one of those moments that crept up when I least expected.

"I'm sure the kids will enjoy it, he's good on the grill." I tried to clear my voice, so he wouldn't know I was crying.

"Hey, you okay Baby?" His voice was low.

I cleared my throat. "Yes, I'm fine. I'm still out, but I won't be gone long. I'm going to take a nap when I get back."

"If you hadn't kept us up all night neither of us would be sleepy." I grinned, I felt a little better. I didn't know what it was about him, but he could bring comfort to me and relax me.

"That's right blame me." I laughed a little.

"Yep, I'm blaming you." He chuckled. "I gotta run, Sweetheart, but you get home and get some rest. And I will see you later."

"Okay, see you soon." I ended the call.

I looked at Dre; he was staring out the window. "Dre?" He looked at me with his eyebrows raised. "I'm sorry, I didn't mean to have a meltdown on you today."

"Nah, don't apologize. I deserved it. I was out of line. I heard how he calmed you down without even trying. I want you to be happy Dawn, and if he does it for you, then I'm cool with it."

I smiled at him. "Thanks, Dre. I do like him. And you're right, hearing his voice is soothing. It's different with him, I feel like we have a connection and I can't explain it. I know we just met, but I've spent so much time with him it feels like I've known him a lot longer."

"That's great Dawn, you deserve it." He reached out and grabbed my hand.

"Thanks, Dre. I do appreciate your friendship, but you know I've been doing this dating thing for years, I can handle it." I squeezed his hand. "So, what if he hurts my feelings later? All I know is that right now, he makes me feel good. I don't want to miss out on something good because I'm protecting my feelings. It's too exhausting." I didn't know if I truly believed what I was saying, but I wanted to believe it.

Dre let my hand go and ran his hands down his face. "I know you're right, I'll chill and give you your space."

I pulled him into a quick side hug and kissed his temple. "Thank you for looking out for me, especially this year."

Dre leaned back to rest his head on the headrest. "You know I got you." He turned to look at me. "But I'm telling you now if Big Baby is playing you..." He shook his head, and my mouth dropped open. I couldn't with him and the nicknames.

"Big Baby? Really? I can't stand you!" We both laughed. "You are so wrong! Let's go so the fruit isn't picked over."

Dre drove across the parking lot to get us back to the street. "Why are you worried? You never buy much fruit anyway."

"I know, but I'm getting some for Macon's kids, he picked them up this morning." Speaking of which I decided to text him to make sure no one was allergic to anything.

"You MUST like him." Dre whistled. "You out buying food for kids and stuff."

"Be quiet." I chuckled and pulled my phone out. "... and yes, I do like him. A lot."

**Do your kids have any allergies to any fruit?**

"How are things with the lady on your block?" My head was down looking at my phone.

**Macon: Hey, no, nothing will go to waste.**

"She's cool for now."

I peeped over at him and gave him a side eye. "I guess that's code for she won't be around long."

**Gotcha. Anything in particular you want? What's your favorite fruit?**

**Macon: Watermelon... and yours?**

**Ditto:)**

**Macon: I see this thing we got going on keeps getting better.**

I giggled, and Dre looked over. "I guess you over there texting with Big Baby now? Didn't you just talk to him?"

"You better stop calling him that. And yes, we just talked but so what." I was all smiles; I kept texting.

**Yes it does:) I'll get you a melon**

**Macon: Thanks, but I have a request.**

**Which is?**

I was smiling so hard my cheeks were starting to hurt. Dre looked amused; he had a half smile.

**Macon: You must feed it to me:)**

I threw my head back laughing. "He is a mess!"

**LOL! I see the Greedy Savage has returned.**

**Macon: He's always around... waiting.**

**Goodbye!**

**Macon: LOL! See you soon Sweetheart.**

I put my phone away, and noticed Dre watching me. "Dawn I've never seen you this ... umm, what's the word... giddy."

"Dre, I told you, he feels good." I wrapped my arms around myself and closed my eyes. I exhaled deeply.

"You didn't seem this happy when you met your ex."

I dropped my arms and opened my eyes. "That's not true, I was very happy with him in the beginning, but this feels different. I can't explain it."

"If Big Baby makes you this happy then I'm all for it."

I stopped smiling. "I'm glad you feel that way because if you say something to him again, I will hurt you." I shook my fist at him.

"It's like that? I thought you were my Day One?"

I turned the volume up on the radio and danced in my seat.

~~~~~~~~~~~~

Later that evening, I was waiting for Macon to come by and pick up the fruit for the kids. I was sitting on the sofa in my family room looking out at the lake watching the sunset. I thought about my argument with Dre again. I knew he was trying to help, but I couldn't understand why he would broach the subject the first time I introduced Macon to the group. He was always protective, but this was a little out of character for him. The doorbell interrupted my thoughts. As I walked to the door, I felt a few butterflies in my stomach. I was excited to see Macon. I could see the outline of his large frame through the frosted side window in the front door. I put my hand on the doorknob and rested my forehead on the door. I took a couple of deep breaths and opened the door.

"Hi Macon, come on in." *Did I sound too excited?*

He came in holding a plate wrapped in foil. He reached for me with his free arm and gave me a one-armed hug. "Hey, this plate is for you, courtesy of Brock." He smiled.

"Well thank you." I took the plate and went towards the kitchen, he followed.

"He put some food on the grill for the kids, and he insisted that I bring you some. You really shouldn't have told him his BBQ is the best in St. Louis." Macon shook his head.

I pulled the foil back and smelled the food. "I didn't lie." I replaced the foil and put the plate in the refrigerator. "He knows his way around a grill."

"I'll admit he's good, but I might be better." He took a seat at the kitchen table and flashed a smile. I saw a dimple; I don't think I noticed that before now.

I gathered the boxes of fruit on the counter. "You grill?" I turned to look at him.

"No, I don't grill, I 'cue." He had one eyebrow up. "You've been out on that east coast too long talking about grilling. You know it's called 'cue-in' in the Lou." We both laughed.

I turned back to the fruit boxes. "You are right about that one." I popped a grape into my mouth. "Well, I'll be the judge of your skills versus Brock's."

He walked over to the counter where I was standing. "Please tell me all of this fruit is not for me."

I looked up at him. "No, it's not all for you, it's for your children." I smiled. "I got there towards the end of the busy time, I was able to get a lot for a good price."

"Thank you, Dawn, I really do appreciate this. The kids will devour this before the week is out."

"Good...now tell me more about your 'cue-in' skills." I placed a few grapes in a paper towel and handed them to him. He took the grapes and ate one. He plucked another grape off the vine and put it up to my lips. I smiled and gladly accepted it. He grabbed my hand and pulled me gently to the kitchen table for us to sit down. He had on a black V-neck t-shirt and dark gray cargo shorts. When he sat down his shorts rode up just enough to expose the bottom of his thighs. Mmmm-hmmmm, all of that jogging definitely paid off.

"Actually, Brock taught me everything I know about barbecue." He ate a few more grapes and then fed one to me. "It's how we ended up bonding after I lost my father." I was all ears, chewing my grape slowly. "My mother had known Brock for years; they went to high school together. His first wife passed a couple of years before my father, and mom went to him for advice about family grief since he had two boys." I slightly gasped and put a hand over my mouth. "One thing led to another, and they started dating. I hated him; I felt like she was trying to find a new daddy for me and I didn't like it. One day he came over with a grill and asked me to help put it together. My mother made me go out in the backyard with him, but I wouldn't talk. He was cool about it, he told me to hand him the tools, and he would do all the talking." I was so engrossed in the story, I didn't realize Macon had a grape at my mouth until he tapped on my lower lip with it. I took it and waited for him to continue. "He talked about all sorts of stuff, and then he told me that he had a talk with his sons about him dating my mother. He told me they didn't like her." My mouth dropped open. "Of course, that broke my silence, and I went off about my Mother never doing anything to them and how they didn't know her, and they better not disrespect her in front of me. I was mad as hell, and Brock stood there looking at me. He told me his boys said the same thing about me, so maybe I should meet them because we seemed to have a lot in common."

My arms were folded in front of me. "Hmmmm, what did you say?"

Macon offered me the last grape, and I shook my head, he popped it into his mouth and chewed slowly. Even his chewing was sexy. I waited with baited breath for him to finish the story. "Well, I went in the house and told my mother. She told me how bad she would feel if those boys didn't like her, and it just clicked for me. I decided to give Brock a chance because I knew I wanted his boys to do the same for my mother. Soooo, I went back outside and helped Brock with the grill. Neither of us said a word."

"Awwww, that is the sweetest story." I playfully dabbed my eyes as if I were crying. "I'm assuming you never had an issue with the boys? You and Donald seemed to be very close from what I saw last Sunday."

"Oh yeah, Dale and Donald are my brothers. And the story Brock told me, and my mother cosigned, was just that – a story they wove." He shook his head slowly and laughed.

"What? Are you serious?" I got up and went to the refrigerator to get us some water. His eyes followed me. I was glad I had on something cute. I was wearing a simple red cotton t-shirt dress. It was slightly fitted and hit me at the knees.

"Yep! They told me about ten years ago that they made it up. We laughed about it." He shrugged his shoulders. "It was something I needed at the time, it's all good." I handed him a bottle of water and gestured for him to follow me into the family room. "I noticed your magnet collection over there." I stopped and turned to look. "I wouldn't have pegged you as a magnet collector."

I continued walking with him trailing behind me. "I wasn't until recently. It's my mom's collection, and I'm continuing it for her." I sat on the sofa and kicked my feet up on the ottoman in front of me. Macon sat next to me and stretched his arm across the back of the sofa. I slid the ottoman over so that we could share. He put his legs across the ottoman; they were so long his feet were hanging off the other side. "Anytime I traveled I would bring her a magnet, and she would put them on her refrigerator. She loved them, but they had to be unique, not the simple magnets." I chuckled. "The last magnet I got for her was from Hawaii. I remember it took about four days to find the perfect one. It was the oddest thing; I probably looked at thirty different magnets during that trip." I took a sip of my water. "After she passed I couldn't get rid of them; a friend suggested I continue with the collection, so that's what I'm doing."

Macon reached over and softly rubbed the back of my hand. "That's a good idea."

I smiled. "It's therapeutic, and I feel like she's traveling with me now. Is that weird?"

He shook his head. "Not at all. You should do whatever you need to do to make you feel better."

I sat up. I completely forgot his kids were in town. "Where are your kids? Do you need to go? Don't let me keep you."

He squeezed my hand and pulled me back on the sofa. He smelled good, like soap with a hint of cologne. "Naw, I'm good. I told you I have to make appointments with them when they are in St. Louis. The boys are at my older sister's house hanging with my nephews. Chloe is at the youngest of my older sister's house with my niece. I won't see them for two or three days, then they will all come to my house for a couple of days. They will rotate around the whole time. You'll meet them before they leave. Chloe has already asked about you."

I laughed. "Not a problem, let me know when." I finished off my water. I was hungry, Brock's plate was calling my name. "I'm hungry, would you like anything to eat or something a little stronger than water to drink?"

He brushed my hair behind my ear. "I'll take a drink, what do you have?"

"I have a bar in the basement, I can make you anything your taste buds desire." I stood up.

"Lead the way."

A couple of hours later Macon and I were sitting at the bar in the basement laughing and talking about all sorts of things. "Okay, old school rap. Who's your favorite?" Macon asked, and took a swig of the vodka drink I made for him. We had been playing this 'favorite things' game for the past hour. We were both tipsy.

I looked at the ceiling as if I were contemplating. "Eric B. and Rakim, hands down."

He choked on his drink a little. "I was not expecting you to say that."

"Why?" I side eyed him. "You think I'm a stick in the mud or something?" I crossed my arms.

"No... well maybe a little." I playfully pushed his arm, and he laughed.

"What did you expect for me to say?"

"I don't know, but I didn't expect you to say Rakim, I figured you for lightweight rap. Not many women I know would say that's their favorite old school rap."

"Uh-huh, your turn." I walked around to the inside of the bar to start cleaning up and putting the bottles away. "I'm listening."

"Hmmm, I would have to say Tupac." I reached for his glass.

"You want another?" He shook his head no. "Okay that's a respectable artist and common, I could see that. But weren't you a little young to be listening to Tupac?" I had my back to him washing the glasses at the sink. A moment later, I felt him behind me. He took the glass out of my hand and turned me to face him. Before I could say a word, his lips were on mine. His tongue was so deep in my mouth I could barely catch my breath. His hands were cradling my face, and I wrapped my arms around his waist. The feel of his solid body against my breast had my nipples pebbling. I tasted the vodka in his mouth and smelled it as he breathed. The taste and the smell of the vodka mixed with his natural manly scent was an aphrodisiac. I knew I needed to end this kiss before it went too far, but I could not find the strength to pull back. It had been a long time since I'd had sex and he was awakening all sorts of closed off feelings. I got greedy and wrapped my arms around his neck and stood on my toes to get closer to him. His hands left my face and traveled down the sides of my body as he pulled me closer. I didn't know how but I deepened the kiss even further. His lips were the perfect size, full and soft. I felt his erection growing on my lower stomach, "mmmm." *Did I moan?* I really didn't care; he felt so good. His hands roamed all over my hips and butt. Something vibrated on my leg. What the...? Oh! His phone was ringing. He ended the kiss and put his forehead on mine. He let out a long breath.

"I'm sorry Dawn, I need to answer this. It's probably my kids."

I smiled up at him. "No, go ahead, it's fine." I moved over and patted my hair down. I had to pull myself together. The sexual tension between us was so thick I could've cut it with a knife.

Macon reached into his pocket and grabbed the phone. "Hey Baby Girl, what's up?"

I turned to finish washing our glasses. I couldn't make out what Chloe was saying, but she was talking a mile a minute. I was glad she called or else I would have been perched up on the counter naked by now. Hmmm, would that have been so bad? I liked Macon, but I wanted us to get to know each other a little better before my judgment became clouded by sex. If our chemistry was this strong from a kiss, I could only imagine what the real deal would be like. I looked over my shoulder at him. His shoulders, his height. I licked my lips. I could climb him like a tree or ride him like a... He continued talking and interrupted my thoughts.

"Do you have to have it tonight Chloe? Where is it?" Macon leaned against the bar facing me. I tried to move around him to put the glasses away, but he grabbed me around the waist and pulled me against his chest. I rested the back of my head against his chest; he put his chin on my shoulder. He whispered to me, "She put me on hold. She left her journal at my mother's and wants me to bring it to her. My sister doesn't allow my niece to drive when it's dark, so she can't bring her."

I turned my head slightly and smiled at him; he gave me a quick kiss. The tip of his tongue grazed my lips. I whispered to him, "Do you need to take it to her?"

"I have..." he paused. "Alright. Are you sure?" He paused again. "Stop being nosy Chloe. I'll talk to you tomorrow. I love you. Bye." He ended the call and kissed my cheek.

He let me go and stood. I went over to the cabinet and put the glasses away. "What happened?" I turned the bar lights off and grabbed Macon's hand. We went to the television area on the other side of the basement.

He chuckled. "My sister fussed at her. My mother must have told my sister that I was taking you a plate and she doesn't want to interrupt us, so she told Chloe to get off the phone."

"Poor baby." I felt sorry for Chloe. "And I see your family rivals mine on gossip." Macon sat on the sofa and patted the seat right next him. I sat, and he draped his arm around my shoulders. The lights were dim; the fountain light was visible from the sliding doors in the basement. It was cozy and very comfortable.

"Chloe's a character and a daddy's girl. She knows she has me wrapped around her finger." I moved a little closer and leaned my head against him; he pulled me in. "My sisters and my mother talk constantly. What one knows the others know. Which means they know all about you from Lady B."

I laughed out loud. I recalled Donald referring to Mrs. Lila as Lady B when I went over last Sunday. "That name cracks me up...by the way, has your mom made any tea cakes since I gave her the recipe?" I felt his heart beating on the side of my arm. It was relaxing.

"Yes, but they aren't as good as yours." He chuckled. "She's doing something wrong."

"You better not let her hear you say that." We were quiet for a few minutes. I was thinking about how much I'd enjoyed getting to know him over the past couple of weeks. He made me feel good and safe. "Macon, I really like you."

He tugged my chin until I turned and looked up at him. "I really, really like you too, Dawn." He kissed my lips.

I turned my body, so we were facing each other. "No, I'm serious. I like you as a person, not just as someone I'm interested in romantically. I can talk to you for hours about anything, and you comfort me." His eyebrows went up. "Why do you look so surprised?"

"Because I am. And thank you for saying that. I've been enjoying our time together, too."

"In the past, I didn't always share what I was feeling if I was seeing someone." I paused to get my words in order. "It's kind of hard to explain. I guess I didn't think I needed to say it if my actions were there."

"Actions speak louder than words?"

"Exactly! See, you get it." I reached out and touched his cheek; his skin was smooth.

He smiled, showing a dimple. "I get it but..." he paused. "It doesn't work for everyone. You can't use the same tactic for different people."

"I know, and I didn't think that was the case but maybe I did treat everyone the same." I thought back to my past.

Macon sat up straight and pulled me over so that my back was lying across his lap. My head was resting on a throw pillow propped up against the arm of the couch. "I'm glad you brought up relationships. I've been wondering why you are divorced. You seem cool, I guess I'm confused about anyone letting you get away." He gave me a suspicious look. "Unless I've only met your representative so far."

I looked up at him and shook my head. "Here we go with the rep talk," I chuckled softly.

"You know it's true. People are nice, and then some crazy woman shows up later."

"You're right, but I'm pretty much the same all the time. Of course, I get angry or upset, and that's not pretty. I don't like when it happens, but I'm human. It actually happened today."

Macon's eyes went wide. "When?"

"I had a meltdown on Dre right before you called earlier today. I was pissed with him for saying something to you."

"I knew something sounded off with you. But, Dawn I can handle Dre. I didn't want you upset, that's why I didn't tell you." He slowly massaged my scalp with one hand.

"I know, but I needed to let him know he was out of line. To my knowledge, he's never done that before, and I can't have him running people off." I was starting to relax. He had magic fingers.

"You have nothing to worry about, I don't scare easily. But enough about Dre, tell me what your ex did so that I don't do the same thing."

I chuckled. "It wasn't quite like that, I don't think we were equally yoked. We loved each other, but I don't think either of us were fully committed for the long haul. You know marriage is work, and I came from a single parent household. I didn't fully understand the requirement to be fully vested in the marriage." I stretched my legs. "I went in with the option of ending it if it didn't work and that wasn't good. I also felt like I had too much responsibility in the marriage."

"What kind of responsibility?"

"In general, I guess. I felt like I always had to oversee everything. I was always the pilot and never the copilot no matter what was going on. It was tiring."

Macon stared down at me listening intently. "What would you do differently if you were to get married again?"

"I'm a lot different now, I realized after losing my mother that I need a husband that can shoulder some of the emotional responsibility when life throws me off my game. I also think I'm still learning not to be so quick to end things." I stifled a yawn. That scalp massage was like a lullaby. "That's always been a major problem for me, hence me getting married with divorce as an out."

"No waiting to exhale moments and burning clothes at the end?"

I smiled. "Nope, not at all. My ex is a good guy; we just weren't meant to be." I looked at him. "What about you and Mia? You get any of your sailor suits thrown out the window?"

He chuckled. "We had our problems, but nothing ever became violent. Mia and I married so young that we wanted different things in life after year ten. She wanted more children, I didn't. I went to college soon after I enlisted, and after I finished, she went. After the kids were older and we were both doing well career-wise that's when the trouble started." He let out a deep breath. "It's very odd that we got along better when we were busy with school and the kids, but when things got easier, we argued more. Eventually, we became like two ships in the night, passing each other by."

"That was the biggest problem?" It didn't seem like a deal breaker. I wondered if he would want children later, he was only thirty-seven

He yawned. "I think that's what started it. Instead of arguing I'd come home late, watch TV or play with the kids. I prolonged everything, so we wouldn't be alone to argue. Then she thought I was cheating because I avoided her."

*Uh-oh.* "Did you cheat?"

"No, I didn't. She didn't believe me. She was mad because she thought I was lying, and I was mad because she was calling me a liar. I hate when my integrity is questioned. I'm not saying I'm perfect, but I'm honest."

I was confused. "You're saying your marriage ended over a misunderstanding?"

He shook his head. "It was a domino effect, and that was the start of it. One thing led to another until we eventually became more like roommates."

"What would you do differently if you married again?"

"I guess communication is key for me. I can't read minds."

"Macon, I know this is new between us, but I always put this out on the table very early." I could feel him tense up underneath me. "I know you mentioned you didn't want more children when you were married, but I want you to know I can't have children anymore. You're only thirty-seven, it may be something you would want later."

"Do you want children?" he asked.

"No, I don't. I did when I was in my twenties, but I changed my mind before I got married. My ex and I sort of decided if they came we would roll with it, but we didn't plan to have any." He seemed to relax again.

"I love my kids, but they wore me out at a very young age. I can't imagine starting over with a newborn."

I sat up a little. "But you're not even forty yet; you could meet a young woman and start all over. When I was in my mid-thirties, I tossed the idea around again."

He brushed my cheek with the back of his hand. "I see you're going to try and convince me that I'll want kids again." He chuckled and smiled. "Dawn I'm clear on what I want. You have to understand that while you were enjoying your twenties, I was chasing the twins around, working and going to school. It wasn't easy, but I did what I had to do to take care of my family. Now, it's time for me to enjoy the fruits of my labor. The kids have two years of high school left, and I plan on enjoying every minute of my forties NOT chasing a baby around." I tried to speak, but Macon put his finger over my lips and looked at me. "I appreciate your honesty about not being able to have kids, but I want you to understand that it is NOT an issue for me, so can we please not make it one?" He removed his finger. Our eyes locked; he didn't blink or look away.

"Okay." I smiled. I guess he told me.

We talked until neither of us could hold our eyes open. I walked Macon to the door and kissed him goodbye. By the time I was settled in bed and almost sleep, I realized I had not received a text from him letting me know he made it home safely. I grabbed my phone from the nightstand. I did have a text from him.

**Macon: I'm home, you were a great bartender tonight. I left a tip on your kitchen table.**

What was he talking about? I got out of bed, and tiptoed down the stairs. There was thirty dollars on the kitchen table. When did he do that? I went upstairs to get my phone to text him.

**Glad you made it home. Why such a large tip?**

**Macon: Fruit ain't free.**

I smiled to myself, I was feeling him. I loved a man who paid attention and wasn't self-absorbed. I guess he knew I wouldn't tell him the cost of the fruit. I didn't mind, and I had offered, but I honestly had forgotten. But, when did he? Oh yeah, I did go upstairs to my bedroom before we went to the basement.

**Well played Mr. James... I will have to keep my eye on you next time I leave the room.**

**Macon: Or maybe you'll take me upstairs with you next time.**

I covered my mouth. "Oop." He was talking under my clothes, but I was game. I was getting warm thinking about those big hands all over me.

**Good idea!**

**Macon: Don't have me coming back over there... I will!**

**LOL! you are a mess. GN**
**Macon: GN Beautiful.**

# Chapter 8 ~ Macon

"You want another beer?" I was sitting on the deck at my place with Donald.

"I'm good, I'm on my bike, I can't be fuzzy." He was laid back in a lounge chair across from me with his legs stretched out. Donald was a little shorter than me at six feet with Brock's thin build. "How is it going with your girl? She met the twins yet?"

I took a swig from my beer. "Not yet, but she'll meet them tonight at the house."

Donald laughed. "Man, you crazy, you are introducing her to the twins and the sisters at the same time?" He shook his head. "The kids been down here about three weeks, right?" I nodded my head. "Why did you wait until now?"

"I didn't wait on purpose. The last few weeks have been hectic for both of us. She's been trying to catch up at work, help her grandmother move, and pack her mom's house. I've been running with the kids." I took another swig. "They decided to use this place as their hub, so the whole teen clan of the family is over here on a regular."

"You haven't seen her?" Donald's eyebrows were hiked up.

I shook my head. "Naw, I see her and talk to her daily. We hang out after I get off from work for a couple of hours. We go to dinner and do other things around the area, but I don't stay out too long because I still have to get my time in with the kids. I'm at work all day, I don't want to be gone all night."

"I feel you, man. But on the real, Maj will be cool but Chloe?" He shook his head. "Plus, the sisters? Are you trying to run her off?"

I chuckled. "It won't be that bad." Chloe would probably end up watching or reading her, whatever she called it. But my sisters were a different story. They were all nosey, but my oldest sister was the problem. That girl had no filter and said whatever came to mind.

"Whatever you say." Donald started messing with his phone. "Speaking of Dawn." *I knew it was a matter of time.* "Did she say anything about me and her friend?"

"She talked to her, she's going to set something up."

He smiled wide. "That's what's up. When?" This was going to be a hard sell. Donald was always eager when it came to women. It was one thing to show interest, but Donald was like a tight suit; all over her.

"Chill man, she's working on it." I pulled out my phone to shoot Dawn a text.

**Hey Pretty Lady, u still up for today?**

"Alright Dude, I'm heading over there now to see if Pops needs some help on the grill." Donald walked towards the door to go inside.

"Okay, I'll see you over there."

**Dawn: Absolutely! I have Brock's cake all ready to go.**

**You're spoiling him:(**

**Dawn: I made one for you too, am I spoiling you?**

I rubbed my stomach and smiled; I loved her cakes.

**Woman you're supposed to be spoiling me!**

I knew she would get a kick out of that. I heard the door slide open, and I looked up. It was Major. "Dad, we're leaving to go to Poppi and Gram's house."

"Alright Son, I'll see you soon." He lingered at the door; he looked like he wanted to say something. "You alright Maj?"

"Yeah, I'm cool. I was going to ask you about Ms. Dawn." My phone buzzed, but I wanted to holla at my boy first.

"What's on your mind?" I put my phone on the side table.

"Well, you've been hanging out with her a lot. I'm wondering if you are getting serious? Chlo said she could feel your energy and all that stuff, you know how she does." Major had a serious look, his eyes were wide and jaw tight. I was surprised because he rarely asked me about anyone I was dating, that was usually Chloe's job.

"I do like her a lot, but if you're asking about marriage, then we are a long way away from anything like that."

"Does she have kids?" *Well damn.* I couldn't believe he was questioning my love life. He stood with his arms folded over his chest and his legs spread apart. He looked like me at that age. It was hard to believe that I was married when I was a year older than he was right now. No wonder my mom was so upset, it made perfect sense now.

"No, Dawn does not have children."

"I can't wait to meet her. She must be cool because Chlo said she's never seen your aura this bright before." He shrugged. "Whatever that means. But she's right, listen to her Dad. She was right about my ex."

I smiled at him. "Yeah, I heard you were dating someone loose. I assumed it was over since I haven't seen you on the phone much and you never mentioned her to me."

Major looked down. "Loose doesn't describe her on a good day." I popped an eyebrow up. "From now on I'm listening to Chloe, these girls ain't loyal."

I laughed out loud. "You may be right about some, but that's not always true. It's best to deal with everyone on a case by case basis."

"Alright Dad, I'm out because you're about to sneak in a therapy session." He walked towards the door.

I shook my head. "Okay, see you later." He closed the door; I heard him calling the other kids. I picked up my phone.

**Dawn: You haven't seen anything yet.**

Oh really? I groaned and looked up at the sky. I thought about the last few make-out sessions we had at her place. I knew it was way past time for us to take that next step, but I wanted it to be right. I didn't want an hour or two with her the first time; I needed hours. I didn't like leaving the kids alone overnight, and I didn't want to chance an interruption. I had to wait until I had a full free day or night. She was so sexy and sensual; I couldn't wait to have her. Last night I kissed her a little too long, and I smelled her essence, I knew she was wet. Her scent had me in savage mode; I wanted to take her right up against the front door. Her eyes were glassy looking, and all I could do was imagine her on top of me, underneath me, in front of me, wherever. Oh, let me text her back.

**You trying to wake-up the Greedy Savage? I'll be there in 45 to pick you up.**

**Dawn: You damn right!... Okay. I'll be ready.**

No way I'd make it another couple of weeks until the kids left. I would lose my mind.

~~~~~~~~~~~~~

I picked Dawn up, and we went around the corner to my parents' house. I had to park on the street because the driveway was full. I tried to get there earlier, but I had to have my feel of Dawn for a little while. Although our sexual chemistry was damn near animalistic, our conversation was on point too. She was caring, and she had the biggest heart. I watched how she pitched in with her family and friends. She was always willing to help out no matter the situation. I liked being around her. I turned the truck off and looked at her. "You cool?"

"Of course, I'm sure it won't be that bad."

She had no idea. "If you say so." I got out of the truck and helped her out. I carried the cakes and led her to the front door. Before I could get the key out, Chloe opened the door.

"Hey, Daddy. Hi, Ms. Dawn." She moved back to let Dawn in the house.

"Hello Chloe, it's nice to finally meet you." Dawn reached out to hug her. Chloe gladly accepted and winked at me.

"Nice meeting you too, would you like to come to the kitchen with me?"

I had to stop her. "No, she wouldn't." I gave her a stern look, and she smiled, then walked off.

"Hey Aunties! Ms. Dawn is here!" she announced as she left the room.

Dawn looked at me and shrugged her shoulders. "Baby I'm fine, don't worry. I have tough skin."

Before we could get out of the living room, I heard footsteps coming towards us. My two older sisters came around the corner.

"Dawn Simms?!" *She knew her?* My oldest sister, Lois, was the same age as Dawn but how did they know each other?

"Oh my goodness! Delores James!?" Dawn looked between the two of us. We favored but didn't look alike. I looked like mom, and the girls all looked like our father. "Macon, I graduated high school with your sister!" *Wasn't expecting this.*

"I can't believe you're the Dawn dating my baby brother." I looked at Lois, but she kept going. "Girl he was like six when we graduated. You straight up robbin' the cradle!"

I had to save my lady. "Lois chill! And I was not six when you graduated." I turned my back to her and reached for my middle sister, Tonya. "Dawn this is my middle, more civil sister, Tonya. Do you know each other?"

Dawn and Tonya hugged. "Nice to meet you, Dawn. Your face looks familiar, but I wasn't in your class." Tonya looked at Lois. "And excuse Lois, she's mad because her husband is Brock's age." I laughed, and Lois rolled her eyes. Dawn wanted to laugh too but didn't know what to do.

"Good looking out T." We fist bumped.

"Well, this must be Dawn." My youngest older sister, Melody, came around the corner and hugged Dawn. "I've heard a lot about you, and you have Baby Bro over here smiling all the time." Yeah maybe Donald was right, they were talking too much.

"It's nice to meet you too Melody, and I'm trying to keep a smile on his face." I was smiling from ear to ear.

"That's right, Baby." I leaned over and kissed her cheek.

The girls groaned. Tonya grabbed the cakes and Melody grabbed Dawn's hand, the four of them went towards the kitchen. I followed behind. I wasn't ready to have them all over her yet. Once I saw my mother in the kitchen, I knew she was safe. She wouldn't let anything happen to her. Dawn hugged my mother, and they all took seats around the island. I stood behind Dawn's stool and whispered to her, "Are you going to be okay? I'm going to go find the boys." She smiled up at me and nodded.

"Get out of here, she's fine!" Should have known Big Mouth Lois would say something. I squeezed her shoulders and left.

I found Major and MJ outside with Brock. I saw Chloe out of the corner of my eye going into the house. I was sure she was going right to Dawn. I shook my head. My Baby Girl was something else. I guess she could be chasing knuckleheads right now, so if this was the worst I had to deal with, I was cool.

"What's up Brock?" I patted him on the back. He had his hands full taking meat off the grill.

"Hey!" He frowned. "Where's Dawn?"

"Why you checkin' for my Lady?" I joked.

"As long as she keeps making' me those cakes I'm gone always be checkin' for her, whether she's your lady or not." I laughed at him.

"She's here. She's in the house with Mom and the girls." Brock froze.

"You sure that's a good idea? You know that Lois will say anything out of that mouth of hers."

"She's cool, I found out they graduated high school together, so Lois has a leg up on the other girls. You know she likes knowing more than anyone else."

Brock handed me a pan of meat. "I guess you're right about that, she loves being in the know."

I called the boys over. "Follow us in the house I want you to meet Dawn."

We went into the house, I watched Brock immediately go over to Dawn, he whispered something to her. She nodded, and he patted her on the back and clapped his hands. Chloe was sitting on a stool right next to Dawn grinning. I assumed she thought she was okay or else she wouldn't be anywhere near her.

I put the pans of meat on the counter and went over to Dawn; the boys were right behind me. "Dawn I want you to meet Major and MJ."

She stood from the stool and once again I almost groaned. She was dressed casually in one of those long summer dresses. It was a little clingy; I could see her figure well. She reached out and hugged the boys.

"Nice to meet both of you. How are you two enjoying your summer?"

MJ and Maj rambled on about something. I barely heard them because I was focused on Dawn. It had only been about five weeks since we met, and I already knew I was catching feelings for her. It seemed like it was fast, but I didn't care. I enjoyed talking to her and being around her. Even through her own sadness, she had a way of making me happy. I realized I wanted to do the same for her.

"Dad?"

I barely heard Maj. "Yeah, Maj? What's up?"

"Ms. Dawn said she made another one of those cakes, where is it?" I looked at Dawn. She smiled and shrugged her shoulders.

"I'll save you a piece." Maj looked at me with his eyes wide. A couple of weeks ago he told me the same thing when I asked if they had eaten the cake she sent over. Of course, when I got home from work it was all gone. The kids and the cousins were eating me out of house and home. But it was nice having them there, and I was happy they enjoyed the new place enough to hang out there.

"Alright listen up everybody." Brock was talking like he had a megaphone. "Your Momma and I have an announcement, Maj go get your uncles from the basement." We all looked around at each other, but no one seemed to know what they were going to say.

"You think Momma is pregnant?" Lois whispered to me. I couldn't help but laugh.

A few minutes later, Maj came in followed by Dale and Donald. It was almost scary how much they both looked like Brock. I slapped hands with them as they came in.

"Alright, now that we have all of our offspring present, we want to announce my retirement." Everyone looked shocked. I didn't think Brock would ever retire, but I guess Mom finally got to him. "I'm retiring in two weeks, and your Momma is planning a party to celebrate."

I looked over at Mom; she was smiling hard. "Yes kids, Dad is retiring, and I'll need your help getting this party together."

We all took turns hugging and congratulating Brock and Mom. I knew she wanted to travel and I was glad she was finally getting it done while she and Brock were still healthy.

As the day progressed, we settled in the family room off the kitchen playing games and watching tv. Dawn seemed to be having fun, it was good to see her so happy. I watched her slip out to go to the restroom. After she was gone a few minutes, I went to check on her and almost ran into her coming around the corner from the hallway bathroom.

"Hey." She smiled up at me. I rubbed her cheek and kissed her lips gently.

"Are you ready to go?" I had my hands resting on her shoulders.

"I'm okay, whenever you're ready is fine."

I took her by the hand and led her through the kitchen to the deck. There was a round table with a few chairs but only one lounger. I sat first and patted my legs for her to sit. She sat on my lap, I leaned back so that I could see her face. "You comfortable?" She nodded. "Good... I think my family likes you more than they like me now."

She laughed. "Are you jealous?" I nodded playfully. "Well don't be because I like you most." She leaned over and kissed me.

"That makes me feel a little better. Chloe has been all over you."

"She's fine, I've been enjoying talking to her. We talked about college mostly. I didn't know she and Major were both interested in science. She's been asking tons of questions. She asked for my phone number. I hope you don't mind that I gave it to her."

I laughed. "Not as long as you don't mind her calling you."

"Of course not, I love to see our young kids interested in higher education, especially any science field." I swear this woman was going to make me fall in love with her. Now that the kids had met her and liked her I was more than happy.

"Remember you said that when Chloe starts blowing your phone up." I tickled her side. "But on another note, I would like to know if you'd be my date to Brock's retirement party?"

She smiled at me. "Absolutely!"

"Thank you, let's say our goodbyes and go. I want a little alone time with you before I go home to the kids." She stood and reached for my hand to help me up.

After Mom prepared us some to-go plates, we left and went to Dawn's house. I told the kids I would see them in a couple of hours. We were sitting in her family room looking out at the fountain and talking. Dawn had her head on my shoulder, and we both had our feet up on the ottoman. Her phone vibrated, it was closest to me, I handed it to her, she answered.

"Hey Dre, what's up?" *Him again?* I'd seen Dre briefly since the happy hour, and he'd called a few times over the last few weeks while I was with her. More like a lot of times. He seemed a little too clingy to be a friend. I wondered if he was like this during her marriage.

"Okay, that's fine, but I'm with Macon right now, I'll have to call you back." *Did I hear that Fool say "damn"?* "Where did you leave it?" Dawn got up searching around the room for something. She went near the window and pulled a phone charger from an outlet. "You need it now?... Okay, come on by." *Why doesn't he have more than one?* Dawn ended the call.

"Dre left his charger over here earlier today, he's going to come by and get it. I'm sorry I know this is our alone time, but it will only take a minute." I pulled her over to the sofa.

"It's fine, Sweetheart." I was lying, but I didn't want her to think I didn't like her friend. It wasn't that I didn't like him, I didn't trust him. He took the friendship thing too far.

"Thank you." She smiled.

A few minutes later the doorbell rang, Dawn took the charger and went to the door. I heard her messing with the locks and opening the door. Dre started talking. The front door was within earshot of her family room. "I'm sorry Baby, I didn't mean to mess with your lil' date." *Baby?* I might have to check him at some point.

Dawn laughed. "Whatever, come on in here and say hello and goodbye to Macon."

"It's like that? You puttin' yo' boy out?" I heard them walking towards me; I stood up.

"You damn right I'm puttin' you out. You're messing with our alone time. You're lucky I didn't leave that charger on the porch." She was teasing, but I got some enjoyment out of her defending me.

Dre walked towards me. "What's good, Macon?"

"Not much, trying to get some time in with my lady." Yep, that was petty as hell.

Dre gave me a slow head nod. "Alright then, I guess I'll let y'all get back to it." He reached and tried to hug Dawn, but she pushed him away.

"Get away from me with all that cologne on." She fanned him away. I knew what he was doing, he was trying to mark his territory, but it backfired.

"Whatever, Dawn." He chuckled and turned towards the door. Dawn grabbed my hand; we walked to the door with Dre in front of us. He turned around after he opened the door. His eyebrows shot up and his jaw tightened. I guess he didn't realize I was standing next to her. "Alright good people, I..." He looked down at our joined hands. "See you later Macon. Dawn, I'll call you later."

"Yeah, good seeing you," I said.

"Alright Dre, I'll talk to you tomorrow." Dawn let him out and closed the door.

I wasn't sure if she noticed his behavior. If she did, she didn't say anything. He behaved more like a jealous ex rather than a long-time friend. And, I saw the way he looked at her. It was the same way I looked at her. We went back into the family room and settled back in on the couch. "Dawn, can I ask you something?"

"Sure." She turned to look at me.

"How did Dre and your ex-husband get along?"

"They weren't really around each other too much because we lived out east the whole time we were married. Dre walked me down the aisle at our wedding, so the times they were around each other they got along great. But, they did share a love for football. Dre came out to catch a couple of professional games with him. Why do you ask?"

I was even more confused now. He was cool with the ex-husband, but he was having a pissing contest with someone she just met? "He seems a little protective of you, just wondering how that worked out when you were married."

"Dre has always been protective but a lot more since I lost my mom. He means well though." I still didn't trust him. He didn't act like a man protecting his friend. He acted more like a man on the hunt.

Dawn had her head on my shoulder and one arm across my stomach. "Sweetheart, I need to get going. I hate to leave you. Unless you want to come over and hang out with the kids and me?" I laughed, no way would she want to hear that noise. I assumed it would be about eight of them over there by now.

"I don't mind Macon, I like your kids."

I was all teeth. "Alright, let's go. I will bring you home later." I kissed her cheek. I moved to get up, but I didn't feel my phone in my pockets. She stood and went into the kitchen to grab her shoes and purse. "Dawn, have you seen my phone? I thought it was in my pocket, I know I didn't leave it in my truck." I was looking around but didn't see it.

Dawn came back in the room. "Let me call it from my phone." She tapped on her phone, and I froze.

*Damn! Please don't call it.* I walked towards her to try and stop her. "Naw, Baby I'll find it, you don't have to call it." It was too late, I heard my phone from the other room. The music was so loud, it sounded like it was hooked up to a speaker. Dawn looked up with her eyebrows up and she smiled. I was embarrassed, I felt like a damn teenager. The music stopped but she called again, and the music played.

She walked towards me with her hands behind her back. "I have a special ringtone?" One eyebrow went up.

"Yes." There was no way I thought she would ever hear it, and if she did, I didn't think it would be this soon. I couldn't even look at her I was so embarrassed. She reached up and pulled my chin so that we were face to face. She stood on her toes and gave me the longest kiss. She pulled back and looked up at me.

"The song doesn't sound familiar. What's the name of it?" I thought she would let it go but that wasn't happening.

"'Booed Up' by Anthony David."

She smiled and tapped on her phone. A few seconds later I heard the song coming through her speaker system. She held her hand out. "Will you dance with me?" I took her hand and pulled her close. We started off slow, and then we moved to the beat. A simple two-step. "You dance well." She smiled at me.

We kept dancing; she felt so good in my arms. "Thank you, my mother taught me how to dance."

"Really?" She had her arms around my neck, and my arms were wrapped tightly around her waist.

"Yep. My mother and father used to go out dancing when I was a kid. After he died, she cried so much that I danced with her at home to cheer her up. I was pretty bad, but she got me together." I chuckled as I thought back to her teaching me how to dance in our living room. "After I got better I would always dance with her when she was sad."

Dawn stopped moving and pulled back to look at my face. "You're going to make me cry. That is the sweetest thing." I pulled her head against my chest and kissed her forehead.

After the song went off, Dawn grabbed my hand and we walked to the front door. She stopped by the dining room to get my phone off the table. I guess I put it there when I came in the door and forgot. She looked up at me and smiled. "Don't be embarrassed, I thought it was sweet of you. I think it's my new favorite song."

"I'm glad you like it, I heard it while I was in my office one day and it reminded me of us. Well, let me say how I picture us in the very near future." Her smile faded. "What's wrong?"

She looked away. "Macon, I have to be honest with you." *What was this about?* "I like you a lot but I'm so scared. I feel like I'm an emotional mess and I don't want to put this on you. I've already exhausted my friends. I don't want to do the same thing to you."

I pulled her chin until she faced me. "Dawn, I'm not asking you to give me a perfect person. I want you." I pointed at her. "I don't care if you're an emotional mess, as you call it. I'm also not asking you to make any decisions about us right now, let's keep doing what we do, and it will all fall into place. Okay?"

"Okay." She was so quiet I almost didn't hear her. "But Macon I..." I put my finger to her lips to keep her from talking.

"Dawn, are you trying to make decisions for me again?" She shook her head no. "Good, because as I've told you before, I am very clear on what I want. Okay?" She nodded and gave me a little smile. "Great, now give me one of those long kisses again before we leave." She smiled and pulled my face down to meet hers.

## Chapter 9 ~ Dawn

Over the last couple of weeks, I'd been spending a lot of time with Macon and the kids. They were great kids and fun to be around, especially that Chloe. I seemed to bond with MJ the most because he didn't have his mother in his life. Apparently, she ran off when he was a baby and only called occasionally. I couldn't imagine my childhood without my mother. My mother's love was one of the best things I felt in my life. Sometimes it saddened me to know I didn't realize how lucky I was until it was too late. OKAY, I didn't have time for tears or a stroll down memory lane. I was busy cleaning and prepping food for my annual drink competition I had with my family and friends. I usually had it during the Christmas season, but this year I decided on a late summer competition. Today would also be the first time Macon met my family; I was excited. My doorbell rang, it was most likely Macon. I ran to the door; I could see his truck in the driveway. I had my blinds open to let the last of the sun in for the day. I opened the door to let him in; I couldn't help the wide smile on my face. "Hey Baby, come on in "

He reached to hug me; I went willingly. "Hey." He held me tight. "Just what I needed today." He released me. "What can I do to help? It smells good in here."

"Thank you." I walked towards the kitchen. Macon followed. "I think I'm done. I finished cleaning the last of the dishes. I need to run up and change my clothes. Can you answer the door for me?" I noticed a bag in his hand. "What's in the bag?"

"Sure, I can watch the door." He held up the bag and went to the freezer. "This is my winning drink for the competition." He opened the freezer door and gently placed the bag in the freezer.

"What? You're entering the contest?" I couldn't believe it. "You know if you win they will swear I cheated. They are serious about this competition; it's like blood in the water around here."

Macon laughed. "It will be fine. Go get dressed." He came over and kissed me; the doorbell rang. "I got it, go upstairs."

I ran upstairs, a few moments later I heard Summer's loud mouth all through the house. I heard her coming up the steps. "Sis, you up here?"

I was changing from my lounge clothes into a blue maxi dress. "I'm in the closet Summer!" She came to the closet door. I looked up; she had the biggest smile on her face.

"Why didn't you stay down and talk to Macon?" I was surprised she passed up that opportunity.

"Your brother-in-law is down there talking to him." Summer's hubby was cool, I knew he wouldn't give Macon a hard time. "But why does he have to be so fine? I don't even know why you're inviting people over with that fine man around." I laughed, she was funny. "Seriously though, do you like him or is he arm candy?"

"No Summer, I like him. We talk for hours and hours. We fall asleep on the phone facetiming. I almost feel like we are in high school. He listens to me, he hears what I'm saying, but he also has enough intuition to know some of the things I can't quite articulate."

"So basically, you're saying he's a unicorn?"

I laughed out loud. "Yes, I guess you could say that about him. He treats me like a queen. He's chivalrous and he is always concerned about my well-being." I looked at the ceiling. "But Summer I'm so scared, he's too perfect."

"Are you kidding?" I shook my head. "Dawn listen, you deserve him. It's okay to be scared but don't let it ruin something good."

"I'm trying, but I hate him seeing me so messed up. I question everything since Momma has been gone. I've cried in front of him a few times and you know that's not me." I went into the bathroom to touch up my hair while Summer looked through my lotions. I had to keep an eye on her, she was known for permanently borrowing my smell goods.

"What did he do when you cried in front of him?"

"He held me until I stopped or fell asleep."

"You are trippin', I don't see a problem. If he ran off or something, I could understand, but the man is holding you?" I nodded. "Girl, bye," she waved her hand at me. "Any other problems you've created in your head?"

I narrowed my eyes at her in the mirror. "Be quiet, my feelings are valid." She rolled her eyes at me and plopped down on my bed. "Dre gave him a hard time too."

Summer sat up straight. "Wait until I see him. I knew Dre was going to be a problem. Momma told me a long time ago that you and Dre would probably end up together."

My eyes went wide, and my mouth dropped open. "Say what!?" This was news to me. "Momma said that!? When!?"

Summer shrugged. "She told me after you got divorced and he kept flying out there checking on you."

"But Dre doesn't like me like that, we've never liked each other like that."

"Maybe you don't, but I know as of late he likes you."

Alright, I had enough of this nonsense. "Whatever Summer, let's go downstairs. I heard the doorbell ring a few times." I wasn't paying attention to her. But I was very concerned about what my mother said.

We went downstairs, a few other guests had arrived, including Janae and Tori. I noticed Macon watching me from the family room while I talked to Janae. "Girl I see your new Boo is manning the door. That's what I'm talking about." I was smiling from ear to ear.

I heard the doorbell ring again, and Macon waved me off to let me know he would go.

A few seconds later, Dre came around the corner. "Wad up?" He was slapping hands with my brother-in-law and hugging my sister. He made his way to the kitchen. He kissed Janae on the cheek and then came over to me. "Hey, Dawn." He leaned in and whispered in my ear, "Big Baby live here now? He's answering doors and what not?"

I swatted him off. "Mind your own business. And I swear Dre if you start with him today." I narrowed my eyes at him.

He threw his hands up and laughed. "You know I'm playing." I smiled at him, and he walked off to talk to Tori and some other guests.

I noticed Macon looking at me, but I couldn't read him. This was the last thing I wanted. I did not want to choose between Macon and Dre. Dre was a jerk to Macon, and I hoped Macon would forgive him and move on, but I couldn't blame him if he didn't. I was not going to let Dre ruin anything for me either; his women came a dime a dozen. And as my sister said, Macon was a unicorn.

"Janae, I'll be back." My eyes were on Macon.

"Okay, I'm going to have a word with Dre. I heard what he said, and if he tries to ruin this for you, I'll toss his ass in that lake." I laughed out loud. Tori was the feisty one, but if you upset Janae, it wasn't pretty.

I made my way over to Macon. He saw me coming and excused himself from my nephew and the others. "Hey, are you okay?"

"I'm fine Baby." He brushed the back of his hand across my cheek and smiled. "Do you need me to do anything else?"

I smiled up at him. "No, I think everything is done. I saw you looking at me and I wanted to make sure you were okay."

"I'm a passive-aggressive stalker remember? I think that's what I'm supposed to be doing." He smiled at me and eased my mind. I'm glad he wasn't trippin' off Dre. And if he was I couldn't see it.

"I guess you have a point. I see you've met Summer?" I smiled.

"Um yes, she reminds me of Lois."

"Sorry, I should have warned you," I said.

"It's fine Baby. Go talk to your people, I'll be okay. Let me know if I can help with anything." I smiled and turned to walk off. "Dawn?" I turned back to him. He whispered to me, "Would you stay with me tonight? The kids are at Six Flags, and they are staying with my sister when they get back."

I could not get my thoughts together. I wanted to send everyone home and go with him immediately. "Yes," I answered. He smiled at me and I walked away. I was warm all over, I fanned myself. This was going to be a long evening.

After everyone arrived, and the food and drinks were flowing I called everyone to the basement for the drink competition. "Alright everyone, thank you for coming to the summer edition of the Annual Holiday Cocktail Competition. Let me spell out the rules because I don't want any confusion at the end." Everyone laughed, and I continued explaining the rules. "The judges will be basing your drinks on presentation, originality and overall taste, equally. The person with the most points wins." There were six competitors, including Macon and Dre. Everyone randomly chose a number, Dre was up first.

"Alright Y'all, I'm the reigning champion so let's continue the tradition." Dre prepped his drink at the bar. "Dawn, can you dim the lights please?" *He was so dramatic.* I rolled my eyes and dimmed the lights. As he filled the shot glasses, the bottom of each glass flashed. The shot glasses had LED lights in different colors inside the bottom portion. Everyone started clapping and talking. Dre looked proud. "I call this drink 'Summer Lights'!" I tasted the drink then helped pass them to the judges and the rest of the guests.

Everyone made a fuss about the LED shot glasses and the taste. I had to admit his drink was pretty good.

My niece, Janae, and Tori presented their drinks after Dre. Macon was having a good time. He talked with everyone and commented on all the drinks. I was happy he was enjoying himself. He was standing next to me, I whispered to him, "Is Donald still coming?"

"He sent me a text and said he stopped to see Brock, but he was on his way. I sent him your address." I invited Donald so that he could meet Tori and neither of them would feel any pressure. "I'll go and see if he's out there." He left to go upstairs.

Summer was finishing up her presentation when Macon came down with Donald. I was standing near Tori, and she whispered, "He's cute, I like him already."

"He is very nice-looking Tori, but I told you he's shy. Please take it easy on him." She rolled her eyes at me. Donald was about six feet even, with a light complexion. He was thin and toned, with a bald head. He had on motorcycle clothes and boots. Tori and a few other ladies were watching him. He came over to where I was standing. "Hi Donald, I'm glad you made it." I hugged him.

"Thanks for inviting me." Donald was usually clean shaven, but he had a low beard today. It looked nice on him.

"No problem, excuse me Donald it's time for Macon to present his drink." I went to the bar. "Okay everyone, it's time for our last, but certainly not least, presenter. Come on up, Macon."

Macon went behind the bar and set up shot glasses. He pulled out some sort of small light fixture and plugged it into an outlet. Everyone was watching; I was very curious. "Dawn, Sweetheart?" I blushed. My friends and family were laughing at me. I wasn't that chick who blushed in public. "Could you assist me please?"

"Of course."

I went over; he handed me his phone. "Can you connect this to your wireless speakers?" *He had music?* I did as he asked and handed him his phone back.

"Can I do anything else?" I was standing right next to him. He was shaking something up in a large metal shaker.

"Just stand there and look beautiful for a second." He winked at me. I was smiling so hard my molars were probably showing.

"I heard that! Go head Macon!" Summer shouted.

"That's what I'm talking about!" Tori yelled and high-fived Janae. Everyone else laughed and giggled.

Macon poured something from a bottle into the shot glasses. He then poured the liquid from the shaker into the glasses. He looked at me. "Lights!"

I turned the lights off, and he started the music. "Flashlight" by Parliament came through the speakers. Everyone started dancing around. As soon as they sang the word "flashlight" the drinks lit up on the bar. The drinks were about four different colors of glow-in-the-dark neon! Everybody clapped and chanted, "Champ! Champ! Champ!" The light fixture was a black light that made the drinks glow in the dark. He turned it off and on to the beat of the music, which made the drinks look like flashlights. It was cool. After a minute or so he cut the music, and I turned the lights on. I helped Macon pass the drinks around. I took a sip, and it was delicious. I tasted all sorts of fruity citrus flavors.

"I'm going to tally the scores while you all mingle," I announced to everyone. I whispered to Macon, "Can you formally introduce Tori and Donald? And please tell me how you made edible glow-in-the-dark drinks later?"

"I got you." I watched him go across the room before I turned my attention to the judges and tallied scores. I heard several different people asking him about his drink.

After a few minutes of adding up scores, I pulled the trophy from a cabinet and stood in front of the bar. The trophy was a liquor bouquet, an oversized shaker filled with a variety of miniature bottles of liquors on skewers. "We have a winner!" Everyone stopped talking. "Macon, you're the winner!" I heard claps and whistles. Macon came up and stood next to me. I gave him his trophy, he leaned over and kissed me on the cheek.

"Thank you." He pretended to be bashful and everyone laughed at him.

"Macon, you can give an acceptance speech," I teased.

Macon cleared his throat. "I'd like to thank the judges for choosing me as the winner. I..." Macon continued talking, and I looked around the room. I saw Tori and Donald talking; he looked like a deer caught in headlights. I chuckled to myself. I looked behind them, Dre stared at Macon; he was mad. I knew he won every year, but this was all fun and games. Could he possibly be mad about Macon winning? This was not going to be a good situation. I liked Macon, but Dre was a staple in my life. I wanted him to be happy for me. "But I would also like to thank our beautiful hostess for inviting me." I smiled up at him. "I've had a few requests for my drink so meet me at the bar if you want the recipe." Macon went to the bar, Summer and a few others followed him.

I walked across the room to talk to Dre; he was standing on the opposite end of the basement near the sliding doors. "Hey, Dre, what's up with you?" He was messing around with his phone.

"Nothing, I see your boy did his thing." Hmmm, I couldn't read him. He didn't have a facial expression.

"Yes, I thought he did a good job. He surprised me." He finally put his phone in his pocket, but he didn't respond. "Is something wrong Dre?"

"I'm fine, but I gotta bounce. I have plans." Yeah, something was off. He never left my house early.

"You have plans? Okay, so that's what we do now?" I folded my arms and raised an eyebrow.

"It's all good, I'm taking the chick down the street to the movies." His mouth was in a straight line.

"Why didn't you invite her over here? You know I don't mind."

"Hey, Baby?" Macon came up behind us, and I turned around. "Do you have some paper? Your sister wants me to write down my drink ingredients." I smiled at his handsome face. Before I could answer, Dre interrupted.

"Alright Macon, congrats on the win." He gave him a manshake. "Alright D, I'll holla at you later."

"Thanks, man, see you later." Macon had his arm loosely around my waist. Dre walked off towards the steps.

"Let me walk Dre out; something is wrong with him. I'll grab some paper on the way back down, okay?"

"Take your time, I'll be here." He smiled at me, and I went to catch up with Dre.

By the time I got upstairs, I heard the front door opening and closing. I went to the door and stepped out on the porch. Dre turned around. He looked mad, but he didn't say anything. I walked over to him and looked at him. "What's wrong? And do not say you're fine." I crossed my arms over my chest.

"I'm cool, ol' girl sent a few crazy texts and it kind of pissed me off."

I knew Dre well, he was lying. "Whatever you say." I turned to go in the house. "I'll talk to you later."

He grabbed me by the elbow. "Dawn, wait." He let me go and rubbed his hand down his face. "Do you really like Macon? Things seem to be moving pretty fast, he's hanging with the fam already."

I knew it! I had to choose my words carefully because I did not want to get upset and ruin the rest of my day. I needed my friend to be happy for me and most of all I needed him to be supportive. "Dre, I need..." I pointed at him, "you to be the best friend that you are and be happy for me. I want this thing with Macon to work. He accepts me the way that I am, emotionally broken. You know better than anyone that I'm going to mess up with him. I need you to check me and tell me I'm wrong. I can't take you not supporting me right now." He looked at me for a long time, but he didn't speak. "Dre? You with me?" I waved my hand in front of his face.

"Yeah, I'm here, and I got you." He gave me a genuine smile, and I smiled back at him. "Now go get Big Baby some paper." He backed away slowly. I laughed and turned to walk back in the house. "Hey, Dawn."

I looked over my shoulder. "Yeah?"

He stopped walking. "I love you."

I licked my tongue out at him. "You better! Because I need my friend." I chuckled and went into the house.

~~~~~~~~~~~~~

About an hour after everyone left, Macon and I were putting things back in order. We were in the kitchen loading the dishwasher. "Is everything cool with Dre? You seemed upset earlier." Macon was rinsing a dish in the sink with his back to me.

"I think so, he's still in protective mode. And he has something going on with a woman that lives down the street from him."

Macon turned around; his face was scrunched up. "He's seeing someone?"

"Yep!" I closed the dishwasher. "You seem surprised."

"I am. I've seen him a few times, and he's never been with anyone."

"That's because Dre never commits to anyone. He does bring women around sometimes but not often." I shrugged my shoulders.

"Interesting. Well, I'm glad he's cool, but enough about him. You're still coming home with me, aren't you?" He caged me in at the counter. We were facing each other.

"Yes, that's the plan." I wrapped my arms around his neck and gently placed kisses around his lips.

"Mmmm... good, go get your things so we can go."

I walked off and he swatted my butt. "I'm going to take a quick shower and change, so I won't have to bring too much stuff." I paused. "Actually, we can stay here if you want?" I was standing on the bottom step, he walked to the family room.

He turned and shook his head. "No thanks."

I put my hand on my hip and pouted. "What's wrong with my house?"

"Nothing, but I want uninterrupted time with you. I know the kids are at Six Flags, so my place is good. Over here people randomly stop by to pick up chargers and things." He turned the tv on and sat on the sofa.

I laughed. "You are so wrong! That was only one time. I see the Greedy Savage is in the house tonight."

"Yep! And he doesn't like to share. Now go upstairs and get ready Woman!"

"Okay, okay!" I ran up the stairs giggling.

After I showered and did a little body landscaping, I made sure I used my favorite body butter that Macon always complimented me on. I decided on a short green sundress and thong sandals. I packed a small overnight bag and went downstairs. "I'm ready."

Macon looked up and smiled. "Don't you look cute, come here." He held his hand out; I walked over to him. "And you smell good." He had his face in the crook of my neck. I giggled. "Let's go."

On the way to his place, we chatted about the party and my family. "You never told me what made your drink glow in the dark." He pulled into his garage.

"I used tonic water; the quinine makes it glow under a black light." He got out and opened my door.

"I never would have thought of that, very impressive."

"I've done enough science projects with the kids; it was easy." He shrugged and held the door to the house open for me. This was one of the things that I truly liked about Macon; he loved his children. He dropped the food bags off in the kitchen and went for the steps. "Let's go upstairs. I'm going to take a shower and then we can talk."

I followed him upstairs, but I had no intentions on talking after his shower. When we got to his bedroom, he went into the bathroom. Macon's bedroom was very masculine, I thought I did a pretty good job decorating, he told me he felt like a king in his new bedroom. He had a large king bed with a tall, dark wood headboard. A nightstand was on either side of the bed with some cool up-lights I picked out during one of our decorating shopping trips. When set low, the up-lights cast a dim light on the large pieces of abstract canvas art above each nightstand. Macon had some nice art, but I added silver floater frames to make them pop. At the foot of the bed, there was a silver metal and black leather bench. It was originally blue fabric, but I went through my stash of fabrics at home and found the perfect black leather to reupholster the bench. My obi belts would have to wait since I used all the fabric for the bench. We mounted the TV on the wall directly in front of the bed and placed his dresser underneath. I took the mirror off the dresser and mounted it on the wall in between his two closet doors. The far wall was mostly windows treated with wood blinds. I added a long curtain rod near the ceiling and hung gray and purple sheers that framed the windows. There was just enough room for one chair on the far side by the windows. I chose a classic black Barcelona chair with a silver metallic leather pillow propped in the center. The walls were a neutral gray. The bedding was steel gray satin with deep purple Egyptian cotton sheets. I'd never stayed overnight, but I felt at home since my stamp was all over his bedroom. I slipped my shoes off and sat on the side of the bed. I realized I had not looked at my phone in a while. I pulled it out, I had a few missed calls and texts.

**Dre: Are you home alone? I wanted to come back by.**

Not tonight my friend. I thought he was with the lady from down the street. I had a text from Tori.

**Tori: You're right, the brother is shy. He's fine though.**

I laughed and shook my head. I heard the shower running and I thought about Macon's naked body right in the next room. I fanned myself. I sure hoped he wasn't sleepy or too tired tonight because I couldn't be deprived anymore. All the kissing and touching over the past six or seven weeks had taken a toll on me. And I knew he felt the same way. The way he looked at me had me all wet and bothered. Mmmmm. Oh, I needed to respond to the texts and then turn this phone off. No interruptions tonight!

**I'm not home. Are you okay?**

**Girl you are a mess, we will chat tomorrow.**

**Dre: What time are you coming home?**

**I'm at Macon's, I'll be home tomorrow. What's wrong? You're scaring me.**

This was so out of character for Dre. I was the one that was usually bugging him when he was on a date, especially on a Saturday night. And why hasn't he responded yet? I waited a few more minutes. My phone buzzed.

**Dre: Cool, I'll holla.**

**Really?**

I heard the water in the bathroom stop. I should have been focused on that fine man in the bathroom and not Dre's behind.

**Dre: I was gone come through and chill for a minute. I thought BB was with his kids.**

I chuckled, he knew I hated that he called Macon Big Baby or BB. The bathroom door opened, I looked up from my phone and saw steam coming out the door. "You alright in there?" Macon yelled.

"I'm okay, I'm returning a few texts that I missed from earlier."

**au contraire mon frère … NOT tonight. LOL! ttyl!**

**Dre: Whatever, I'm out.**

**Dinner this week?**

**Dre: cool**

I powered my phone off and put it on the nightstand. I turned around and saw Macon coming out the bathroom in shorts and no shirt. I was speechless. I had felt all over that chest, but I didn't expect it to look that good. He was muscular, but he didn't have a body builder's type of body, it was more natural looking. I referred to his body type as country strong or sturdy. I knew he could lift just about anything; hmmmm, maybe even me. But the way my weight was set up, I settled for only being lifted up in prayer a long time ago.

"Dawn?"

How long had he been calling me? "Ummm, yeah?"

Macon sat next to me on the bed. "Is something wrong?"

I looked at his tattoo on his upper arm. This was the first time I had a full view of it. "No, I'm fine. Tell me about your tattoo?" The tattoo looked tribal. They looked like thorns; they wrapped around the top of his bicep area like an armband. There were three of them close together, and each one was about a half inch wide.

"They represent my children, one for each child, including the one we lost." He rubbed his arm.

I felt bad that I asked. "I'm sorry Macon, I didn't mean to bring up any bad memories." *Way to go Dawn! Guess you ruined it for tonight.* I looked away.

"Dawn, it's fine. Sadness is a part of life; no one escapes it." He palmed my cheek and kissed me gently then pulled back. "Okay?"

I nodded and smiled. He smelled good, I tasted the minty flavor of mouthwash when he kissed me. We sat there for a moment and stared at each other. I could feel the heat coming from his body. I didn't know if it was from the shower or if I had caused it. He grabbed my hand and kissed the back of it. He was trying to be a gentleman, but the way he was looking at me told a different story. I leaned over slightly and kissed him and that was all it took. His tongue was in my mouth, he was forceful, but I kept up with him. He grabbed me around the waist and pulled me closer, but I wasn't close enough. I put my arms around his neck and turned my body so that I straddled his lap; our lips never broke contact. His hands were under my dress unhooking my bra from the back. "Dawn?" I had moved past his mouth and was nibbling on his ear and neck like he was my last meal. He pulled back and chuckled. "Baby, slow down, we have all night."

I cocked my head to the side. "Where's the Greedy Savage?"

He laughed and quickly flipped us over so that I was on my back on the bed and he was on top of me. "Give me a minute." He kissed the tip of my nose and got off the bed. I was on my back with my legs hanging off the side. "Move over to the middle of the bed."

I moved across the bed so that my head was on a pillow; I was in the middle on my back watching him. He turned the lights down, but it wasn't completely dark. His phone lit up, and music came through the speakers in the room. *Was that Al Green?* "Simply Beautiful"? Alright now Macon! I felt the bed dip, he raised one of my legs and kissed my ankle. He barely touched me, and I was about to explode. I needed to touch him and feel him. I reached out to pull him closer, but instead, he pulled me so that I was sitting up. He lifted my dress over my head and then pulled one bra strap off my shoulder. He kissed my shoulder and continued to the other side.

I looked at him and smiled. "You need music?"

He took my bra off. "No... but you will." He kissed me and guided me until my back was on the bed.

I was so aroused from his touch. "Oh Really?"

He pulled my panties down my legs, I was completely naked. I could see that he had lost his shorts at some point and I was quite impressed with his package. I'd felt him a few times, but unclothed was a little different. I was slightly worried too, but I planned to take every inch of him like a soldier. "Yep, remember the ice cream shop?"

He was on top kissing me hard. I couldn't get close enough to him, I wrapped my arms and legs around him. "Uh-huh," I said in between breaths.

He kissed his way down my body and stopped at my breast. "Well, your two senses will be touch and sound." He had one of my breast in his mouth.

"Uh-huh." I couldn't pay attention to what he said because he was looking at me while he sucked my breast. My hands were wrapped around the back of his head. My nipples were hard as rocks. He moved down to my stomach and slowly placed soft kisses from the top to the bottom. He inched down further, I was on fire, I felt myself getting wetter. My legs were open, and he slowly kissed the inside of my thigh on one leg, then the other. I was so sensitive even the air he breathed out of his nose onto my inner thighs turned me on. My legs were over his shoulders, and his face was centered directly between them. His arms went up under each of my legs and wrapped around them like a vice grip. He held my legs apart so tight that I couldn't move. Our eyes were locked on each other. He gave me the most seductive grin, then dipped his head and swiped his tongue slowly from the bottom of my lowers lips to the tip of my clit. Mmmmmmm, that felt good! His eyes were still on me, but I had to look away, it was too damn erotic. His mouth covered me completely, I threw my head back and closed my eyes. He settled in on my clit; he sucked and ran his tongue over the very tip at the same time. Back and forth; back and forth his tongue went over my clit. My back arched, and my eyes closed tight. I tried to move my legs to reduce some of the intensity, but he held my thighs; I couldn't move. I fisted the sheets. Back and forth; back and forth his tongue went. I finally found my voice; I panted and moaned, "OH-OH!" I concentrated on the music; it helped relieve some of the pressure. But as soon as I felt a little relief he picked up the pace. He let one of my legs go and slipped a finger inside me. I couldn't take it, "MACON! MACON!" My head was going from right to left. I was moaning, Al was moaning. I lost track of time, I had no idea how long I'd been in this state of euphoria. He added a second finger and my legs started trembling; I knew I was about to cum at any moment. "MACON Please! I can't take anymore!" He released my leg. I attempted to turn over on my stomach, but he caught me in mid-turn and turned with me. He was on his back with his face between my legs and his tongue still working magic; I was on my stomach with my butt in the air. Back and forth; back and forth his tongue went again. My face was smashed in the pillow; I exploded all over him. My energy was gone, I trembled uncontrollably. Macon finally slid from underneath me and pulled my knees down. He turned me over on my back and gently kissed and rubbed my legs.

"Dawn?" I heard him calling my name, but I was too weak to answer. "Dawn? Baby say something."

"Something," I whispered.

# Chapter 10 ~ Macon

I kissed my way up to her face. I had worn my baby out with just an appetizer. Her eyes were closed, she looked peaceful. "Sweetheart are you okay? Because we aren't done."

She slowly opened her eyes. "I know, give me a minute."

I chuckled. "I don't think so. You've been talking smack for weeks, and now you need a break? You just asked about the Greedy Savage."

She covered her mouth and giggled. "You're right, but I'm rusty. It's been a while. Once I get my mojo back, I'll be able to keep up."

She was so beautiful. Her hair was all over the place, her eyes were glazed, and her skin glowed. I couldn't keep my hands off her. She was on her back, and I massaged and kissed her breast. I'd been waiting to hold these in the flesh for the longest. I kissed her neck and licked her earlobe. She wrapped her arms around my neck and kissed her way to my mouth. "Can you taste yourself?" I said between kisses.

"Mmm-hmm." She wrapped her legs around me.

"You taste good Baby." I was hard as a rock, and we were lined up perfectly. I needed to grab a condom, quick. I had to control myself or else this would be over before it started. I tried to pull back, but she held on tight. "Dawn, hold up Baby, let me grab a condom." She let me go, I reached and got one out of my nightstand. I sat back on my knees and rolled it on while she watched. She licked her lips slowly, and I almost moaned. Before I could get back to her, she had gotten on her knees and reached for me. We were wrapped up in each other's arms kissing like crazy. I tried to move us back down on the bed, but she damn near crawled on top of me. Oh yeah, I loved a team player, but I needed to slow her down a little bit. "Baby..." She didn't hear me. "Dawn?"

"Hmm?" She pulled back and looked at me. Her eyes were half closed.

"I'm taking care of you right now, okay?" She smiled, and I guided her back to the bed. I got on top with my upper body weight on my forearms. She tried to wrap a leg around me, but I caught it in the crook of my arm and slid inside her. *Damn!* She was so wet that I didn't move for a few seconds. She kissed me, and I stroked her slowly. She was so warm and tight; I felt her muscles making room for me. "You feel so good." I let her leg go, grabbed her hands and stretched her arms above her head. I slid in deeper and picked up the pace. She wrapped those long legs around me and joined in with my movements. She started grinding, and I went harder. We were both breathing hard and moaning. I knew I wasn't going to last long for the first round, but no way was I going first. Her legs were tight around my back. I slowed down and pulled out just enough to unwrap and straighten her legs between mine. The moment I slid back into the hilt I knew she felt it; I sure did. Her eyes were wide open, and her mouth formed a perfect "O." She wouldn't last long. The friction with her legs closed damn near made me scream.

She grabbed my shoulders, "OH! OH!" I picked up the pace and got lost in her. She started screaming, "MACON! OH! OH!" Her legs were vibrating, and she squeezed my arms. "AAAAHHHHH!" she screamed.

I was almost done too. Her walls tightened up as she clamped down to ride out her orgasm. I drove in deeper and harder then went stiff and released. I held on to her for a while, until she stopped trembling. I kissed her shoulders and neck until she was completely relaxed again.

"You okay?" I whispered in her ear. She nodded yes but didn't say anything. I got up and went to the bathroom to clean myself up and get a warm towel for her.

By the time I went back to the bedroom, she was still on her back, but her eyes were open. I gently wiped her legs down. "You want something to eat or drink?"

"Yes, that sounds good." I kissed her lips and grabbed my shorts from the floor.

I went downstairs to the kitchen and grabbed a couple of bottles of water and some grapes. When I got back to the room, she was sitting up in the bed with the sheet over her breast trying to pat her hair down. "Don't worry about your hair, it's going to look that way for the rest of tonight and most of tomorrow." I got back in the bed and pulled the sheet down, I wanted to see her body.

"You're going to keep me held hostage?" She smiled and tried to pull the sheet up again, but I blocked her.

"More like posted up." I fed her a grape. "I've seen you covered up for weeks so please don't deny me." She laughed. We were quiet for a few minutes while we ate and drank. I sat with my back against the headboard and my arm around her waist. Her head rested on my shoulder. "What's on your mind?"

She must have been in deep thought because she jumped. "Not much, thinking how nice this was tonight." She fed me a grape.

I grabbed her by the chin and pulled her face to me and kissed her. "I hope you don't think I'm finished with you yet. Should I turn Al back on?" I put the water bottles on my nightstand.

She laughed, then turned around and straddled me. I pulled one of her nipples in my mouth. "Not yet, but I do think I'll drive this time."

"Will this be a driving lesson?" My hands were full, I had an ass cheek in each hand kneading and massaging.

She kissed my ear, then my jaw. "I don't think you need any lessons, this will be more of a demonstration or performance, if you will."

"But what if I want to take over the wheel?" I tried to flip us so that I was on top, but she grabbed the headboard and stopped me, I chuckled. I loved a woman who knew how and when to take control in the bedroom.

"Not this time." She reached over to the nightstand and grabbed a condom. "Now, sit back and enjoy the ride."

"Yes, ma'am!"

~~~~~~~~~~~~~

The next morning, I was showered and in the kitchen making breakfast while Dawn slept. I was exhausted and didn't have the energy to take my morning run. We were up most of the night giving each other orgasms. She was a generous lover in every way; I was spoiled already. But I loved pleasing her too, watching her cum was a turn on, and those screams... I needed to chill before I woke her up again for more. My phone rang. I picked it up, it was my older baby sis. "What's up, Mel?"

"Hey Baby Bro, I'm surprised you answered."

I put the phone on my shoulder and flipped the bacon. "What are you talking about? Where are my children?"

"The kids are still sleeping, you know they were up all night after we got back from Six Flags. But don't try to change the subject." She laughed.

"Whatever Mel, what's up?" I needed to finish cooking and get back to my woman. I thought I heard the shower running upstairs.

"I talked to Lois and Tonya, we want to all chip in and send Momma and Brock on a cruise as a gift for his retirement. It won't be too much if all six of us do it."

"Sounds good to me. You know Momma has been waiting for him to retire." I put the eggs in the skillet and grabbed a couple of plates from the cabinet.

"Good, I'll call the boys now. But umm, where is Dawn?"

My sisters never stopped. "Why Mel?"

"You don't have to answer because I hear those pots and pans going over there. She must have put it down if you're up cooking." She laughed extremely loud.

"Why couldn't I have more brothers instead of sisters?" I shook my head.

"Because your sister takes kids to Six Flags and not those lame brothers. And your sister is keeping your kids another night, not your brothers."

My eyebrows shot up. I would not complain about having another day and night with Dawn. "Word?" I paused. "Wait, what does my Baby Girl have to say about this? You know she loves her daddy?"

"Well, she loves her Aunt more right now. They may have tricked me into going back to Six Flags again today for some event."

I laughed and began plating the food. "They got you. But look I have to go and thanks for taking the kids to Six Flags."

"Da-yum, well let me let you go, we don't want Dawn's breakfast cold." She was laughing hard.

"Whatever, Mel. You just mad because ain't nobody bringing you breakfast in bed." I closed my eyes; I didn't mean to say that, Damn!

She laughed even harder. "Yeah Dawn! I might have to get some tips from her if you over there serving breakfast in bed. You got some flowers and fresh squeezed orange juice too?"

I couldn't help but grin; I handed her that one. "Goodbye Mel. And you know what they say about payback."

"Goodbye, Mr. Bentley...I mean Baby Bro." She laughed, and ended the call.

I grabbed the serving tray of food and went up the steps. I looked real domestic, but after the things that woman did to me last night and this morning, I didn't care. I'd make her breakfast in bed every day if she wanted it. As soon as I went into the room, she came out of the bathroom in some kind of thin robe that barely covered anything. I loved my kids, but I would not complain about having one more day of Dawn.

She covered her mouth with both hands. "Oh my goodness, breakfast in bed? I may never leave." She sat on the bed and put her feet up.

I put the tray on the bed and got in beside her. "You can stay as long as you want." I leaned over and kissed her. "Good morning, Beautiful."

She smiled and helped me get the plates together. I had bacon, eggs, toast, and fruit for us to eat. "Macon, thank you so much, this looks good. I'm starving."

"Good, because you're going to need your energy. The kids won't be home today." I wiggled my eyebrows.

She laughed. "I am not fooling around with you all day."

"Baby I'm joking. But if you don't have plans today I would love to spend the day with you. We can go out."

"I'm sorry, but I do have plans today." She put a strawberry in my mouth.

"That's cool, we can catch up later." I wasn't trippin'; I could hang with the fellas.

She giggled. "I plan to spend the day with this handsome man who brings me breakfast in bed."

Now that I'd tasted every inch of her there was no way I was letting this woman go.

~~~~~~~~~~~~

I sat in my office working, but I could not stop thinking about the last few days. My weekend with Dawn couldn't have gone any better. We went out for a little while but ended up back in my bed for the rest of the day and night. That woman was freaky, horny, and all the above; and I was not complaining. I knew she had a lot on her plate, but I didn't care because I liked her a lot. I was pretty sure I was in love with her, but I wasn't speaking on that anytime soon. She was cool, but she still had a wall up. It made sense because she didn't have any constant positive men in her life other than that clown, Dre. I was sure he'd been there for her, but still, he wasn't a family member or someone in the house where she grew up. I knew that was important for women and their relationships with men. It was one of the reasons I liked Mike, Mia's husband. I wanted Chloe to have good men around her at all times, so she would know how a man was supposed to act whenever she started dating. I was all about Dawn, but I knew it would take some time for her to let me in fully, I had plenty of time. My phone alarm went off reminding me I had a meeting in fifteen minutes. I decided to call Dawn. After a few rings, she answered.

"Hey Baby," she said.

"Hey Beautiful, how are you?"

"I'm okay, how is your day going?" I could tell she was smiling.

I leaned back in my office chair. "It would be better if I were with you. What are you doing this evening?"

"I'm meeting the girls for dinner and drinks. I'm sorry."

"It's all good, I'll try to catch up with you when you get back."

"Alright, what are you doing after work?" I could hear her typing on her keyboard.

"Nothing now, I'll go see what the kids are up to."

"Okay, I'll call you when I'm on the way home and I'll come by."

"Sounds good. I gotta run to a meeting I'll see you later tonight."

"Okay, see you later." We ended the call.

I was just about to put my phone on silent before going to the meeting when a text came through.

**Lisa: Surprise! Guess who's landing in the Lou in a few hours? Can you pick me up? Or should I get an Uber to you?**

What? This was a surprise. I wondered if she talked to my mother? No way, she would have told me, she couldn't hold water.

**I can pick you up, send me your flight info.**

**Lisa: Sending it now, can't wait to see you!**

## Chapter 11 ~ Dawn

"Dawn, I like Macon for you. And not because he looks good." Janae chuckled. "I see how he looks at you and how you two interact. It's nice, and I haven't seen you this happy in a while."

I grinned. I was in the West End at the vodka bar with Tori and Janae. "Thanks. He's cool, and I like him a lot, but you know I'm scared to death. He seems too good to be true." We were seated at a booth near a window, and Tori and Janae were across from me.

"All I want to know is what's happening between the sheets?" Tori sipped her martini and stared at me. Janae shook her head.

"I'm not telling you, Tori." I paused, "Because I don't want you jealous." I popped an eyebrow, and she almost choked on her drink.

"I knew it! I could tell by his walk!" Tori smacked the table. We all laughed.

I stopped laughing and jokingly pointed my fork at Tori. "You better stop checkin' for my man."

"He's your man now? When did that happen?" Janae asked with a smug grin.

"We haven't talked about titles and all that stuff, but we have become inseparable." My smile faded as I noticed a couple outside the window. Was I dreaming or was I actually watching Macon walk down the street eating ice cream with a woman? He was across the street, but it was definitely him. As Tori said, I knew that walk from a mile away. I could hear Janae and Tori going on and on about something, but I couldn't speak. I couldn't decide on an emotion either, was I mad? Was I sad? Was I pissed? And he took her to my ice cream shop! I'd recognize that purple colored lavender ice cream anywhere! Yep, I'm pretty sure I was pissed off! I had no idea what I was going to do. I watched him stroll down the street laughing and talking. I hoped he choked on that damn ice cream! The woman was cute too, of course.

"Dawn, what's wrong?" Janae asked, but I couldn't say anything, I pointed to the window.

"Is that...?" Janae said.

"Hell naw, that's Macon!" Tori covered her mouth. "Who in the hell is that woman?"

I finally spoke. I shrugged my shoulders "I don't know. I talked to him earlier and he said he wanted to see me, but I told him I was meeting you guys." I had a blank look on my face.

"And I guess he decided he would take someone else for ice cream since you were busy?" Janae said as we watched them turn a corner and leave our view. "What do you want us to do to him?"

I chuckled a little and tossed my napkin on the table. "It won't matter what you do to him, I'll still feel the same way." I looked up at the ceiling. "You know if this had happened a year ago, I would have chalked it up to the game, but now I'm pissed and numb. I swear I can't win this year. I..."

Tori interrupted. "Okay, now before we go off the deep end," she eyed Janae. "There could be an explanation. Maybe it's one of his sisters or family."

"Nope, I've met all three." I turned my glass up and finished off my drink.

"Talk to him first, Dawn."

"I'm really surprised at you Tori. You know good and well that's not his sister on a damn ice cream date." Janae was mad; she rolled her eyes as Tori.

I smiled at them and reached into my purse for my wallet. "Ladies, I have to go."

"Well wait a minute, let's all go, we can trail you and come to your place." Tori was signaling for the waiter to come over and gathering her things.

I got up and tossed some money on the table. "I'll be fine, I always am. It was fun while it lasted." I walked off. I could hear Janae calling my name, but I couldn't stop. I didn't know if I was going to cry or scream. This year had taken my heart and stomped on it; I was pretty sure an extra stomp might send me over the edge. I should have gone with my first mind and not dated anyone. My car was parked in front; it only took me a minute to jump in and pull off. Before I could get to the highway, I heard my phone ringing. I didn't feel like talking to anyone. I ignored it and turned up the volume on the radio for the rest of the ride home.

By the time I got home I finally looked at my phone, I had five missed calls from Dre. Great! I forgot to tell Janae not to tell him. I knew I had to call him back or he'd be banging on my door shortly. I kicked my shoes off, plopped down on my sofa and called Dre's number. It barely rang.

"DAWN!" He was on ten, yelling into the phone.

"Dre I'm fine, okay?"

"I swear if I didn't have a security clearance I would kick BIG BABY'S ASS! I TOLD HIM! I SPELLED IT OUT FOR HIM! I told him that if he wasn't serious he needed to leave you ALONE! But you know what?" He didn't wait for me to answer. "I'm glad he did it now rather than later. I never trusted him! I KNEW IT!" I could hear him moving around.

"Dre this is not my first rodeo, I'll be fine. And do not come over here. I need a moment to myself." He was quiet.

"You don't want to see me?" *Why was he so dramatic?*

"It's not that, I want a minute alone." My phone buzzed, I had a new text.

**Macon: I have to stop at my mom's house, can you come there instead? Or I can come to you when I leave.**

*Wow, he was stunning.*

"Dawn, you there?"

"Yeah, I'm here." I didn't bother telling him Macon was texting me. He would get angrier.

"Please let me come over, I want to make sure you're okay, then I'll leave."

**I'm already home, not feeling well. I'll call you tomorrow.**

I couldn't talk to Macon tonight.

"Can you give me about an hour?" I knew he wouldn't rest until he laid eyes on me, but I needed a moment to myself.

"Okay, I'll be there in an hour. Let me know if you need anything." I heard the relief in his voice.

"Okay, bye." I ended the call, and another text came through.

**Macon: I'll be there in a minute.**

This evening kept getting better. I threw my head back on the sofa. I guess I would talk to him tonight after all. But what do you say to someone you've been seeing almost two months and you're not exclusive? If he wanted to see other people, then why do the family intros? And why introduce me to your kids? Could he be this messy? Could I be mad at him? I sat and stared at the ceiling until the doorbell rang. I walked to the door and unlocked it. I decided I would play it cool and let it go. I opened the door and let him in. He rushed in and tried to hug me, but I stepped back and closed the door.

"Baby come here, what's wrong? You don't look sick." His eyebrows knitted together.

"I'm okay." I folded my arms across my chest. *So much for playing it cool.*

"Why did you tell me you weren't feeling well?" I stared at him, but I didn't say anything. "Dawn, what's wrong?" He gave me a small bag. "I got you some of that lavender ice cream you like."

This was classic right here. *I couldn't believe him*! "Macon are you dating other people?"

"What?" he paused. "What are you talking about?"

I shrugged my shoulders. "It's an easy question."

"Dawn, I've been with you or my kids for the past couple of months. When would I have time to see anyone else?"

*Now he was lying*! "From what I saw, it looked like you had time today." I cocked my head to the side. My attitude was stank.

His eyebrows went up, and he smiled. "Okay, you think you saw something today, and instead of asking me a direct question, you're playing this game?"

"I think my question was very direct. I asked if you were dating other peo...." He cut me off.

"No, I'm not!" *Did he get loud with me?* "But maybe you should have asked me who I was with at the airport or the west end or wherever you saw me." He had his arms folded across his chest.

"The airport? Wow! You flew her in?" I shook my head. "I can't do this right now." I turned and walked away; defeated. Macon followed me into the family room. I sat on the sofa, and he stood. *Why did he look so mad?*

"You know Dawn, you're right, I can't do this either." I looked up at him. "I've bent over backward to spend time with you. I've been completely open and honest with you, and you treat me like some random ass dude the first time you smell smoke. You couldn't even give me the benefit of the doubt." And he still hadn't identified the woman. "I'm going to go, but could you do me a favor before I leave?"

I let out a deep breath. "Sure, why not?"

"Can you come outside and meet my cousin Lisa?" My eyes went wide. "She flew in for Brock's party, and I've been talking about you nonstop. She wanted to meet you today."

I had to look away I was so embarrassed. "Macon, I didn't know, I..." He cut me off.

"I know you didn't know, but it would have been nice if you had picked up the phone and asked."

I stood and walked over to him. I put my arms around his waist, but he didn't return the hug. "I'm sorry."

He grabbed my face and kissed my forehead. "I guess you were right, we did move too fast. You're not ready." *He didn't want to see me anymore?* "Grab your shoes and meet me outside." He let me go and walked towards the door.

"This is it? We aren't going to see each other anymore?" I was still standing in the same spot.

He turned around slowly, his eyes looked sad. "Isn't that what you planned to tell me after you saw Lisa?"

I didn't respond. He opened the door and went out. I felt awful. I did it again; I assumed the worst in a man. I put my shoes on slowly and went outside. Macon stood by the passenger door, I saw Lisa, the woman from earlier, getting out of the truck.

"Well hello! You must be Dawn." She had her arms stretched out to hug me. "My cousin cannot stop talking about you. We were on the way to Aunt Lila's, and he said you weren't feeling well. He almost turned the truck over trying to get here," she laughed, and I smiled.

I looked at Macon, he didn't have an expression on his face. This was not good. "Nice meeting you too, Lisa, you could have come in."

She waved her hand. "I was facetiming my husband, it's bedtime for the kids, and I wanted to say goodnight."

I felt worse. "I see." I had no idea what to say to her and Macon was quiet.

She looked at Macon, then at me. "Is something going on here?"

Macon cleared his throat. "Dawn isn't feeling well, let's go so she can get some rest." He opened the passenger door.

She got into the truck. "I hope you feel better by Saturday so that you can come to the party."

I had forgotten about the party. I guess that wasn't happening either. "I hope so too." I couldn't believe I'd made such a fool of myself and I completely disrespected Macon. He was right, he had been the most honest man I'd ever met, but I treated him like he stole from me. I watched Macon as he started the truck. He slowly backed out, and I waved. Lisa waved, but Macon would not look at me.

I went back in the house and stretched out on the sofa. I stared at the ceiling and thought about nothing. I missed him already, it had barely been thirty minutes since he left. The doorbell rang, and I jumped up. Maybe he came back to let me apologize. I ran to the door and opened it. Dre rushed in and hugged me; he held me tight. I hugged him back just as tight and cried. "It's okay, I'm here." He closed the door. "Come sit down." We walked into the family room and sat on the sofa. I cried hard; it wasn't pretty. Dre rubbed my back, but I couldn't get any words out. "I swear if I see that dude..."

I shook my head. "It's not his fault..." I lifted my head from his shoulder.

"What? How is this not his fault?"

I wiped my eyes. "It was his cousin, not a date."

Dre stared at me with a blank expression. "Is that what he told you? He on some for real bullshit if he thinks I'm fallin' for that one."

"No Dre, it's true. He brought her over to meet me."

"What? If it was a mix up why are you crying?" His face was scrunched up.

"Because he broke up with me or doesn't want to see me anymore." I threw my hands up. "I don't know, whatever we had going on... is over." I was still sniffling. Dre looked confused. I told him the whole story from the beginning.

"Forget about him." He blew out a breath. "Listen, yeah I see where you were wrong, but if he's going to end it over something this simple that's on him."

"Dre, it's not that simple. He told me I wasn't ready and he's right in a way. I never gave him a chance to explain, I assumed the worst about him. I basically called him a liar and questioned his integrity."

He pushed my hair away from my face. "There will always be problems, but if he runs off at the first sign of trouble, then he's the one that's not ready."

"You're not being fair to him. We've been inseparable for almost two months. I should have handled it differently." I laid my head on the sofa. "I was so arrogant about it too. Instead of telling him I saw him, I tried to give him the option to lie. It's like that's what I expected him to do."

"I'm sure you did, I know you have a little baggage you carry around." I side-eyed him, and he chuckled. "All I'm saying is that you're not perfect. If he can't give you a pass on this then it's good he bounced. You need someone that understands you and won't run off at the first sign of trouble."

I kicked my feet up on the ottoman. "Maybe you're right."

He kicked his feet up next to mine and put his arm around me. "I know I'm right."

~~~~~~~~~~~~

A few days after the situation with Macon, I was miserable. I was on autopilot, and I hadn't talked to my girls or Dre since that night. I told the girls the story and they offered some advice, but I didn't know what to do. He had not reached out to me, and I didn't think he wanted to hear from me. One thing I realized over the last few days was that at some point during the last couple of months I was falling in love with him. I didn't know how far but there was something there. I was so focused on trying to manage my feelings that I didn't realize my feelings for him had grown. I had to figure out a way to get him back. Even if it didn't work, I would try. I decided to call him. I reached for my phone and pressed his number. The phone rang, but he didn't answer. His voicemail picked up, then beeped. "Hi Macon, it's Dawn. I'm so sorry I didn't trust you enough, and I hope you will forgive me." This was harder than I thought. "Please call me." I ended the call. My phone rang, I was excited, but it quickly went away when I saw Dre's name. I answered, "Hey Dre."

"I've given you almost three days of space. I'm taking you to dinner tonight, be ready at seven."

I smiled, Dre was such a good friend. "Okay. Where are we going?"

"That was easy... I have to go to a work thing first, we won't stay long. Then we can go to dinner."

I rolled my eyes. "A work function? I'm not up for that."

"You're going, it's not formal. We will stay about thirty minutes, then we can go."

The last thing I wanted to do was dress up. But, I needed to get out of the house and Dre wanted me to go so I'd go. "Dang, alright. See you at seven." We ended the call.

I went upstairs to my bedroom to look for something to wear. I had a jumpsuit picked out to wear to Brock's party with Macon. No need to let it go to waste. It was fitted, sleeveless, and bright yellow. I loved bright colors; I paired it with multicolored strappy heels. It was only noon; I decided to shampoo my hair and give myself a manicure and pedicure. Might as well look good on the outside.

~~~~~~~~~~~~

Dre and I walked to the door of the hotel where the party was held, I felt like a million bucks on the outside. The inside was a different story. Too bad Macon wouldn't see me in my new outfit, I had chosen it for him. He always complimented me when I wore bright colors.

"You good?" Dre held the door open for me as we entered the lobby.

"No, I'm not. But I don't want to ruin your evening."

"You could never ruin anything for me, Dawn." He led me inside with his hand at the small of my back.

"Ms. Dawn! Hi!" I turned and saw Chloe walking towards us. *What was she doing here?* Shouldn't she be at Brocks' retire... Oh NO!

"Hi, Chloe." I hugged her. "How are you?"

She looked at Dre. "I'm fine. Hello, I'm Chloe."

Dre extended his hand. "Hi, Chloe. I'm Andre."

Chloe eyed Dre a few seconds longer and then turned to me and smiled. "My Daddy is going to be so happy you are here, he said you were sick. I'll go find him." She walked away. Guess I couldn't run away now.

"Umm, why is a child that looks like Big Baby at my coworker's retirement party?" Dre had his eyebrows knitted.

"Apparently, your coworker is Brock, who is Macon's stepfather." This week just kept getting better.

"For real?" I nodded. "Brock is a cool guy, I've known him from day one. We can go if you don't want to see Big Baby."

Why was St. Louis so damn small? You couldn't go anywhere without bumping into someone you knew. "I can't leave now, Chloe saw me." Macon was coming out of the ballroom. He looked so good it almost brought a tear to my eye. He wore a dark gray suit with a white shirt and a tie with yellow in it. Are you kidding me? His tie matched my jumpsuit. And what was that on his face? Was he growing a beard? This was way too much for me to handle. He came over to where we were standing.

"Hello, Dawn." He looked at Dre. "Dre."

"What's up? I didn't know Brock was your stepfather." Macon looked at me while Dre continued. "He's cool, I've known him for years..." Neither of us said anything, we stared at each other. "Okay, let me give you two a minute." Dre walked away. I heard him speaking to a few people in the distance, but my eyes were glued to Macon.

Macon broke the silence. "You look beautiful." He had his hands in his pockets.

"Thank you, you look nice too." It was awkward. A week ago, we were in each other's arms and now we could hardly find words. "Macon, I didn't know this was Brock's party until I saw Chloe."

He gave me a small smile. "You sure you're not passively aggressively stalking me?" My eyes went wide. "I'm joking, Dawn."

I smiled. I didn't know what to say to him. It was obvious he was only talking to me because I was here. "Ummm, I'm going to go, I'm glad I got a chance to see you." That was so lame.

"You don't have to leave." I heard someone call his name and he turned. "Stay and enjoy yourself. I have to go and check on something for my mother. I'll come find you later." He walked away slowly with his eyes on me. I held my breath until he was gone. No way I could stay here.

Dre came up behind me and touched my elbow. "You alright?" I shook my head no and had to check myself before I ruined my mascara. "I'm sorry, I had no idea. Let's go. I'll holla at Brock later."

"No, I'm fine. This isn't about me. Let's do what we planned and stay for a while and then go." I gave him a fake smile. "I'm a big girl."

We went into the ballroom, Dre talked and mingled with coworkers as we looked for a table. I tried not to look for Macon, but I saw him watching me from across the room. Dre found seats with a few of his coworkers. I excused myself to go to the restroom to catch my breath. I slipped out of the ballroom and walked down the small hallway to the bathroom. I went to the mirror and checked my makeup. I stood there for a minute and stared at myself. I needed to get through this evening without crying. I heard the door open, and Mrs. Lila came around the corner.

"Hi, Mrs. Lila! You look so pretty." I smiled and went to hug her.

"Thank you, Dawn, you look good too!" I blushed. "Well, let me cut to the chase." She put her hand on her hip. *Was I about to get reprimanded in the bathroom?* "I don't know what's going on with you and Macon, but my boy has been moping around for the last few days." I tried to talk but she raised her hand, I closed my mouth. "You young people run around here playing with each other not realizing life is short." *Please don't make me cry, Mrs. Lila.* "Did Macon tell you how we lost his father?" I nodded. "Well, then I know you understand how hard that was for me. I was about your age when he died. You don't know how many times I thought about the silly arguments." She looked at the ceiling and blew out a breath. "All that time was wasted! You don't think about it until they're gone, then you live with regrets."

I grabbed a napkin and dapped my eyes. "You're right, Mrs. Lila."

She crossed her arms over her chest. "If I'm right, why are you in here and not out there talking to my son?"

"I messed up, and he's not talking to me."

She put her hand on her hips and leaned towards me. "Then fix it! Go ahead and go!"

Ummm, okay. "Yes, ma'am." I hugged her and left the bathroom. As I walked to the table I thought about what Mrs. Lila said, she was right. How many times during this year had I thought about all the things I never got to say to my Mother? I missed her every day, and I felt robbed because I didn't get to say goodbye. The thoughts were always there, why didn't I do this while she was here? Why didn't I do that while she was here? I guess the honest answer was, I never thought about time running out until it was too late. Well, I wasn't letting my time run out with Macon. I reached the table and put my purse next to Dre. "Can you watch my purse?"

He looked up. "Yeah, but where are you going?"

"To get my man back!" I turned and walked off. I saw Macon mingling close to the dance floor; I kept my eye on him as I walked across the room. I knew he was watching me too; I made sure I had my cute stroll on. Well, as cute as I could be in four-inch heels without falling. I stood in front of the DJ booth, he removed his headphones. "Can I request a song?" I yelled over the music.

"Yeah, but I've already been told to play all the slides a little later."

I laughed, yeah St. Louis did get down with the slides. "It's not a slide. The song is "Booed Up" by Anthony David."

He stared at me, and I shrugged. "Alright, I'll play it next."

"Thank you so much." I turned to walk off then I stopped. "And when you do play the slides can you play the 'Wobble'?"

He laughed. "You know that's already on the list."

I gave him a fist bump and left to find Macon. I didn't have to go far; he was coming towards me. Did he have to look that good in a suit? We met right on the edge of the dance floor. The current song was coming to an end.

"How are you enjoying the party?" he asked.

The intro to "Booed Up" began and I held out my hand. "Will you dance with me?"

He smiled and took my hand. "Of course."

He led us to the middle of the dance floor. Most of the people were leaving the floor; maybe they didn't recognize the song. He gently put his hands around my waist, and I put my arms around his neck. We slowly swayed from side to side. He wasn't looking at me. I took a minute to get my words in order. I knew I needed to apologize, but I didn't know what to say beyond that. "Macon?" He turned his attention to me. "I'm sorry."

"I'm sorry too, but can we talk later?"

Ordinarily, I would have agreed, but that wasn't happening tonight. I wasn't sure I would have the nerve later anyway. "No." He pulled his head back and his eyebrows went up. "I want to talk right now because later isn't promised."

He relaxed and smiled. "I see my Mother got to you too."

I laughed. "Yes, she did, and she's right. Macon, I was wrong. You've been good to me and the minute I thought you were trying to play me I went into defensive mode. I completely ignored all the chivalry and honesty that you've shown since we met. I handled it wrong. What can I do to make it right with us again?" I let out a breath, I hadn't planned to say all that at once. Our song was still playing, and we were the only couple left on the dance floor.

"Sweetheart..." That was music to my ears. "It's always been right with us." He pulled me closer. "I'm sorry too, I was pissed off that you didn't trust me."

"I guess we are both carrying a little baggage from the past." I thought about his problems with Mia which led to their divorce. I did the same thing to him; I felt bad.

He brushed my hair behind my ear. "Maybe, but I think we can handle it."

I was so relieved because I didn't have a backup plan. "Can we start over?" I asked.

He stopped moving. "Hell no!" *What!?* My mouth dropped open. "You think I'm waiting another two months for sex? Nope, we are picking up right where we left off." We moved again.

I threw my head back and laughed out loud. "Really? Are you serious?"

His forehead wrinkled. "I'm very serious. I plan on gettin' real indecent with you..." he looked at his watch, "in about three hours."

I could not stop laughing. Our song came to an end and we stopped moving. "Best of Me" by Anthony Hamilton started playing. Everyone slowly came back to the dance floor. Macon pulled my hands to his lips and kissed the back of each one. We stood staring at each other.

"I'M GLAD Y'ALL MADE UP!" Lois yelled over my shoulder. I jumped, and Macon pulled me next to him. She was dancing with an older guy that I assumed was her husband. "He's been listening to Lenny Williams for the last few days... *Cause I looooove you!*" she sang, then danced away.

I looked at Macon and he shook his head. "She talks to much. Let's go." He grabbed my hand and led me off the dance floor. My Baby really missed me if he had been listening to Lenny. I smiled to myself.

We walked out of the ballroom and into the lobby area. A couple of the staff members stopped him to ask questions. I tried to let his hand go, but he held on tight. We went down the hallway that led to the restrooms; he stopped abruptly and turned around and kissed me. It wasn't long, but enough to get me all hot and bothered. "I've wanted to do that since you walked in the door." He held my face. "You're leaving with me, okay?"

He read my mind. "Okay, but let me go find Dre and let him know."

"No need." *What the...?* Macon and I both turned; Dre was standing a few feet away. He stared without an expression. "I was bringing your purse. I'm headin' out."

"Hey, Dre." *Why did he look so sad?* He couldn't be upset about me leaving with Macon. We'd done this plenty of times over the years. But, it was usually me getting a ride with someone while he took a random home. "You okay?" I asked Dre.

"I'm cool." He handed me my purse and flashed a smile. There was my friend; he had me worried for a second. "Alright, Macon." He gave him a manshake, then grabbed my pinky finger. *What was he doing?* "Alright Baby, call me tomorrow."

I snatched my hand back and gave him a side-eye. I couldn't believe him. I wasn't back with Macon five minutes, and here he was trying to pull rank. Yeah, I'd table that tongue lashing for tomorrow. I would have never done that to him! "I'll talk to you later."

"Be easy, Dre." Macon grabbed my hand. "And you bring your fine self with me, I'm ready to dance with my woman again." I couldn't help blushing. We walked off and left Dre standing there; I'd deal with him later. For now, I had my man back, and I planned on enjoying him for the rest of the night.

## Chapter 12 ~ Dre

His woman? I didn't like that dude, and he wasn't about to lay claim to my damn friend. I'd been with Dawn through everything, and he thought he was taking her from me? She was mine. I watched them walk into the ballroom all cuddled up. He acted like this was his first piece or something; simple ass. I knew I should have left, but curiosity got the best of me. I went back into the ballroom and walked around for a minute. Too Short's "Blow the Whistle" was bumpin' when I spotted them on the dance floor. I didn't even pay attention to him dancing all over her like a young boy, but I did pay attention to her. She was happy out there dancing, her hair was bouncing, and she had the biggest smile on her face. She looked good in that outfit too; I couldn't keep my eyes above her waist. I knew I was wrong, but I couldn't help it, and I had no idea how it happened. One day she was my best friend, then out of the blue I was noticing body parts and wanting to touch her. I rubbed my hand down my face; I had to get out of here before I did something I regretted.

"Andre Brown? Is that you?"

I turned around. "Delores?" *Why was she here?*

"In the flesh... I saw you earlier with Dawn. I can't believe you two are still tight after all these years." She hugged me.

"Umm, yeah we still tight, did you talk to her tonight?"

"I did, but she's dating my baby brother, so I've seen her a lot lately." *What?* She never mentioned that to me. But when did she have time with Big Baby around?

"Macon is your brother?" She nodded. "And Brock is your father?"

"Yes, how do you know him?" Delores was crazy in high school but always cool. Who would have guessed she was related to Big Baby?

"I've worked with Brock for about twenty years. He's good people." Maybe she could tell me something about her brother. "But um, yeah so Macon is your brother? Small world."

"Yeah that's my baby brother and from what I can tell..." She glanced at the dance floor. I turned in the same direction and saw the damn love birds still dancing. "...he's all wrapped up in your girl."

"I see, but you know they just met, so you know how that goes." I tried to play it down like it wasn't much to it.

"It's been a couple of months, and she's been at family stuff. Macon doesn't bring anybody around the family, especially his kids. My niece, Chloe, is in love with her. Got me feeling all jealous," she laughed.

She wasn't making this any better; I needed to leave. "That's cool, but I'm on my way out, it was good seeing you." I reached to hug her.

"Good seeing you too." She walked towards the dance floor, and I took one last look at Dawn.

I talked to a few coworkers and Brock, then left the party. I sat in my truck with my head back and my eyes closed. If I had skipped this party, Dawn would be with me right now. I had no idea what I was going to do, but I knew I could not hurt her. Was I trippin' because I was used to having all her time? Or was I really feelin' my best friend? This was crazy, I needed to talk to somebody because I had been trying to figure this out by myself for weeks now. I tried to be her friend and accept Big Baby, but it wasn't happenin'. When I thought he messed her over I was mad as hell at him, but I was more relieved because I thought he would be gone; for good. I had to call my boy; Rob was level-headed. I found his number and called.

"What's up Dre?" Rob said. I heard Serena in the background.

"Wad up Rob, tell the wife I said hello."

"She heard you... What's good? I thought you and D were at that retirement party."

"We were, but it turned out to be Big Baby's people and now she's in there with him." I tried to keep it cool.

"Ah for real? That's crazy...I guess they back together, huh?" He didn't say anything for a minute. "You cool though?"

I didn't know how to answer even though I had called him for advice. I didn't want to sound like a kid whining about someone taking their friend. Maybe calling Rob was a bad idea. "Yeah, I'm good. Why would I be trippin' off them?"

"BECAUSE YOU LIKE HER!" Serena yelled.

"Damn man, you got me on speaker?" This was the last thing I needed. I did not want the girls knowing anything. Hell, to be for real I didn't know what was going on myself.

Rob laughed. "My bad, she walked out the room I didn't know she could hear, let me take you off."

"What is Serena talking about anyway?" If I didn't know how I felt, how did she know?

"Dre come on, real talk."

I rubbed my hand down my face and blew out a breath. "I don't know man, it's like something is different now. I'm thinking about her all the time. I'm checking her out... It's crazy. And why didn't you say anything?"

Rob chuckled. "Me? So, I'm supposed to tell a grown ass man that he likes his childhood friend?"

"I don't know. My head is all messed up and now she's back with Big Baby." I couldn't believe I was sitting out here all shook up over Dawn. I couldn't get that image of them dancing out of my head. "I gotta go. I'll holla at you later."

"Cool, but ummm, are you planning to tell her?"

That was a good question, but I had no idea what I was going to do. "I don't know."

"A'ight man." He ended the call.

I knew what I needed to do to get my mind off all this. I'd hit up ol' girl from down the street. I pulled up my text app.

**You up for some company?**

**Stacy: I thought you had plans tonight?**

**Change in plans.**

**Stacy: See you soon.**

Cool! I started my truck. I was about to drive off when Dawn walked out of the hotel. Big Baby was right behind her. What were they doing? Maybe he did something to piss her off; he couldn't handle her for real. I kept watching, his daughter came out next. What was going on? Where were they going? The party wasn't over for another couple of hours. There was a fountain in front of the hotel and Dawn posed in front of it, Big Baby was all over her. His daughter took pictures of them. I sat there and watched them, I couldn't move. I thought about everything she'd been through this year, I'd never seen Dawn so fragile. But now she was happy, and it was all because of Big Baby. I had been trying to make her feel better for months, and he came along and did it in two. Maybe he did deserve her.

~~~~~~~~~~~~

My alarm went off early the next morning. I was in bed staring at the ceiling. I called Stacy on the way home and told her I couldn't make it. After watching them take all those damn pictures and kissing all over each other, I didn't want to be bothered. Stacy was cool, but I knew she would want to talk before sex and I wasn't in the mood for talking last night. If I couldn't get right in it, I wasn't interested. My phone vibrated, it was Dawn.

"What's up?" I asked.

"I'm surprised you answered, I was expecting to get your voicemail. I figured you were with one of your women."

"Nope, not today. What are you doing up so early?"

"I'm cooking breakfast for Macon."

*Whatever.* "That's cool, but it's like seven in the morning, you don't get up this early." See this dude had her doing stuff she didn't usually do; this wouldn't last.

"I know, he's still sleeping. I want to surprise him with breakfast."

Yep, that was what I wanted to picture this morning. "That's what's up... so what's up?"

"I have to have a reason to call you now?"

She was right, I was trippin'. "Naw, never that, I thought something was up."

"Dre, what's going on? Last night you were trying to pull rank. And now you sound like I'm bothering you. Am I missing something?"

"I'm good, D." I had no idea what to say. "You know I'm happy you and Big Baby cool again. And I wasn't trying to pull rank as you call it." That was a lie.

"Good, because I'm happy, Dre. And I'm sorry about dinner last night."

"Ain't no thing, you know how we do."

"Hold on." She moved the phone away, but I could hear her talking. "Good morning." I heard her moving around giggling. "Stop it... go get back in the bed. I'm on the way up with the food."

Big Baby started talking. "You better be, I'm not finished with you yet. I need my morning fix." More giggling. This was pissin' me off.

"Dre? I'm sorry. Macon is up, but I'll call you later."

"Cool."

"And Dre, thank you so much for making me go to the party."

"You know I got you. I'll holla at you later."

"Bye." I ended the call.

That was the last thing I needed to hear this morning. I got out of bed and put on my running clothes. I needed to clear my mind. Usually, I would run to Dawn's and eat breakfast with her, but not today. I couldn't believe that dude was over there laid up eating breakfast in her bed. I had to figure out a plan; my mind was running wild.

I went out of the house through the garage and decided I'd run to my folks' house. I put my earbuds in, cranked up some Jay-Z and took off. Moms was probably getting ready for church, but I knew Pops was most likely getting his meat together to put on the grill. Pops was funny, he went to church every other week and grilled on the Sundays he didn't go. I had no idea why he did it, but that was his thing from May to November. I was close to the end of my street when Stacy's garage went up. I wasn't trying to talk to her right now, but it looked like I didn't have a choice. She walked down her driveway, she looked good too. Stacy was short, brown and curvy with long hair. Well, long hair they put in at a shop. I hated weave, but I was hard-pressed to find a woman that didn't wear it, so I got over that years ago. "Hey Sexy," I called out when I was in front of her house.

Her head jerked up. "Hey, why are you out so early?" She ran her hands over her hair. She had on some small shorts and a tank top.

"Trying to get it in before it gets too hot." I held my arms out to hug her. She felt good, and I felt like a fool for canceling on all this last night. "What about you?"

"I didn't get my mail yesterday and I'm expecting something. You want to come in?"

As good as she looked right now I couldn't be that dude. Dawn was all over my head. "I'm on my way to my folks' house right now. I'll call you later though." Stacy's ex-husband had her kids for the weekend; I knew they were coming back later today.

She frowned. "Dre, you don't have to give me excuses, we are both grown. If you don't want to see me anymore, it's fine."

"It's not like that." *Where was this coming from?*

"Then what is it like?" She had that stance, arms folded across her chest and hip stuck out to the side.

"Stacy, I don't know what you're talking about. I was trying to see you last night, but I got sleepy on the way home and didn't want to fall asleep on you. And I'm headed to my folks' house now." This was the reason I didn't get involved with relationships; it was too much trouble.

"If you say so, but we've been hanging for the last few months and now you're different, blowing me off, canceling. It's not cool, and like I said I'm fine if you want to end it."

Truth be told, I didn't know what I wanted. But was I acting differently? "I'm cool, I got a lot going on right now." I reached for her chin, and she smacked my hand away. I looked down and shook my head... women.

"I'll see you later." She turned to walk away, but I grabbed her by the waist.

"I will call you later, okay?"

She moved my hand. "Whatever, Dre." She walked off.

I stood there for a minute and looked up at the sky. What was happening to me? I had this fine woman asking me to come in her home, and I was standing in her driveway thinking about another woman. And the other woman, a.k.a Dawn, was probably feeding

Big Baby that damn French toast I loved. I took off running to my folks' house.

My parents lived about ten minutes from me; it didn't take me long to get to their house. I used the code on the garage to get in. I expected to see Moms at the kitchen table when I went in, but she wasn't there. I went into the tv room and found both of them on the couch. "Your favorite child is here," I announced.

My father looked up from whatever he was reading. He had on his reading glasses, and as usual, he looked over the rim of the frame. "You don't have much competition for that spot." He was grinning at me. I was an exact replica of my father; only he was completely grayed out. We even shared the same haircut and goatee.

Moms laughed. "Leave my baby alone, I'm glad we only had him. He was all I needed." Pops rolled his eyes and shook his head.

"Thanks, Mom. Good to know one of you like me." I went into the bathroom to wash my face. It was humid out, and I was wet from my run. I usually kept a few clothes here for the days I ran and stopped by. I had stuff at Dawn's too for the same reason... not for long, I guess. After I cleaned up, I went back into the tv room with the folks and sat across from them. "No church today?" I looked at my Mother, but my Father answered for her.

"We thought we would have a morning alone, but I guess that's out the window."

I laughed, Pops was always on joke time. "No one else lives here, you're always alone."

"Doesn't look like it right now," Pops said, and Moms giggled.

"Larry, leave my boy alone... Why are you here so early? Is something wrong?" My Mother worried all the time. She had the prettiest brown skin and long grey-black hair. She was short and almost too thin.

I leaned back in my chair. "Nothing's wrong, can't I visit my parents?"

They looked at each other and Pops closed his magazine. "Alright, what's going on, Son? And don't say nothing. It's Sunday morning, which means whatever date you had last night ended early, or you didn't have one. Either way, something happened." He stared at me.

I had a good relationship with my folks, but I wasn't sure if I wanted to talk to them about Dawn. They loved her, and always hinted around to us dating. "I'm cool Pops, I wanted to get a run in this morning. I thought you had some food on the grill."

Moms looked at me and smiled. "You know your Father and I were single before we were married, we may be able to help."

Maybe this wasn't a good idea. "Would you two stop it," I laughed. "I'm fine, I'll make sure I don't come over here early again." I got up and walked towards the kitchen.

"Well Larry, I guess this early morning visit has nothing to do with that guy we saw Dawn holding hands with in the grocery store last week." I stopped dead in my tracks.

"Yeah Barb, I guess he's fine."

I turned around. "When did you see Dawn and where?"

Pops smiled. "Oh, you want to talk now?" I sat back down and waited. "Like your Momma said, we saw her at the grocery store holding hands with some tall guy. She introduced us to him, he seemed nice enough."

"And very handsome." Pops looked at her and frowned. "Well, he is nice looking, I see why she had his hand."

*Not her too.* "He's cool, Dawn seems to like him, it's all good," I lied.

"And how do you feel about him?" Moms asked.

"I'm not dating him, Dawn is." I had to change the subject. "Are you going to cook anything today?"

She shook her head. "Boy, when are you going to stop being foolish and tell her how you feel?" I tried to talk, but she raised her hand. "Andre Brown, I've been your mother for forty-four years, and I know when you're lying. I've watched you run after Dawn since you were kids. Now that your brain has finally caught up with your heart, you better tell her before it's too late." She pointed to a picture on the mantel of Dawn and me at her first wedding. "Like last time."

I looked at Pops for help, but he shrugged and picked up his magazine. I guess I needed to come clean. "Okay, you're right, I don't like her dating this guy because I may have feelings for her."

Pops put his magazine down and took his glasses off. "Since when?"

I ran my hand down my face; this was hard to explain. "Since a few weeks ago, I guess. I know you thought I always liked her, but I honestly didn't look at her like that. Something changed, and all of a sudden, I saw her differently. I don't know how it happened."

"That's because you equate love to lust." I looked at Pops again for help, but he sat back in his chair with his hands behind his head. "Who do you call when you're sick? Who do you call when good things happen? Who do you call when bad things happen? Who knows your secrets?"

"I know that Dawn is the answer for everything, but..." She cut me off.

"Then that's the person you spend the rest of your life with, not running around chasing anything in a skirt." *Damn, is that what she thought of me? Was I that bad?* "Your Father is my best friend; you think we would have made it all these years on sex alone?"

I threw my hands up. "Alright, I need a timeout. Can we not talk about sex?"

Pops chuckled. "Look Son, what your Momma is trying to say is that what you have with Dawn is the same thing we have in our marriage. I love your Mother, but she's my best friend too, if she weren't it wouldn't have worked."

I understood what they were saying, but this was different. "I hear you, but I guess I'm a little late realizing it. And Dawn doesn't feel the same way."

"Have you asked her?" I shook my head no. "Then I guess you better talk with her before that handsome young man steals her heart. Maybe I'll tell her," Moms said.

I looked at Pops, he finally came to the rescue. "Barbara, you will not get involved." She looked at him, and half smiled; her way of conceding. "I'll thank you after he leaves." He winked at her.

I laid my head back on the chair and closed my eyes. I knew they meant well, but they didn't understand. They married in their early twenties; Dawn and I were in our forties. We had thirty-something years of friendship at stake, and I knew I didn't want that messed up. I had to figure out how I felt about her before I considered talking to her anyway. Man, this was a lot. I never had this much head space dedicated to one woman. But I knew no matter what happened I could not lose her as a friend. I couldn't even handle her being mad at me.

"Andre?" I opened my eyes. Moms stood next to my chair rubbing my head the way she did when I was sick as a kid. "It will be okay, I know things will work out for the best." She was right about that one, but who was best? Big Baby or me?

~~~~~~~~~~~~~

I was in my office working; I heard a knock at my door. "Come in." After a few seconds, the door opened, and Brock came in carrying a big box. I stood to help him, I grabbed the box and put it on a table. "What's good, Brock?" We shook hands. "I guess this is your last official day? Have a seat." I closed the door and sat in my office chair.

Brock had the biggest smile on his face. "Yes, Sir. I'm on the way to turn in my badge and I'm done."

"Good for you man, you deserve it." Brock was one of the first people I met when I started working here a little over twenty years ago. I was fresh out of college, and I was scared to death on my first day. Brock took me under his wing and showed me the ropes. "What are your plans?"

"Whatever my wife tells me to do," he laughed. "She's been on me about retiring for years, I owe her at least five years of whatever she wants. I'm leaving for a cruise in a few days."

I chuckled. "Sounds good, Brock. I'm happy for you."

"And thanks again for coming to my party, the wife and kids did it up for me."

I didn't want to think about that party. "No problem, I had a good time."

"Oh, and thanks for bringing Dawn. We didn't think she was going to make it."

*Where was he going with this?* I'd known Brock for years, and he was a man of few words. "Anytime, Dawn is like family."

"So I've heard... But exactly what kind of family are we talking about?"

*Damn Brock, straight with no chaser.* "What's on your mind Brock?" I had a lot of respect for him, I wanted to hear him out. I leaned back in my chair and gave him my full attention.

"Let me tell you a little story." *This was serious.* "My wife, Lila, and I went to high school together, but we didn't get married until after both of our spouses passed. Macon was about thirteen when his father passed, and Lila came to me for help with him. We eventually got close and started dating. I proposed, but she turned me down." *Why was he telling me this?* "You know why?" I shook my head. "Macon didn't like me, and Lila told me she couldn't put her son through any more pain."

"I'm guessing he came around since you're married now," I said.

"Yes, he did come around, but it was up to me to get him to come around, if I wanted his Momma." I didn't say anything. "In other words, my wife had a fit when she saw you come to the party with Dawn." Now, this was making sense, but not really because she left with Big Baby; not me. "And she had a bigger fit when she saw you watching them on the dance floor."

"Listen Brock, Dawn and I have been friends since we were about ten; it's all good." I couldn't promise him I wouldn't take her from Big Baby.

"Heard that too, but Momma Bear will do anything to protect her boy, including sending me in here to talk to you. I hate to get into you young folks business..." *Too late for that.* "But, I saw you with her, and you didn't look like a man out with his friend."

I had to kill this conversation. I couldn't believe he was in here trying to feel me out on behalf of Big Baby. What parents still ran interference for their middle-aged kid? I chuckled to myself; this was something my Moms would do too, I couldn't trip. "You can tell Mrs. Lila she has nothing to worry about; as long as Dawn is happy, I'm happy."

Brock gave me a suspicious look, then stood. "Alright, I'll let you get back to work. Don't be a stranger, you'll keep in touch?"

I stood and shook his hand. "No doubt. And thanks for all you've done for me over the years." He grabbed his box and left.

I sat back in my chair and took my cell phone out. I looked at the pictures of Dawn. I couldn't believe after all these years I had fallen for a woman I wasn't sure I could have. Next to Moms she was the only woman I trusted, it made sense that we should be together. But what if it didn't work out? I could not lose her. A knock on the door interrupted me again. "Come in."

Janae stuck her head in the door. "You got a minute?"

"Yeah, come on in." Janae usually called me at work. She rarely stopped by my office because she worked in a different building.

She closed the door and sat in Brock's seat. "I talked to Serena." She rested her head on her fist and stared at me.

*What the hell was going on today?* "Okay?" I stared at her.

She sat up straight and squinted her eyes. "Dre, I swear if you mess this up for Dawn with your foolishness I will hurt you."

"Mind your own business Janae. Dawn is grown, and so am I. I don't need you or Serena telling me what to do."

"You are so damn selfish, that's why you're by yourself now!" She rolled her eyes and stood to leave.

*Did she really just cut me like that?* "I'm selfish because I want to go after the woman I want?" My eyes were wide, and forehead wrinkled.

She crossed her arms. "It's selfish because you know what she's been through this year. She's finally happy about something, and you're trying to take it from her. Leave her alone, Dre." She tilted her head to the side. "Please?"

"Am I that bad? And you think he's better for her?" I was mad, I stood and paced back and forth behind the desk. "I was the one picking her up off the floor and holding her until she was asleep! I was the one at her house every day making sure she ate! NOT HIS ASS!" I stopped and pointed to the door. "Don't come up in here tellin' me that he's better for her!"

Janae was quiet. "I never said he was better than you."

"That's what it sounded like to me." I ran my hand down my face, I was tired of talking to everyone about Dawn. I sat down in my chair and blew out a breath.

Janae sat down again. "My concern is Dawn. You're so caught up in trying to be better than Macon that you're losing sight of what's best for her. Are you ready to be in a relationship, Dre?"

"You know I would do anything for Dawn."

187

"But this wouldn't be for her, this would have to be what you wanted as well."

I didn't have an answer. "All I know is that she's on my mind all the time. I see her differently now." I blew out a long breath. "I'm attracted to her."

Janae smiled. "It takes more than that, Dre. If you're going to drop this in her lap, you better be damn sure about what YOU want. This can't be about having a pissing contest with Macon."

"What am I supposed to do? Watch her with him and say nothing?"

"All I'm saying is that either way, she's going to lose. You're going to make her choose between you and Macon. I don't think she can take another loss right now. What will you do if she chooses him?"

I hadn't thought about the consequences of her not choosing me. "I don't know."

"See that's what I'm talking about. If she stays with Macon, your relationship will change, and she loses her best friend. If she chooses you, it would only be out of fear of losing you, but she'll still suffer by losing Macon. Did you see how upset she was last week when they broke up for three days?"

This was too much for me to think about. Janae put a spin on the whole thing. "I don't know what I'm going to do, but either way I can't lose her." I was hurt, but I wasn't about to admit it to Janae.

Janae stood and walked to the door. "It's your decision, but make sure you know what you want before you talk to her." She opened the door and left.

My phone vibrated.

**Dawn: After work dinner at my house?**

Maybe I would tell her today.

**Of course, you want me to bring anything?**

**Dawn: Just yourself.**

**I'll be there.**

# Chapter 13 ~ Macon

"How is it going with Tori?"

"She finally called, we're going out this weekend." He sounded relieved.

"That's good, the conversation went well?" I knew Donald; he was capable of running a woman off with his shyness.

"It was cool, we didn't talk for long. But enough about me, what was all that drama with you and Dawn I heard about?"

I didn't want to talk about that, but I guess my mood gave it away last week. And Chloe. "It was a misunderstanding, it's all cleared up now."

"But Lady B said something about her coming to the party with one of Brock's coworkers."

I shook my head. "Naw man, it wasn't like that, he's like a brother, they grew up together." Speaking of Dre, why was his truck in Dawn's driveway? Just the person I wanted to see after work. I pulled in and parked next to him. "D, man I just got to Dawn's house, I'll talk to you later. Let me know how it goes with Tori."

"Alright man, talk to you." He ended the call.

I had to get my mind together before I saw Dre. That stunt he pulled at the party on Saturday had him about to catch my hands. I got out of my truck, and her front door opened. Dre came out and closed the door. He saw me walking towards the porch and made a face. "What's up Dre?" I stopped when he was a few feet in front of me.

"Not much, Dawn cooked dinner for me." He stared at me with a slick grin.

"Good, that means she's ready for our dessert." I figured that comment would make that grin disappear. It did.

"I've been meaning to tell you, that break-up or skit or whatever it was you performed had my girl upset. She's not used to dealing with dramatic men."

I chuckled. "I think that's all she's used too, I should fit right in."

His jaw was tight, mouth in a straight line. "Whatever, man. Stop upsetting my girl, and we'll be cool."

I looked down at him and leaned in; I had him by about four inches. "She might be your girl, and you're her boy. But, she's MY woman, and I'm HER man. As long as you remember that, we'll be cool."

He was mad, his nostrils flared, and his jaw clenched. He opened his mouth to speak, but the door opened and interrupted. Dawn came out on the porch smiling. "Hey Baby, I didn't know you were here. I thought you were working late?"

I walked around Dre and went to her. I gave her a loud kiss, and she giggled. "Hey Sweetheart, I needed to see my woman."

"Well, your woman is ready for her man." She smiled and moved past me to Dre. He looked at me but didn't say a word. "Dre, you left your charger again." She handed it to him.

"Thanks, I didn't realize I left it." *I bet.* "Alright, I'll catch y'all later." He turned and walked away. "And Dawn?" We both looked back. "Thanks again, we need to start doing our weekly dinners again."

She laughed. "Yeah right, you'll start canceling when you meet someone new like you always do."

"Not this time." He held his hand up. "I promise."

Dawn moved in front of me to go in the house. I held the storm door open for her. "Whatever you say." I looked back at him, and we went into the house. "Are you hungry? I wasn't expecting you this early. I put your plate in the refrigerator."

"I'm starving and thank you. How was your visit with Dre?" I didn't trust him at all.

She moved around getting my food together. I could get used to this. "It was fine, I kind of felt bad about leaving him on Saturday."

"Was he upset about it?"

"No, he was okay, but I know he's feeling like I'm ignoring him lately."

Dawn was such a good friend to that punk. She didn't realize what was going on and I was not going to tell her. They had been friends for too long, and I knew she was protective of him. I had to be careful with what I said about him. "Whatever you need to do Baby, I know he's your family."

She stopped and smiled. "Thank you for being so understanding, you are so good to me." She brought my plate to the island and handed me a glass of water. "Now that the kids are gone are you missing them yet?" She sat next to me.

"They just left yesterday, but yes I miss them." Mia and Mike were down for Brock's party, and the kids went back with them. "School starts next week, and since I am closer now, I want to make sure I'm there for their school activities."

"That's right, volleyball and drama for Chloe, and track for Major."

"Yep, would you like to go with me sometime?"

She smiled. "Of course, I was hoping you would ask me. And speaking of Chloe, she introduced me to Mia at the party."

I shook my head. "I saw but couldn't get to her in time. Mia is cool, I wasn't worried anyway. But, I wanted to do the introductions. What did you think of her? She likes you a lot."

Her eyebrows went up. "Really?"

"Anybody that gets along with Chloe is an angel." We both laughed.

"She's not that bad... But Mia was nice, and over a foot shorter than you. You told me you like tall women."

I nodded. "I do, but you have to remember I was fourteen when I met Mia and I was only about five-seven."

She threw her head back and laughed. "Get the hell outta here, no way!"

"I'm telling you I didn't grow until I was about seventeen. Then I grew a couple of inches a year until I was about twenty." She kept laughing. There was something I wanted to say, but I didn't want to complicate things. Might as well do it. "You know we never really talked about last week. We just made-up. Not that I'm complaining. I enjoyed your apology." The things that went down after that party had me back over here last night and again today.

"I know." She turned away. "I was embarrassed."

I grabbed her chin. "Don't be." I kissed her. "I didn't bring it up to rehash it, I brought it up because I don't want it to happen again. I want you to understand that I don't want to see anyone else."

"I don't either. But..." I cut her off with a kiss

"There are no buts. We decided we are seeing each other, and that's it, okay?"

"Just like that? No questions or talking about it?"

"Yes, just like that. I don't have any questions, do you?" *Why was she making this hard?*

She tilted her head to the side. "I think we both have to try to let go of past relationships. I know I was wrong, but if we are going to do this, I can't have you breaking up with me when I mess up."

I pushed my plate to the side and grabbed both of her hands. I looked into her eyes. "Sweetheart, please forgive me. I was trippin', I may have had a flashback or two. But trust me when I say I had already decided I was coming for you as soon as the party was over that night." I let her hands go and started eating again.

Her mouth was wide open. "You mean I could have waited and not said anything?"

I leaned over and kissed her cheek. "Yep! Now, any more questions about you officially being my woman?"

"I guess I haven't done the exclusive thing since I was married." She shrugged.

"I've done both since I divorced."

"You mean you ran around?" She side-eyed me.

"I did." I drank some water. "I'd been with Mia since high school. After we divorced, I umm, tried to play the field. But, it wasn't me, I didn't have time to figure out all those personalities and moods. I don't see how people do it, I'm a one-woman man."

She smiled. "Good to know."

"I'm all yours, Baby." We both laughed.

"After I got divorced I..." I cut her off, I put my finger to her lips.

"Dawn you know I'll listen to anything you have to say, but I don't want to know anything about your past sex life."

She moved my finger. "You just told me you were a whore after you got divorced."

I laughed. "That is not what I said... But, I only want to picture you with me, no one else." I tapped her nose with my finger.

She shook her head. "I guess as far as you're concerned I've only been with my ex and you."

"What ex?" I asked.

She laughed. "Alright, I guess I've only been with you then?"

"Now you got it, Baby." We both laughed.

~~~~~~~~~~~~

The last few weeks were great. Dawn and I were together on a regular basis. We stayed at her house during the week and my place on the weekends. And true to his word, Dre had been by for dinner once a week. He was usually leaving by the time I got there after work. He was still up to no good, and if I wasn't sure before, I knew for a fact that he was feeling Dawn. I caught him looking at her on more than one occasion, and there was nothing friendly about it. Dawn and I were good; if he wanted to hang out on the sidelines and watch, that was his prerogative. But if he crossed the line I couldn't promise I wouldn't hurt him. We were on our way to her sister Summer's house for her great nephew's birthday party. I knew I was officially whipped if I was going to a toddler's party on a Saturday. She told me I didn't have to go, but I didn't mind. It was more of a family thing anyway, a couple of kids but mostly adults. She had a cool family, and I liked being around them. As soon as I parked, Dre pulled up behind me. He didn't miss anything.

Dawn took her shades off and turned around in her seat. "I didn't know Dre would be here, I guess Summer talked to him." I didn't say anything, I got out of the truck and went to help her out. She went to the back door to get the gifts. "Hey Dre, I didn't know you were coming."

He walked up to her and kissed her cheek. "I guess you didn't since you forgot to tell me." I took a deep breath. "What's up, Macon?"

"What's up?" *Who in the hell wore dress clothes to a kid's birthday party?* I closed the doors and took the gifts from Dawn.

"I'm sorry, I didn't think you would want to come." We walked to the porch. I made Dawn get in front of me; I didn't want him looking at her.

"That's cold D, but you brought Macon?" He laughed from behind me.

"He's my man, of course, I did," she yelled, and laughed. I looked over my shoulder at him and smiled.

The front door opened, a young guy came out of the house. "Hey, Ti-Ti."

"Hey, where are you going?" She hugged him.

"Momma needs something from the store, I'll be back."

"Okay, I want you to meet someone." She introduced us, and I shook his hand. I remembered her mentioning a younger nephew that was away at school.

"What's up, man? How is school going?" Dre was slappin' hands with him and puttin' on a show as usual. Dawn and I went in the house and left him outside talking to her nephew. I locked the door behind me. I knew it was childish, but he brought out the worst in me. We went to the back of the house into the kitchen and connected family room area and spoke to everyone. I went outside on the patio off the kitchen with the rest of the fellas. Summer's husband, son, and son-in-law, plus a few family friends were sitting around talking.

"Hey Macon, good to see you again, grab a brew and have a seat. Hey everybody! This is Macon, he's a friend of Dawn's," Summer's husband said. He was manning the grill.

I said what's up to the fellas, grabbed a drink from the cooler and took a seat. They were talking about football, I joined in. A few minutes later, Dre came out and eyed me. Of course, he knew everyone, he started slappin' hands and talking loud.

"Dre, why are you always in church clothes man?" I wasn't sure who asked, but everyone laughed. "We are all out here chillin', and here you come with wingtips on."

"Hate the game, not the playa." Dre popped his collar and laughed.

"You do keep 'em lined up though," the guy said.

"Naw, man it's not like that."

Summer's husband turned around. "Whaaat? You turned your player's card in Dre?"

"I don't know about all that." He had a slick grin. "But, I do have my eye on a prize."

"You need to ask Macon over here for some advice if you got your eye on someone. You see how fast he pulled Dawn."

I knew I liked her brother-in-law, I wanted to laugh. Instead, I took a swig from my bottle and leaned back. "Not a problem Dre, anytime you need any advice let me know. As the man said, I got Dawn on lock."

Everyone laughed, but Dre kept his mouth shut for once.

~~~~~~~~~~~~

The following day, Dawn and I were on our way to get the last few things from her Mom's house. "Baby how are you feeling?"

She stared out the passenger window as I pulled into her Mom's driveway. "Not good, this is the last time I'll be in her house." Her eyes were wet.

I turned my truck off and grabbed her hand. "I know this is hard, but I'll be here with you, okay?"

She smiled. "Thank you, it means so much that you would come with me."

"Where else would I be?... Come on, let's go in." I got out and went around to get her out. She fumbled with the keys and seemed to be shaking, so I rubbed her shoulders. "I'm here," I whispered.

She unlocked the door and went in to turn off the alarm. I'd been here a couple of times before with her, but this time was different. We weren't moving and packing, everything was quiet. The kitchen was right off the living room. A hallway led to three bedrooms and a bathroom. Dawn walked into the kitchen and leaned against the counter. She slowly slid down to the floor and screamed. *Whoa, okay.* I ran into the kitchen and pulled her into a tight hug. "I CAN'T DO THIS! IT'S TOO HARD!" she cried.

"Baby, I'm so sorry, let it out." I was on my knees holding and rocking her. She calmed down a little, but she continued crying. I hated seeing her like this; I knew how she felt. It reminded me of the days after I lost my father. The pain was constant.

She tried to stand, but I held her. "I thought the worst part was over." She pulled back and looked at me. Her eyes were red, and her face was wet. I grabbed the roll of paper towels from the counter. I tore off a few and wiped her face. "It's just the beginning, and I don't know how I'm going to make it."

"I'm here for you, whatever you need, okay?" She nodded.

"You know the worst part is that I didn't get to say goodbye." She sniffled. "All the years I took for granted. I thought that she would always be here. I didn't get a good father, so I subconsciously thought that God gave me a good mother to compensate. I thought that I would have her for a long time because I only had her."

My poor baby, she needed grief counseling. "Dawn, it's okay, I understand. Maybe we can get you some counseling. It may help." I wiped the new tears from her face.

She tried to stand again, I helped her up and stood with her. "You might be right, but I know it can't take the pain away. It's almost unbearable."

I pulled her into a hug and rubbed her back. "Whatever you need, I got you."

She looked up at me. "Can we go? I thought this would be more nostalgic, but it's torturous."

"Sure, let's go." I grabbed the last few boxes and loaded them into my truck, and we left.

# Chapter 14 ~ Dawn

I was finally feeling somewhat normal. This year had been rough for me, and I didn't think I would ever find a comfortable place in time to rest. We had packed my Mother's home and put it on the market. That was the hardest part of the process. I always thought that we would pack her house with her fussing over our shoulders about what she wanted to keep. I had it all worked out in my mind; she would move to a senior apartment, and then with me, once she couldn't live on her own anymore. But, I guess God had other plans for her that I couldn't question. Although I missed her, I had a good family and good friends; I also had Macon. I was in love with him, and I wanted to tell him, but I didn't want to scare him. I also didn't want to say it and he not say it back. My self-esteem wasn't set up to handle that kind of awkwardness. The doorbell rang. I looked at the clock; it had to be Dre coming over for our weekly dinner. He was about an hour earlier than usual. I went to the door and looked out the side window. I opened the door. "Hey, you're early." I moved back to let him in. He came in and hugged me tightly, he didn't let go. "Dre, what's wrong?" He didn't say anything, he just held me. "You're scaring me."

"I need to talk to you, can we sit?"

Oh my goodness, what happened? "Okay, let's go sit." I closed the door and followed him to the tv room. I sat on the sofa; he sat in front of me on the ottoman.

He grabbed both of my hands and looked at me. "You know I love you, right?" I nodded. My heart started beating fast. "I need you to promise me that no matter what I say, you won't be mad at me, okay?"

I narrowed my eyes and tried to pull my hands away, but he held on. "What did you do?"

"Dawn, I didn't do anything." He let my hands go and ran a hand down his face. What happened? He was nervous; his hands were shaking. "I've been trying to figure out how I wanted to tell you, but I couldn't come up with a good way to say it."

"Would you just say it!" *Geez.*

"I love you."

Okay, he was making me mad. "Yes, you said that already."

"No, I mean... I'm in love with you, Dawn."

*Say what?* My eyes went wide. "What are you talking about?"

"I have feelings for you." I sat back on the sofa and stared at him. "I don't know how it happened. And I've been fighting it for weeks." I couldn't say anything. What was going on with my life? Why was my best friend of thirty-four years telling me he was in love with me? How did this happen? And why? "Dawn I'm sorry, please say something."

"Why now? Why tell me this when I'm in a relationship and in love with someone." My voice was so low I barely heard myself.

"You're in love with him?" he asked in a low voice. His forehead was stretched.

"Yes, I am, and is this why you're saying this to me? Because of Macon?" I knew he wasn't all that crazy about Macon, but really?

"NO! This has nothing to do with him, this is about you and me."

"There is no you and me, what are you talking about?" I was confused. I was on the verge of tears. He tried to wipe my eyes, but I smacked his hand away.

"Please don't cry, I'm sorry." He tried to hug me, and I let him. I thought my life had taken a turn for the better and now this. A few tears slipped from my eyes, and I pulled away from him.

"Dre, I need you to leave." I couldn't do this right now. I wiped my eyes.

"What? Dawn, please don't push me away. Talk to me." His eyes were sad; he was hurt.

"When?"

He dropped his head down. "I honestly don't know. I thought I was losing my mind. It came out of nowhere. I tried to fight it." He lifted his head and looked into my eyes. I stared back at him.

"Are you sure this isn't jealousy blown out of proportion because of the time I've been spending with Macon?" I knew I was grasping at straws. I knew him well, and I could see it in his eyes for the first time. But, I wasn't sure if he understood what all of this meant. Dre was a wonderful friend, but he was not a relationship person.

"I'm positive this isn't jealousy."

We sat staring into each other's eyes for a moment. "What are you asking me to do? Break up with Macon and be with you?" This was crazy.

"I'm not asking you to do anything. I want you to think about it and make your own decision. I know my timing is bad, but I couldn't control it."

"But how are we supposed to be friends now? You're asking me to choose between you and Macon." I threw my hands up.

"I will always be here for you, no matter what happens. If you stay with him, I'll deal with it. I know things won't be the same for a while, I'll need some time to get myself together."

He was killing me, I didn't know what to say. I couldn't brush what he said under the rug and pretend he didn't say it. I loved him, I never imagined he would have feelings for me after all these years. "If I stay with Macon I will lose you." A few tears dropped. "You know it."

He wiped my eyes with the pads of his thumbs. "I'm not giving you an ultimatum, I want you to do whatever makes you happy. If he makes you happy, then that's what I want for you. But, I know I can make you happy too." I felt like I was in the twilight zone.

"This is too much, I need to go lay down." I stood, and he stood with me. He hugged me, but it felt different this time. Was I saying goodbye to my childhood friend? Or was I embracing my future mate? I was used to protecting Dre, it was natural for me to do whatever I could to make him feel better. But could I be with him romantically?

He pulled away. "I'm going to go and give you some time. I'm sorry." He kissed my cheek and left.

I put the food away and went upstairs to my bedroom, I was on autopilot. I got in the middle of my bed and propped my pillows behind my head. I smelled Macon's scent, it provided some comfort. He made me happy, and I loved him, but Dre was a permanent fixture in my life. What would I do without him if I stayed with Macon? I knew he said we would remain friends, but I knew things would be different. I wanted to be mad at him, but Dre would never do anything to cause me harm. And, Summer told me Momma thought we would end up together. Was she sending me a sign that I was supposed to be with Dre? I had to call my girls, I needed help with this one. I grabbed my phone and called Janae.

"Hey, what's going on with you?" I had a lump in my throat, I couldn't talk. "Dawn? You there?"

"Janae." Tears flowed.

"Dawn what's wrong!? What happened?" She was frantic.

"It's Dre, he..." I could not get my words together.

"What happened to Dre?"

"Nothing. Give me a second, hold on." I got up to get some tissue to wipe my eyes. "Okay, Janae, I'm sorry. Before I tell you can you call Tori?"

"Umm, okay. Hold on." I wiped my face and got back in the bed. "Dawn? Tori?"

"I'm here," Tori said. "Dawn what's wrong?"

"Dre just left, he told me he is in love with me," I blurted out.

"What the hell?" Tori said.

I told them the whole story and waited. Janae was surprisingly quiet. Tori started in again. "You're telling me that Andre Brown has a thing for you?" She didn't wait for my answer. "This is bizarre, I don't get why after all these years. And Janae why aren't you saying anything?"

It was very odd that she hadn't commented. "Janae, did you know?" I asked.

"I did." *I should have known.* "And before you ask why I didn't tell you it was because I didn't think he was serious. I thought he was jealous. I told him not to tell you unless he was sure, because what's happening right now is what I didn't want to happen."

Janae was a protector too; I understood her reasoning. I was sure she had a few choice words for Dre during their conversation. I chuckled to myself. "I understand Janae, and I wish he hadn't told me. I have no idea what I'm going to do."

"Hold up. I know you aren't about to leave Macon's fine ass for Dre. That's crazy."

Leave it to Tori to focus on looks. "Tori that's not what I'm saying. I'm saying that either decision is going to be painful."

"There is no decision, you're with Macon. Dre will get over it like he said."

Before I could answer Janae jumped in. "It's not that simple for her Tori. She's known Dre for over thirty years and no matter what he says their relationship will not be the same if she stays with Macon. I..."

Tori cut her off. "Whatever! I hear what you're saying, but if you're true friends, which I know you are, your friendship will survive it."

"She's actually right Dawn. Don't make a decision for fear of losing Dre or out of obligation. It might be hard at first, but things will work themselves out. You need to be true to yourself and do what makes you happy. And from where I'm sitting, Macon does that for you."

I blew out a breath. "Summer told me that my Mom thought Dre and I would end up together." The line went quiet.

Finally, Janae spoke. "Dawn, I know you miss your Mom, but you know she wants you to be happy. You have to make your decision based on the present and what you know to be true. Your Mom probably said that because you were going through a divorce and Dre was there for you. Macon wasn't around then so don't use that for your reasoning. If you want to be for real, how do you know she didn't send Macon in your direction?"

*I never thought about it that way.* "You're right Janae, and what I know is that Macon makes me happy and I'm in love with him, but..."

Tori cut me off. "So, it's settled then! You'll stay with Macon, and forget about what Dre is saying."

"Really, Tori?" Janae snapped.

"What I was trying to say is yes, I love Macon, but I was in love with my ex, and we know how that ended." I sighed. "Dre would never hurt me. Janae, you remember how he was when I first separated? He was at my side the whole time."

"I remember, and I'm not saying you shouldn't try to explore things with him. All I'm saying is that you shouldn't make your decision based on fear of getting hurt. Don't end it with Macon because he might hurt you later. And don't be with Dre because you think he will never hurt you. Nothing is guaranteed."

I knew she was right, I'd been living by that rule for the longest, but it was easy when there was only one man; not two. "I know what you're saying, but you know I've been so indecisive since my Mom passed. It's like I can barely decide on shoes half the time. And y'all know this is not me, at all."

"You damn right it ain't you!" Tori yelled. "I swear I should kick Dre's ass for doing this to you."

I chuckled. "Don't be mad at him, he did struggle with telling me."

"Whatever!" Tori snapped. "This is what he does! He always has to manage you and be in control of you at all times. Now, I know I haven't been in the group since grade school and college, but it's been long enough to make an assessment. And I say that his ass needs to FALL BACK! Let you be happy for once. Better yet, why doesn't he get someone for himself and leave you alone! He's like a damn puppy, always following you around!"

Well damn, my eyes were wide, and I said nothing. Janae was quiet too.

"Are Y'all still there?" Tori asked.

"Yes." Janae and I said in unison.

"Well Tori, I didn't know you felt so strongly about the situation," I said

"Right!" Janae quipped.

"You both know I love me some Dre, but I think you need a win in the love department - with Macon. You light up when you're around him, you both do. And the sexual tension is so damn thick I feel like a voyeur whenever I'm in the room with the two of you." She giggled.

"Okay good, I thought it was just me that was uncomfortable around them," Janae said, and we all laughed.

I blew out a breath. "I hear both of you. No matter what, it feels like I'm choosing between my best friend and my boyfriend. Macon is wonderful, I have the pillow he uses across my face right now, so I can smell him." They both laughed. "But Dre is my boy; he's been my safe place for years. I don't want to smell him, but I don't want to live without him either. I've already lost the most important person in my life this year, I can't lose Dre too."

"You won't lose him," Janae said.

It felt like he was already gone. Whenever I felt bad, he was the person I went to, and now I couldn't call him. "I'm not so sure... I have to go. I can't let Macon see me like this and I can't tell him what's going on right now."

"You better not ever tell him," Tori warned.

"I agree," Janae said.

"I can't tell him right now. I don't want him to hate Dre." I paused, "I will tell him something. Eventually, I'll have no choice if Dre stops coming around. And I don't want to lie to him."

"This ain't the time for honesty in my opinion, but do what's best for you, we will check on you later," Tori said.

We said our goodbyes and ended the call.

I laid in bed for another thirty minutes. I got up and washed my face, then headed to the wine fridge to get a bottle of wine. I went out on my deck, poured a large glass of wine and kicked my feet up. I sent Macon a text to let him know I was on the deck.

About twenty minutes later I heard footsteps coming up the stairs. "Hey, Sweetheart." Macon walked over and leaned down to kiss me.

"Hey, how was your day?" I reached for his hand and guided him to sit on the ottoman in front of me.

"Busy, how was yours?"

That was a question I didn't want to answer. "It was fine. Are you hungry?"

"Not right now. I thought you were having dinner with Dre."

*Do not lie to this man.* "He couldn't stay, so I came out here to relax."

"Are you okay? Your eyes are red." He brushed my cheek with the palm of his hand.

"I'm fine." I gave him a weak smile. "I'm ..." I couldn't do it. "Macon I've had a rough day and I can't talk about it right now." His eyebrows were knitted together. "I'm not going to pretend I'm okay because I'm not, and by the way you're looking at me you already know something is wrong."

He let out a breath. "Yeah, I know something is up, I can see it in your face, and you've been crying."

"I will talk to you about it, but I can't right now. I need to process it for myself first."

He blew out a long breath, he seemed disappointed. "Okay... Is there anything I can do?" I smiled and shook my head no. "Do you want to be alone? I can stay at my place tonight."

My eyes went wide, that was the last thing I wanted. "No, of course not, I want you here." I sat up and grabbed his face. "Okay?" I had to pull myself together, I did not want to run him off. Dre may have put something on my mind, but Momma didn't raise a fool. I'd battle this out in my head and not mention a word of how I felt to Macon. If Momma taught me anything, it was that you always kept some things to yourself when it came to men.

He smiled and then kissed me. "I know, you can't sleep without me anyway." He tickled my side, and I laughed.

"With all that snoring you do?" He tickled me again. "Stop!" I laughed.

"I do not snore!" he yelled playfully.

He finally stopped tickling me. "I was joking." Macon always knew how to make me feel better. I stood, and he grabbed me around my waist and hugged me.

He looked up at me. "Whenever you're ready to talk, I'm here for you."

I smiled, he was so good to me. "Thank you for being understanding." I pulled him up from his seat. "Let's go in."

As wonderful as Macon was, Dre and I had been through a lot over the years, and I couldn't ignore our past. I owed him the courtesy of considering his words. Honestly, I owed it to myself. I needed to be one hundred percent sure my heart and my mind were aligned.

~~~~~~~~~~~~~

### Landscape Elementary School – fourth grade

*I was excited about being at a new school. It was a single-story brick building in the shape of a horseshoe with a large playground at the center. I was sitting in music class in the second row staring out the window at the kids having recess. A boy named Cedric, sitting to my left, smacked my arm hard. My eyes went wide, I turned and punched him in his arm even harder. He grabbed his arm and yelled, "Dang! I was only testing you since you're new!" I turned away from him without saying one word. The teacher was at the front of the classroom banging on the piano singing the 'Do-Re-Mi' song; he never heard our little spat.*

*After music, my class went to lunch. We were in the gymnasium, which doubled as the lunchroom for a couple of hours per day. We sat at long tables with matching benches on either side. I was opening my Strawberry Shortcake lunchbox when Cedric plopped down across from me and said, "Hey! What's your name again?"*

*"Get away from her Cedric!" a voice yelled over my shoulder causing me to turn around. A skinny boy about the same height as me with brown skin and a tiny afro had a scowl on his face. He had on one of those Adidas tracksuits in dark blue with white stripes running down the sides of the legs and arms. Cedric was chunky and much bigger than this boy, so I*

*didn't understand why he would yell at him. My head swung back and forth between the two of them, waiting to see who would move.*

*"I'm only talking to her, Andre." Cedric stood and picked up his tray.*

*"I saw you in music class, leave her alone or I'll never sell to you again," he said.*

*"Okay, okay, I'm leaving." Cedric walked away and never looked back. I was confused.*

*Andre walked to the other side of the table and took Cedric's seat. He held out his hand and smiled. "Hi, I'm Andre."*

*I smiled back at him and shook his hand. "Hi Andre, my name is Dawn. Thank you for helping me get rid of Cedric. I don't know why he keeps bothering me."*

*He shrugged his shoulders. "He probably likes you, but he won't mess with you again."*

*I took a sandwich bag from my lunchbox and offered it to him. "You can share my cookies since you helped me."*

*He took the bag and inspected the cookies before taking one out. After tasting a small piece, his eyes went wide. "Hey, these a good! What kind of cookies are these?"*

*"They are called tea cakes. My Momma makes them." I took one out of the bag and ate in silence with him.*

*He put his elbows on the table and leaned towards me. He looked from side to side and then whispered, "You think you can get your Momma to make enough for me to sell?"*

*I scrunched my face up. "Sell? What are you talking about?" I did remember him scaring Cedric off with something about selling.*

*He leaned back and crossed his arms. He grinned. "I run an empire, I sell stuff."*

*"Like what?"*

*He unzipped his jacket and revealed a row of colorful pencils taped to the inside. "Mostly pencils, but as good as those tea things are I might expand."*

He was funny; I liked him already. "Well if you sell my Momma's tea cakes, how much do I get?"

"I'll have to think about it, but for now..." He snatched a purple pencil from his jacket. "I want you to have this pencil for free. I'll even add on the insurance." He handed me the pencil.

"This is pretty, but what's insurance?" I didn't know what a pencil had to do with insurance. I only knew about the insurance card my Momma took out whenever we went to the doctor.

Andre smiled and popped his collar. "My pencils cost ten cents, but it's an extra five cents if you want insurance. If you get the insurance and you lose your pencil, I will give you another one for free."

"But what if you never lose it? Do you give the five cents back?" I stared at him.

He cocked his head to the side and chewed on his bottom lip. "It doesn't work like that; my Daddy says once you pay insurance the company keeps it to pay for the bad drivers."

"Huh? But we can't drive." He was confusing me.

He stood. "Meet me after school at the stop sign on the corner. I need to hire you for my empire, you're smart." He popped the last piece of the tea cake in his mouth and walked off. I shrugged my shoulders and decided I would meet him after school. Maybe I'd get a new friend at my new school.

### *Central Missouri – Junior year of college*

I was rolling down the highway exhausted. After a week of grueling finals, I should have been heading east on my way to St. Louis to start my winter break. Instead, I was going two hours south of my school to visit a very sick Dre. I'd talked to him several times during the week, and he sounded awful. He was coughing, and his usual smooth tenor voice had morphed into something like a robot. I attempted to come down earlier in the week, but he lied and told me his voice was off due to a common cold. However, he was in bed sick, according to his roommate, Rob. And, he refused to go to the doctor. I knew something was off, and Rob confirmed my suspicion when I spoke to him this morning.

About an hour later I stood outside their apartment knocking. Rob opened the door with a big smile.

"What's up, Girl?" He stepped back to let me in and shook his head. "Dude in trouble now, I didn't know you were coming down."

I took my coat off and reached to hug Rob. "You know I couldn't let him be down here sick. Aren't you leaving to go to STL soon anyway? And what's going on with your hair?" I frowned. Rob was usually well groomed, but he had a small unkept afro today.

He ran a hand over his head and smiled. "Ya boy about to start some locs."

I rolled my eyes and put my hand on my hip. "Here we go... you'll start, but I'll give you six months, you'll be faded up again. Where's Serena? Has she agreed to these locs?" Rob and Serena met freshman year; they were inseparable.

Rob walked away laughing. "Gone somewhere Girl... when I commit, I commit. I'm going to pick her up on the way out. But you mark my words, when we all forty I'll still have Rena by my side and dreads down my back."

I laughed and yelled to his retreating back, "Whatever Rob! I'll see you and Rena, as you call her, back in the Lou." I walked in the opposite direction and went to Dre's room.

I heard him coughing before I got to the door. I knocked lightly and barely heard him say come in with all the coughing. I opened the door and gasped, what the hell? His eyes were puffy, his nose was red, and his natural caramel color skin had a white film over it.

"Dre?" He was in bed propped up on pillows. He tried to smile but couldn't.

"What are you doing here?" More coughing. I walked to his bed.

Boxes and bottles of cold medicine were tossed around on his nightstand and bed. The blinds filtered light from outside, but it was a little dark in the room. "I'm here to check on you." I ran the back of my hand across his forehead and jerked it back. "You're burning up! You're going to the ER right now!"

He shook his head. "Naw," more coughing. "I'm good, I need a nap then I'm going to go talk to my Professor about my last final I missed."

"You missed a final?!" My eyes were wide. "I thought you finished a couple of days ago? And you didn't talk to the professor?"

He shook his head. "I tried to go take it this morning, but I couldn't make it."

I rummaged around the room looking for clothes and shoes. "You're going to the ER or else I'm calling your Mother. After that, we will get this final situation together." I knew once I mentioned calling Mrs. Barbara he would start moving. I planned to call her anyway.

"Ok." He didn't put up a fight. He pulled the covers back and started slowly putting on the clothes I gathered.

I stuck my head out the door and yelled, "ROB!"

A few seconds later Rob came running into the room with his face in a scowl. "Damn! What's going on? You all loud."

"I'm taking Dre to the ER; can you please get him into my car!?" I was in full-blown drill sergeant mode; tossing things around and gathering the empty medicine containers to take to the ER. Rob and Dre knew not to question me whenever I barked out orders. I saw them eye each other out the corner of my eye. Rob stood at the door and didn't move. I stopped what I was doing and looked at both of them with my hands on my hips. "Robert and Andre, you have two minutes to get him dressed and into MY CAR! I am not playing with y'all today! Rob this is your fault anyway, you should have called me." I yelled because I was nervous, I wasn't set up to handle sickness.

They both moved around quickly. "How is this my fault? Dude is grown, I told him to go to student aid two days ago, but he only went to get the meds and never saw the doctor."

*"I DON'T WANT TO HEAR IT! GET HIM IN MY CAR NOW DAMMIT!" I side-eyed Dre and left the room to call his parents.*

*I shouldn't have yelled at him while he was sick, he didn't like me angry with him. I wasn't angry, I was afraid. He looked awful, and it scared me to think about what might have happened if I had gone home instead.*

*An hour later, Dre was in a hospital bed with an IV drip. He had pneumonia, and they wanted to keep him overnight due to an extremely high fever. His natural coloring was returning, and he talked a little more.*

*"Thank you for coming down," he said.*

*"You're welcome." I sat next to his bed in a chair with my feet propped up half sleep. I was exhausted from finals; I could barely keep my eyes open.*

*He held his hand out to me. I grabbed it and squeezed. "I'm serious, I appreciate it. I didn't realize I was this sick. I need to call the folks and then reach out to my professor."*

*"Done and done." He furrowed his brow. "I've talked to your parents twice, once in the apartment and then a few minutes ago when I went to the restroom. I told them I would have you call once you got into your room, prepare for your Mother." He rolled his eyes and looked at the ceiling. "I found your syllabus in your book bag and called your Professor. I told him you were being admitted and that you would bring a formal doctor's note before you left for winter break. He said he would give you an incomplete once you've turned in your doctor's slip."*

*He released my hand and scrubbed his face "What would I do without you, D?" He smiled in my direction. "Thank you again. And I'm sorry for scaring you."*

*"You're welcome, but why didn't you tell me you were sick?" I stared at him waiting for an answer, my chin resting on my fist.*

*"Dawn you know how you are, you start worrying and what not. You've had a tough time academically this semester. I wanted you to focus on your finals and nothing else."*

"Ok, I'll concede to that but, this can never happen again. You have to go to the doctor; you could have died in that apartment. And Rob was leaving too." I shook my head. "You know I'm not set up for losing my friend."

He chuckled and coughed. "You aren't set up for losing anyone."

I laughed. "Oh be quiet." I stretched my arms out and yawned, standing from my chair.

His smile faded. "I know you're tired, but you can forget about leaving. I'm not staying in this hospital alone in this little town."

"What?" I stared at him. "Dre I'm exhausted, I'm going back to your place and fumigate your room then I'm getting me some shut eye. I'll be back in the morning to get you."

The nurse walked in gathering IV bags and reading his chart. "Alright Mr. Brown, we have a room ready for you now. I'm going to roll you out as soon as I get you unhooked from the monitors."

"Thanks, will I have a roommate?" he asked.

"Oh no, all the college kids are gone, we are pretty empty. You'll have a suite all to yourself." She smiled.

"Good, is it ok if she stays with me?" He pointed at me. "Her dorm is closed, and I think she's too sleepy to drive to St. Louis today. I don't want her getting into an accident on the highway." He gave her a big smile.

"Well, who could say no to that handsome face?" She chuckled. "I'll be right back, let me make sure you're in a room with two beds." She walked out of the room.

I stared at him with a blank face. "You know I can't stand you? And why did you lie to that nurse? I don't even go to school here."

He had a smug grin on his face, obviously feeling much better. "I did not lie. I told her your dorm is closed, which is true. And I never said you went to school here. And I do think you are too sleepy to drive home."

I blew out a breath. "I'm too tired to even argue with you. I guess I'll stay."

*A couple of hours later we were both tucked in our beds barely watching tv. Mrs. Barbara and Mr. Larry called and yelled at him for a while about not going to the doctor. Rob and Serena stopped by on the way to St. Louis to check on him as well.*

*"Dawn?" he said faintly, fatigue taking over.*

*"Yeah?" I answered, eyelids partially open.*

*"I love you."*

*I smiled. "I know you do. I love you too."*

*A few moments later we were both fast asleep.*

### St. Thomas, U.S. Virgin Islands – Wedding Day

*"Momma, I hate this makeup." I looked at my form in the full-length mirror assessing my wedding day look. My white strapless A-line gown and mass of ringlet curls were gorgeous, but I was side-eyeing the makeup. The hues complimented my dark brown skin, but it seemed too heavy, like birthday cake icing heavy.*

*Momma chuckled and brushed lint off my dress. "Cut it out, you look beautiful, but I would like to know why you're so calm?"*

*Summer laughed from across the room. "Momma you know how she is, nothing bothers her! Always got those emotions and feelings in check."*

*I rolled my eyes at her in the mirror. "Anyway, I'm not nervous because I know I'm doing the right thing. We love each other, there's no need to be nervous." I watched Momma tear up through the mirror. Really? If I wasn't crying why was she crying? I rubbed her shoulder; she was a lot shorter than me at only five-two. She was plump, as she called it, with short curly brown hair. Her brown skin and big expressive round eyes matched mine. "Momma why are you trying to cry?"*

*She dabbed at her eyes with a tissue. "I'm happy, I always wanted my girls to get married and have families. I'm proud of you... both of you."*

*"Aww thanks, Momma." I leaned over to hug her. She knew I wouldn't cry; it wasn't me. I rarely cried, and I wasn't going to start today.*

*I glanced over my shoulder and caught Summer wiping a few tears from her eyes. Geesh.*

*A few minutes later, a knock on the door interrupted our conversation. "Come on in," Summer yelled.*

*The door opened, it was Dre. "What's up good people? Y'all ready to get this wedding started? I got a couple of ladies waiting on the beach for me."*

*We all groaned. Dre stepped into the room looking as handsome as ever in his black tuxedo and crisp white shirt. His black hair was faded up perfectly, along with his goatee. I couldn't believe he was the same skinny kid that took me under his wing all those years ago. Where had all the time gone?*

*"Andre Brown if you don't act like you have some sense! You are not about to rush my baby's wedding so you can get back to the beach." Momma had her hand on her hip.*

*Andre laughed and walked to her. He kissed her on the cheek, and she fanned him away. "Come on Momma, you know I'm playing. My girl is getting married, and I'm here to send her off right."*

*Summer and Momma walked towards the door. "Alright, we are going down to get in place. Andre, you get my Baby down there and no playing, or I'll hurt you," she teased.*

*After they left, Dre came up behind me while I stood at the full-length mirror. He rested his hands on my bare shoulders, his eyes locked with mine in the mirror. "Baby you look beautiful... You good?"*

*I placed a hand on his hand and smiled. "Yes, I'm good. Thanks for walking me down the aisle today, it means so much to me."*

*"Of course I'm walking you down the aisle, that was never a question. You're my girl." He gently kissed my cheek.*

*"And thank you for being nice to my soon-to-be husband."*

*He moved his hands and put them in his pockets. "He's a cool dude, this is only my third or fourth time seeing him in person, but I like him."*

*I was happy, I always wanted Dre and whomever I married to get along. "I'm glad you like him, he's a good guy. He likes you too, he wants to invite you out for a football game. He has season tickets."*

*Dre's eyebrows went up. "Word? Oh, he should have told me that last night when I was giving him last words."*

*I laughed. "What did you say to him?"*

*"I didn't say much, I told him I was having a hard time handing you over because I've been taking care of you since the fourth grade." His smiled faded.*

*I reached to hug him. "Aww, that's so sweet. And I thank you for being my best friend all of these years."*

*He held me for a few seconds longer then pulled back. "You took care of me just as much, if not more. Now, let's go get you married off so I can get back to the beach."*

*We both laughed out loud. He grabbed my hand and led me to the door.*

*We were quiet during the elevator ride down to the main lobby. When the doors opened Dre squeezed my hand and whispered, "I love you and you know I always got you."*

. . . . . . . . .

My mind was clouded, I could barely catch my breath. I was on my back with my ankles on Macon's shoulders. I was two orgasms in and trying to go for a third. He felt so good sliding in and out of me; he was forceful and gentle all at the same time. "Baby you with me?" he grunted.

"Mmmmm-hmmm." I couldn't get much out; my legs were trembling. "Macon, I..." He stretched my legs towards my face and leaned in closer to me; I knew it was over then. He found my spot on the inside while he rubbed my clit from the outside at the same time. "AHHHHHHHH!!" My body exploded.

"Baby hold on, I'm right behind you." I could feel him picking up the pace and growing inside me. "You feel so good." I barely heard him grunting out his release; he sounded so far away. I trembled uncontrollably, and I had the chills. Macon let my legs down and pulled my back against his chest. I felt like I didn't have any problems when I was in his arms; almost euphoric. He rubbed and kissed my arms and shoulders until my body settled. "You back?" he whispered.

I laughed a little. "You are so cocky." I peeped over my shoulder.

He grinned. "I can't help I know how to put it down."

I laughed harder, but he wasn't lying. He knew how to satisfy me. He got out of bed and went to the bathroom. I heard the tub filling, and I smiled. He was always considerate and knew what I needed. A few minutes later the scent of my lavender and vanilla bath bombs filled the air. "Get in here woman!" he yelled playfully.

"Alright, Chief!" I was a little sore as I moved out of the bed, but I felt a lot more relaxed. I hadn't talked to Dre in over a week, and it bothered me; I missed him. I had never gone this long without talking to him, especially in the last couple of years since I'd been back in St. Louis. I needed to see him and talk to him. Over the past week, I had gone back and forth in my mind, but there was no doubt where my heart belonged. I loved Dre with everything in me. He always made me feel safe and protected. His presence was like home to me; comfortable and stable. He was as handsome as ever, and as a woman, I could appreciate it. However, I watched him grow from a boy to a man, so my appreciation was not in the romantic sense. No matter how much I loved my friend, I knew I wanted and needed Macon. He gave me those butterflies that every woman desired. Our chemistry was amazing; I felt desired and sexy. His presence consumed me; whenever our eyes met, it was as if we were the only two in the room. The relationship was still new, but I had to take my chances with him. I could not let him go because I feared him hurting me later.

Macon was sitting in the tub when I went into the bathroom. He looked like a model all stretched out with that smooth dark brown skin. And that beard he'd been wearing for the last few weeks blew my skirt up, literally. I loved it, that soft beard hair running across the inside of my thighs was enough to make me cum on the spot. Mmm-hmm. He held his hand out to help me in the tub. The water was warm, I sat in between his legs and leaned my back against his chest. We were quiet for a few minutes.

"Sweetheart, are you ready to talk?" I stiffened up. "You've been doing a good job of pretending you're okay, but I know something is still bothering you. You've been initiating sex every day and more than once." He raised his hands, "not that I'm complaining, but I do need you to tell me what's going on."

He was right, I was on him as soon as he came through the door every day. I even woke him up during the night for sex. I used it as a coping mechanism. I felt good when Macon made love to me. I was upset about not having my friend, and I didn't want to feel empty. I turned to see his face. "I'm sorry."

"Hey, don't you ever apologize for needing me, okay?" I nodded. "But, I don't want sex to replace our conversation. I can't believe I said that, I'm breaking all sorts of man laws." He chuckled. "I must be in love with you to be talking like..." he stopped, and I turned all the way around to face him. He rubbed his forehead and blew out a breath. "Okay, that's not how I planned to tell you."

I smiled at him; now this made me happy. "How did you plan to tell me?"

"I wasn't. Not anytime soon."

*Wait a minute, what?* "Why?"

"I didn't want to scare you off. You've been through so much, I didn't want to pressure you or make you uncomfortable if you didn't feel the same way."

219

I damn near went under water trying to hug him. "But I do feel the same way," I blurted out. I pulled back and looked at him.

"Say it," he challenged me.

I leaned and gently kissed him. "I, Dawn Simms, am in love with you, Macon James." I kissed him again.

"I love you too, Baby." He kissed me. "Sooo, we love each other now?"

I felt like a teenager, I was smiling from ear to ear. "Yes! I guess we do."

His smile faded. "Good, now tell the man you're in love with what's been going on with you for the past week."

Oh yeah, about that. Did I need to tell him now? My heart and mind couldn't be more aligned. I could say that Dre and I were mad at each other. But, I hated lying, and I could not start off this relationship with a lie. "Dre and I are having a few issues."

"I figured it had something to do with him." I looked at him with my eyebrows knitted together. "He hasn't been over here, and you haven't mentioned him."

*Okay, well so much for not telling him.* "He told me he has feelings for me."

Macon didn't flinch, he stared at me. "Is that it?"

*What?* "What do you mean is that it? We've been friends for over thirty years."

"I'm not surprised, it was obvious to me."

"Obvious?" *What was he talking about?*

"We've had a few words." My mouth dropped open. "Dawn he looks at you the same way I do. And he's to protective to be a friend."

"What do you mean you've had a few words? When? Where was I?" I couldn't believe it.

"Just man talk, nothing for you to worry about. I'm more interested in what you said to him."

"I haven't said anything to him. I was so confused and sad. He's been with me for years and now I'm not sure what's going to happen with us."

"Baby I can't really help you with this one... I love you and I do NOT share what's mine, okay?"

"I know and I'm not asking you too. All I know is that I miss my friend and I can't lose him too."

Macon was quiet. "Let's finish up and get out of here."

After our bath, I noticed I had a few missed calls from Janae, Tori, Rob, Summer and Mrs. Barbara, Dre's Mom. Something was wrong. I called Mrs. Barbara immediately. She answered right away. "Mrs. Barbara is everything okay?" I said before she could say hello.

"Hey, Dawn." *Was she crying?* "Andre is in the hospital."

"WHAT!? WHAT HAPPENED TO HIM!? IS HE OKAY?" Macon came running out of the bathroom. I couldn't do this again, I could not lose Dre.

"I'm not sure, he was in a car accident. They called from the hospital and didn't say much over the phone. We are almost at the hospital." I sat on the bed and dropped the phone. My heart couldn't take another blow, I wouldn't survive this time. Macon grabbed my phone and talked to Mrs. Barbara.

I heard him talking, but it sounded like gibberish. "Dawn, can you hear me?" I couldn't talk. "Baby I need you to get dressed... come on." I finally stood. Macon grabbed my chin. "We don't know what's wrong yet, I need you to stay with me, okay?" I heard him, but I didn't. I went to my closet and somehow managed to get my clothes on. The next thing I knew I was sitting in Macon's truck riding down the highway. I was in a daze, I couldn't talk. I couldn't process what was happening. Dre had to be okay, there was no way this could happen. I hadn't talked to him in over a week, and now he was in the hospital? I wanted to cry, but nothing came out. I wanted to scream, but nothing came out. Was I dreaming?

I wasn't sure how much time had passed. Macon pulled into a parking spot and helped me out of the truck. He held my hand tight; we went into the emergency room. Mr. Larry was coming down the hallway towards us.

"Hey Dawn, Andre…" I cut him off.

"Where is he!?" He rattled off the room number and I almost took off running. Macon tried to slow me down, but I had to see him. I got to the room and opened the door. Mrs. Barbara turned around and gave me a sad smile. I looked past her at Dre lying in bed and…

## Chapter 15 ~ Dre

I knew my girl would come and see about me. She stood at the door with her eyes wide and her hand over her heart. I'd seen that look on her in the past; she was scared. I held out my arms, and she came to me and broke down. Dawn wasn't wired for this type of stuff, she hated death and sickness. She wasn't the person you went to if someone died, she would zone out. The last thing I wanted to do was cause her pain. She leaned over my bed, I held her as best as I could. My left leg was hoisted up in a full cast. "It's okay, I'm alright." I tried to soothe her, but she was too far gone; she was trembling. This would take a minute. I rubbed her back and held her tight. Her hair covered my face, I couldn't see anything. I smoothed it down with my hand; Big Baby was standing by the door. What was he doing here? He had his hands in his pockets, and he stared at me. I didn't have time to entertain him because I had to focus on my girl. She seemed to calm down a bit. "Baby I'm fine, it's alright."

She moved a little, and I let her go. She stood and grabbed some tissue to wipe her face. "What happened!? Are you okay!? What's broken!?"

"Dawn," I cut her off. "I need you to take a breath and relax."

She sat on the bench next to my bed. She looked at Macon and held her hand out. He came and sat next to her and put his arm around her. If I thought my leg was hurting, that was nothing compared to watching this scene. Watching her reach for him, and not me? I won't lie, it stung. "Yeah, ummm, so some fool ran a light and hit me. When I got to the hospital they had to do surgery to reset my leg. The folks' number was on my emergency contact list, but you know the hospital can't talk about my business. And my phone broke in the accident."

She stared at me, Big Baby had her wrapped up like she was a damn toddler. Rubbing all on her arms and kissing the top of her head. I couldn't watch this... "Now this makes sense." She seemed to be coming back to life. I hated that he could relax her. "What did the doctor say? Is it just the leg? Or is there anything else wrong?"

"Naw, just the leg. It's broken in one place and fractured in another."

"But he's going to be in that cast from four to six weeks. Once the fracture heals they may put him in a short cast," Moms said. She had already turned into a doctor, reminded me of back in the day when I got sick.

"How long will you be here?" Dawn asked.

I hated to watch it, but I had to give it to Big Baby, he could get her together. She was relaxed. "I'll be here at least until tomorrow, they want to keep me for observation."

"Where's everybody else? I know Rob, Tori, and Janae called me."

"They were all here but left when they found out it was just a leg, you know how they do me," I laughed.

"But why didn't anybody call me back to tell me you were okay? I know my blood pressure is probably through the roof." She had her head on his shoulder, she looked so peaceful.

Moms cut in. "We all tried to call you, but you didn't answer."

Dawn looked at Big Baby. "We left your phone at home, Sweetheart. I was so busy trying to get you out of the door I forgot to grab it." She smiled at him and put her head back on his shoulder. I wanted his ass outta here.

Pops walked in with a bottle of water and handed it to Moms. "Alright, they told me visiting hours are over, and they have a room ready for you upstairs." He looked at Moms. "Barb, are you staying here with him? I know how you are."

She looked at me, silently asking what I wanted her to do. "I'm good, you can go with Pops." I wanted Dawn to stay. I hadn't talked to her in a week.

"Larry, I'm going to stay. He can't fend for himself." I looked at the ceiling. "Well, you can't." She put her hand on her hip. "Anyway, who do you think stayed with you last time you were in the hospital?"

"Dawn stayed with me." Big Baby looked at me, his jaws tight. If looks could kill, I'd be in a body bag.

Before Dawn could say anything, Moms cut in. "Dawn is here with her friend, there's no need for her to stay when I'm here."

"Alright, now that it's settled, I'm leaving." Pops hugged me. "I'll be over in the morning, Son." He kissed Moms and Dawn. "Good seeing you again, Macon." They shook hands and Pops was gone.

Dawn came over and hugged me. "I'm glad you're okay, but please don't scare me like that again. I'll come over tomorrow if they keep you another day." She hugged Moms.

"Alright Dre, take it easy. I'm glad you're okay."

"Thanks, man." I didn't know what else to say to him.

He hugged Moms, she was smiling hard. What was it about this dude that had the women all silly? "It was nice seeing you again, Mrs. Brown." He grabbed Dawn's hand. "Let's get you home, I know you're tired." He rubbed the side of her face.

I thought I knew Dawn, but I had never seen her like this with anyone. She went along with whatever he said, completely trusted him. I didn't like it, and I didn't like him. She turned and waved at me like I was six, then left.

"Andre?" Moms had her hands on her hips. "I didn't raise you to be a manipulator."

"What are you talking about?" I already knew.

"You know exactly what I'm talking about!" Moms was mad. "That poor girl came in here scared to death, and you tried to use it to your advantage."

I didn't say anything, but she kept staring at me. "Okay, you're right, that wasn't cool. I hate seeing her with him. He's always touching her."

"You're jealous... And you better hurry up and fix your attitude towards him if you don't want to lose her as a friend. I watched them, I think it's too late for you to tell her how you feel. They love each other, it's all over them."

I blew out a breath. "I already told her."

She sat on the bench next to my bed. "Baby, I'm sorry." She rubbed my hand and gave me a sad smile. "I'm guessing it didn't go well?"

"Today is the first time I've heard from her since I told her about a week ago. It's cool though."

"No, it's not cool as you say. You've been sowing your oats for years, and when the love bug finally hit you, it didn't end like you wanted it."

"Who says it's the end?"

She shook her head. "I know you're middle-aged, but you're still my son. Let me give you a little advice. Whatever God has for you, is for you, okay?" I understood it, but I didn't want to hear it. "If you're meant to be with Dawn then it will happen when it's time, you did your part by telling her. But, watching them today told me that God has someone else for you." She patted my arm. "I might get me a grandbaby or two after all."

I shook my head. "You know Dawn can't have kids, why would you say that?"

"I know that! But she doesn't want kids. I believe in my heart that you do. You're still young enough to have a couple."

This lady and the grandkid talk had been a subject for the last twenty years. "I don't care about having kids." I looked up at the ceiling. I pictured all the years I spent with Dawn and never once felt anything for her. Now, I was sitting here with my ego shook and my heart on the damn floor. "I just want her."

Moms looked at me. "I know you do, but you have to settle for her friendship or nothing. Let her be happy with Macon, Lord knows that girl needs some happiness. Be her friend and give that to her, don't make her choose; you won't win."

"I hear you." I knew she was right, but there was something that kept telling me I still had a shot with her. My pain meds were kicking in, I needed to sleep. I'd figure Dawn out later.

~~~~~~~~~~~~~

I was getting settled at the folks' house. I was only in the hospital overnight. Mom insisted that I stay with them because my house had stairs. Rob stopped by earlier with my new phone. I couldn't last another day without it. I sent Stacy a text with a picture of my cast.

**Stacy: Is that your leg? Or are you joking?**

I was in a car accident.

My phone rang. It was Stacy. "What happened? Are you okay?" She was almost yelling.

"I'm good, someone ran a red light and hit me, broke my leg."

"Wow, how are you getting around with all that on your leg? I can come down if you need anything."

Stacy was cool, and I enjoyed her company. "I'm not home. I'm at my folks' place for the next month until I get the cast off. Or until I learn how to get up steps in it."

"Okay, well if you need anything let me know."

"I could use some company if you're free." I knew she was feeling me, so there was no harm in a friendly visit. I hadn't heard from my best friend, she was probably with Big Baby since it was the weekend.

"Sure, I can stop by now, I'm on my way out anyway. Send me the address."

"Okay, see you soon." I ended the call and sent her the address. Maybe this was what I needed to get my mind off Dawn. She obviously wasn't concerned about me. I'd been home for a couple of hours, and she hadn't bothered to call to check on me since she left the hospital yesterday. I guess Big Baby had her drinking his Kool-Aid. "Hey, Pops!" Moms was at the store.

I heard him coming towards the room, he was all smiles when he came in. "Let's get some rules established around here." I shook my head and laughed. "You're not going to run my wife and me in the ground while you're here."

"Pops for real? She's my Mother."

He rearranged the pillows under my leg. "She was my wife first, and I know how she is about her only child. She's already out buying up half the grocery store for you."

"I'll be good Ol' Man," I laughed. He hated when I called him old. He was in good shape for his age, probably better than most guys my age. He still jogged a few times a week.

"Maaan you better pray you look as good as I do when you're my age." He looked in the mirror and rubbed his gray goatee. We both laughed.

"I know Pops... But I wanted to tell you I'm expecting a friend to come through. Her name is Stacy, can you bring her back here for me?"

His eyebrows shot up. "I guess that thing with Dawn was short-lived."

"You saw her with dude at the hospital. And where is she anyway? She's not over here checking on me."

He ran his hand down his face. "Yeah, I saw them... So that's it? You're going to let him have her?"

I laughed to myself. I guess I had a lot of ways like Pops; territorial. "She had a choice, and she didn't choose me. I thought about going harder, but I changed my mind after she ghosted me today."

"This is why all of you young fellas are single these days. As long as she's not married, you ain't supposed to be worried about her seeing someone. You make her want to see you. How do you think I got your Momma?" *Here we go.* I blew out a breath. "Your Momma thought she was in love with some guy until I showed her I was better for her. If I had given her a choice, she would have stayed with him."

I laughed at him. "I hear you, but you and Moms were like nineteen or twenty when you met. It doesn't work the same way when you're older."

He threw his hand at me. "See that's your problem. Ain't no difference between a young woman and an old woman but her body. And with all these Kuma classes they take nowadays the old ones lookin' as good as the young ones. Look how fine your Momma is."

Pops was crazy, I laughed him. "It's called Zumba, not Kuma."

He shrugged. "I know what you're saying, but I know Dawn. I can't tell her what to do, she's independent... you know how she is."

He opened his mouth to say something, and the doorbell rang. "Well, I guess that's your friend." He walked off but stopped at the door. "I hope you don't regret not going after Dawn like you should." He left.

I ran a hand down my face. Pops didn't get it, I couldn't make Dawn be with me. I also didn't want to risk losing her for good. I knew I'd eventually get over wanting her, but I didn't think I could live without her as a friend.

Pops and Stacy walked into the bedroom. Her hair was a lot longer than I remembered, but a quick visit to the shop could get you any hair you wanted. I hated all that hair. But I sure didn't mind those jeans and all that ass. Too bad I wasn't at home, I wouldn't be able to pass this time.

"Son, I'm going to the basement. I have my cell, call me if you need me." He turned to Stacy. "And nice meeting you, young lady."

"Nice meeting you too, Mr. Brown." Pops left, and Stacy walked to the bed and kissed me.

I couldn't believe I'd been passing her up the last couple of weeks. She tried to move, but I held on to her and copped a few feels. "Thanks for coming to see me." I kissed her again then let her go. She sat on the side of the bed.

"You're welcome. Other than this..." She pointed to my leg. "how have you been? I haven't heard from you."

"I've been working and kind of taking it easy. I'm sorry I haven't been in touch, but I plan to change all of that." Maybe I would try to make things work with her.

She smiled. "That's nice to hear. I hope it's not because your leg is broken."

I swear I couldn't win with women lately. I was trying to give her what she wanted, and here she was questioning my motives. I had a phone full of women I could have called to come through. "Now why are you being like that?" She shrugged. "What are you getting into today?"

"I have to do some shopping for my kids, that's about it."

The garage door opened. Good, Moms was back, I was getting hungry. "That's cool." I heard Moms talking to someone, but I couldn't hear the other voice. Probably one of my aunts, they were always over here gossiping or having a hen session as Pops called it.

Someone was walking towards the room. "Dre!?" *What!? What was Dawn doing here?* She came around the corner smiling with a big bag in her hand. She saw Stacy sitting on the bed. "Oh... Hi." Stacy looked at her. "I'm Dawn." She reached out to shake her hand.

Stacy had a blank expression, she sized Dawn up. She took her hand. "Hello, I'm Stacy."

Dawn looked at me, I didn't know what to do. "Hey Dre, I'm sorry I didn't know you had company. I brought you some stuff, I'll leave the bag here."

She turned to leave. "Thanks." I couldn't let her leave. *Why did I call Stacy?* "Hold up, D." She stopped and turned. She was beautiful. Her hair was in a ponytail today. I loved that ponytail; it always reminded me how long I'd known her. She wore that same ponytail when we were kids. "What's in the bag?"

"A few things for you to pass the time. I'll catch up with you later... and nice meeting you Stacy."

Why was she trying to get out of here? "Is Macon with you?"

She gave me a look I couldn't read. She didn't roll her eyes or give me a side eye. Was she mad? "No, he went to KC to see the kids for the day."

Damn! He was out of town. I could have had her to myself all day "Why didn't you go? I thought you all were inseparable." Stacy's head was like a pendulum going back and forth between Dawn and me.

Dawn gave me a side eye and half smile. "I wasn't sure if you were getting out of the hospital and I wanted to check on you. But let me go, I'll talk to you later. You two have fun, and Stacy, he cheats in any game." Stacy smiled. "Later, Dre."

"Alright, D." She left. I was mad, but I could only be mad at myself. Dawn had been there for me through everything. I didn't know why I decided she wouldn't this time. I wondered what was in the bag? "Stacy, could you hand me that bag?" She passed it to me, and before I looked in I could smell the tea cakes. I felt bad; she had baked for me. I dug into the bag and found a couple of bottles of my favorite juice, my favorite chips, candy and all kind of stuff. Even a few magazines.

"Who was that?"

I forgot Stacy was here. "My best friend, we grew up together." I hoped she didn't start asking questions.

"Andre, why did Dawn..." Moms came into the room and stopped talking when she saw Stacy. "Hello." She looked at me then Stacy. "I'm Mrs. Brown, Andre's mother."

"Hello Mrs. Brown, my name is Stacy. It's nice to meet you." Stacy stood and shook her hand. "Dre, I need to get going, I'll call you later."

"Thanks for stopping by, I appreciate it." She leaned over and kissed my cheek.

"Stacy, I'll see you out." Moms walked out behind Stacy. She gave me a long stare. A minute later she came in and sat in Stacy's spot on the bed. "Who was she?"

"A friend, she lives down the street from me." I knew Moms was going to trip.

"You have a lot of growing up to do young man."

"I need to grow up because I have female friends?" This was the worst part of being stuck in the house. I couldn't leave if I didn't want to talk.

"Yesterday you were all sad because of Dawn. Now you're smiling up in some woman's face with lipstick on your mouth."

I tried to wipe my mouth. "Didn't you tell me to move on? That Dawn wasn't meant for me?" I needed my pain meds.

"Yes, I did say that, but I didn't intend for you to use someone else to get over her."

I looked at the ceiling. "We were cool before this thing with Dawn. And did you know Dawn was coming over?"

"Of course I did, she's been calling since last night for updates."

*What!?* "What do you mean? And why didn't you tell me? She never called me." Why was she talking to Moms and not me?

"Your phone broke in the accident, remember?" *Oh, I forgot about that.* "She told me she was coming by, but I forgot to tell you. Had I known you'd be in here keeping company with some woman..."

My leg was hurting. I wanted to sleep and forget about what happened. "Could you get my pain meds for me?" She didn't say anything. She got up and left the room. I needed Dawn to come back over. I hoped she wasn't mad. I grabbed my phone off the nightstand.

**Hey, are you coming back over today?**

**Dawn: Hadn't planned on it. Do you need something?**

**Do I have to need something for you to come?**

Moms came back to the room and handed me a pill. "Get some rest, I'll come back and check on you later."

"Thanks, Moms."

**Dawn: I'll come over in a couple of hours.**

~~~~~~~~~~~~

I wasn't sure how long I had slept. I could hear Dawn talking to the folks in the kitchen. A few minutes later she walked into the room and sat on the side of the bed. She was upset, she crossed her legs and folded her arms across her chest.

"What's up Dre? Why are you staring at me?"

Yep, she was mad. "I know you're mad at me. I guess it's about Stacy?" Might as well get it out now.

"Now why would I be mad about Stacy?"

"Dawn come on, I know you're mad at me, I'm sorry okay?" I didn't know what else to say. I'd been apologizing a lot lately.

She got up and closed the door. I closed my eyes and tried to brace myself. "You damn right I'm mad at your ass!" She yelled and whispered at the same time. I didn't say anything, I stared at her.

"You feed me this BS about you loving me and having all these damn feelings! I'm walking around confused about who and what I want for a week. Barely talking to Macon and worried about you! Then I find you over here with a woman!?" Her eyes were wide, and her mouth was tight. She was pissed.

"But it's not..."

"SHUT UP!" *This was bad.* "Don't sit there and tell me it wasn't anything! I saw the lipstick all over your mouth earlier, that's now on your pillow!"

I looked at my pillow, and sure enough, there was lipstick smeared on it. Could this get any worse? But why was she mad? Wasn't she still with Big Baby? "Are you saying you planned to choose me?" I knew she didn't, but I didn't get it.

She seemed to calm down a little, she was back to her regular voice. "You know, as long as we've been friends this is the first time I've realized how selfish you are." *What!?* "You knew I was happy with Macon and you decided that your feelings mattered more than mine. I, on the other hand, sent the man I love to KC alone today because I was so worried about you. Which means I put your needs before mine. Do you see where I'm going with this?" I ran my hand down my face. "And to top things off, you're over here with your tongue down some woman's throat, after claiming you're in love with me."

That pissed me off! "Are you for real!?" Her eyes were big. "I tell you I'm in love with you and I don't hear a word from you for a week! Then you show up at the hospital with HIM! And you're damn near sitting in his lap in front of me. How do you think I felt watching that!?"

"It's always about how you feel isn't it!?" *If I didn't love this woman I would put her out of here.* "I'm sorry, but I don't remember much from the hospital. You know I would never do anything to hurt you on purpose!"

"Whatever, Dawn!" I didn't want to talk to her. She had a lot of nerve blasting me.

She jerked her had back. "Whatever!?" She walked to the door and grabbed the door handle but stopped. "You know what?... I'm done with you. I can't believe you are being so selfish right now." She stood at the door and looked at me. She was pissed but looked more hurt, her eyes were glassy. Well guess what? My feelings were hurt too, so I didn't have much to give her. I turned my head, I couldn't look at her. She walked out the door.

Damn, was this love? Why in the hell were people searching for this bullshit!? I didn't want any parts of it.

# Chapter 16 ~ Macon

"Hey Baby." I hugged Dawn, I had just returned from seeing the kids in KC.

"How was your trip? How are the kids?" She grabbed me by the hand and pulled me into her family room.

"They are good, we can talk on the way. Are you ready?" I was exhausted, but I wanted to take my woman out dancing.

"Yep, I'm ready, but you haven't told me where we're going."

Those jeans. She leaned over to grab her purse, and I almost changed my mind about going out. "Umm," I couldn't stop staring, "a place Donald told me about. Let's go before I take you upstairs and peel you out of those jeans."

She laughed. "You can do that when we get back, but for now I'm ready to turn up."

We left, and I followed the directions Donald had given me, I was slightly confused because so much had changed in St. Louis. I was driving around the area he mentioned and didn't see anything that looked like a club. "Oh, I see where we are going." She had a big smile on her face. "Turn in here."

I turned into the parking lot, there were quite a few cars. "Are you sure this is it?"

"Yep!" She threw her hands up and bounced to the music. "We are about to kick it in here."

I found a space and pulled in then looked at the building. "Wait a minute, didn't this used to be Showbiz Pizza Place back in the day?"

She laughed out loud. "You're showing your age now, but yes it was Showbiz, but it's a club now."

"And you've been here? The people seem a little older." I was a little surprised.

"They are, and that's why I like it." I looked at her with my eyebrows up. "We'll have a good time, and we won't have to worry about anything poppin' off. Aaaand they have catfish baskets."

"Say no more, let's go." I got out of the truck and went to Dawn's side to help her out. It was a little chilly out, she had on a leather jacket and some sort of high heel boot shoe thing with the toes out. I was comfortable in jeans and a button-up. I grabbed her hand and went to the door.

After I paid the fee to get in Dawn started dancing, she pulled me towards the dance floor.

"Dawn! Macon!" someone yelled.

I looked in the direction of the voice, it was Donald. *What was he doing here?* He was sitting at a table near the dance floor. Dawn and I walked to the table and Tori came off the dance floor. "What's up, D?" I slapped hands with him. "I didn't know you would be up here tonight, and with Tori?" I looked to the side and saw Dawn and Tori talking. "Hey Tori," I yelled over the music.

She hugged me "Hey Macon, good seeing you again." Dawn hugged Donald.

The women started talking again, so I went back to Donald. "What's going on man?"

Donald was smiling real hard. "I hadn't planned on coming up here until Tori called and asked me to meet her. You can sit with us; we have space at our table."

Donald sat down, and I went behind Dawn and gently touched her hips, she looked up over her shoulder at me. I couldn't help myself, I gave her a quick kiss. "Baby, you want to sit and order drinks or food?" She nodded.

We took a seat at the table and ordered drinks and a couple of catfish baskets. I was hungry; I hadn't eaten since I left KC. The ladies were in deep discussion about something, so I turned to Donald. "So, what's up with you two?" He shrugged. "What do you mean you don't know?"

"I'm not sure, we've been out a few times."

"Do you like her or what, man?"

Before he could answer one of those slides or line dance songs came on, and Dawn and Tori were up. "I'm going to the floor Baby, you want to come?"

I shook my head. "You go ahead, I'll wait for the food." She and Tori hit the floor and fell in line with the other people. She was laughing and moving to the beat; I couldn't stop watching her. I loved to see her having a good time and letting loose. Donald was talking, but watching Dawn in those jeans and high heels had my mind on pause. Damn, she was beautiful, and she was mine.

"Man, you ain't even listening," Donald laughed. "But the Dre dude…"

My head turned real fast when I heard that name. "What happened?"

"I was saying that Tori had to get off the phone with me earlier because Dawn stopped by her house. I heard her talking loud about something the Dre dude did to her. As soon as Tori opened the door Dawn was going off, she was mad."

"What!?" *What the hell was he talking about?* "When?"

"She told me she would call me back and when she called me later to invite me here, I asked her if Dawn was cool. All she said was that Dawn and Dre had words." He shrugged. "Is this the same dude from Pop's party?"

I was sick of him. "Yeah, that's him. They've been friends since they were kids and she treats him like a damn baby. He got into a car accident yesterday, and she was a mess."

Donald's eyes were wide. "Did they date or something? He sounds clingy like a chic."

"I know man, but they never dated. But, he does like her now."

"For real? How do you know?"

I shook my head. "Long story short, he's been throwing salt since I met her, and he told her he wants her."

"Damn!" Donald shook his head. "So he straight up trying to pull up on your girl?"

"He can try all he wants, but Dawn is mine! And she's the only reason I haven't knocked his ass out." I had to relax, I didn't want that fool ruining our date night. But I was curious about what happened today. Hopefully, he shot himself in the foot and I could stay out of it. It was bad enough that she didn't go to KC with me because of him, but I understood her reasoning. I didn't like it, but I didn't trip either. Good to know he messed up the day all on his own.

The food and drinks arrived as Dawn and Tori came off the dance floor. They were laughing and having a good time. "I hope you saved some energy to dance with me," I teased her.

She sipped some of her drink. "*I get filthy when that liquor get into me...*" she sang and danced in her chair.

I laughed, "And I want you dancing like Beyoncé since you're singing her song."

She laughed and fed me a French fry, I ran my tongue over the tip of her finger as she pulled her hand back. Her mouth opened, and I winked at her.

"Would you two get a room!" Tori yelled.

We all laughed and started eating and drinking. The food was great, I missed fried catfish with pickles, onions, and a slice of white bread on the side. That kind of meal was only available in St. Louis. The conversation flowed, and I noticed Donald and Tori were talking more like friends. I didn't know what was going on with them and apparently, he didn't either.

After a couple of hours of dancing, we said our goodbyes and left to go to Dawn's place. We were showered and in bed talking. She had fun, but she seemed a little distant. "What's on your mind?" I asked.

She had her eyes closed with her head on my chest. "Not much, thinking about the day." She looked up and smiled. "Thank you for taking me out dancing, I had fun."

"Anything to keep a smile on your face." I was exhausted from the long drive and going out, but I wanted to make sure my woman was good before I dozed off.

"Confession time?" she asked.

I'm sure this had something to do with what Donald told me about Dre. I hope I didn't have to break his other leg. "What's up, Sweetheart?"

"I had an argument with Dre today, it was pretty bad. We aren't talking to each other." She was still on my chest with her chin resting on her hand looking at me.

"What are you going to do? Because I know you, and you aren't going to end your friendship with him."

"I don't know. It's like he's a different person now. I know I've kind of spoiled him..." she paused. "What was that look for?"

"Kind of?" I knew I shouldn't have said anything, but I couldn't help it.

"Is it that bad?" She sat up and looked at me.

"Baby it's not the most normal friendship, he depends on you for everything."

"No, he doesn't. You act like I pay his bills or something."

I knew this conversation was going to happen at some point. "Before you get defensive, all I'm saying is that he depends on you emotionally. And, it's probably the reason he's never had a damn girlfriend." She pushed my arm and smiled. "I'm serious, this is a classic case of emotional dependency. Do you see how you and I are talking right now?" She nodded. "He does the same thing with you, so he doesn't need the women he dates for that, which is why nothing lasts."

"I guess I never thought about it like that." She smiled. "Look at you, slingin' therapy around."

I laughed. "You got jokes, but it's true, and you don't see it because you're in it."

She stopped smiling and pulled her bottom lip into her mouth. "Does my friendship with Dre bother you? Be honest."

I had to tread lightly. "No, your friendship doesn't bother me at all, because I trust you. But, he has feelings for you, and that, I don't like. But there's not much I can do about it. As long as he respects what you and I have, I'm good."

She was quiet for a minute, she chewed on her bottom lip and stared past me. I tugged her lip from her mouth, and she smiled. "You're right, but I think he and I need some time apart to sort of regroup."

I knew Dawn, and there was no way she would leave him with a broken leg. "Whatever you say."

"Well, you know what I mean. I'm going to check on him and take his snacks and stuff."

I chuckled. "That's a good way to have time apart."

She poked her lip out. "You know how I am about my friends, I can't leave him with a broken leg."

I smiled at her. "I know, and that's one of the reasons I love you, you're a good person."

"Awwww, thank you Baby, I love you too." She leaned over and kissed me.

"Are we finished talking because I'm sleepy?" I yawned.

She smiled and kissed me again. "I know you're tired, get some rest. I'll make you breakfast in the morning."

"I can't wait." I pulled her to my chest and closed my eyes.

~~~~~~~~~~~~~

I was sitting in my office reading through some notes from a group therapy session. It had been about two weeks since my talk with Dawn about Dre. We were getting along great, but her Mom's birthday and her birthday were approaching. As much as I hated to admit it, she needed more than me to get her through the rest of the year. She had not talked to Dre since their argument, but I knew she missed him and she needed her friend. I tried to do as much as I could, but we didn't have the longevity because our relationship was still new. I thought about contacting that clown, but I would probably end up making the situation worse. A knock on my office door interrupted my thoughts.

"Come in." I closed my folders.

My coworker stuck his head in the door. "What's up Macon, you have a minute?"

"Come on in, Perry." Perry was one of the physical therapists in the hospital. We had a few overlapping patients that we discussed on occasion.

He came in and took a seat in the chair in front of my desk. "I was hoping you could do me a favor?" he asked.

"What's up?"

"My wife wants us to see a counselor. I thought that maybe you could do it."

My eyebrows went up. "I'm not a marriage counselor. My area is PTSD and grief. I do some counseling for transitioning into civilian life also."

Perry wiped his forehead. "Counseling is counseling, and I don't want to talk to some stranger. I don't want to go at all, but I figured if I agreed we could have a session with you and get it over."

I laughed and shook my head. "Perry, I would love to help you out but it's not my area."

"Man, all she needs to know is that you're a counselor and she'll be cool with it. Aren't you married anyway? Ask us a few questions from what you know."

I chuckled and shook my head. "No, I'm not married, I'm divorced. And, counseling doesn't work like that, I can't just ask questions."

"If you're divorced I know you can do it," he paused. "Wait a minute... who's the woman that brings you lunch sometimes?" His brows knitted.

I smiled. "That would be my girlfriend, Dawn."

"Daaaaamn, you doin' it like that?" His eyes were wide. "I know if you have women bringing lunch you can get my wife off this counseling kick."

I laughed. "There's only one woman that brings me lunch, not women. But seriously, why are you opposed to counseling?"

Perry was a couple of years younger than me. He favored Martin Lawrence and was just as funny most days. "I don't think we need to go."

I shook my head. "Can I give you some advice?" He shrugged his shoulders. "If your wife wants to go to counseling I suggest you go and you take it seriously; if you want to keep your marriage."

He blew out his breath. "Sooo you're not going to help me out?"

"Did you hear anything I said?"

"I heard you, but I'm not trying to tell all my business to a stranger."

"Listen man, sometimes you have to do things in a relationship that are uncomfortable and goes against your nature. Even if you believe it won't help you, it will help your wife. Which means it ultimately helps the relationship and you."

He crossed his arms. "You're saying that if the Lunch Lady asked you to go see a counselor, you would go? Even if you didn't think there was a problem?"

I laughed. "You not gone call my woman Lunch Lady. But yes, if she asked me to go I would go in a heartbeat." He shook his head. "She could ask me to do anything, and if I were capable of doing it, I would. It's about pleasing your woman. Simple as that."

A huge smile came across his face and he stood. "Why didn't you tell me I would get some special occasion sex if I went with her?"

"What are you talking about?" I laughed at him.

"You said it's about pleasing her. And whenever she's pleased I get special occasion sex. You know the kind they give you when you do something nice, or you get her a big birthday present." He walked to the door. "I didn't even think about it that way. I'm going out and finding the best marriage counselor in St. Louis, might even take it a step further and ask the Pastor at church." He turned and came over to my desk to dap me up. "Good lookin' out."

I couldn't stop laughing at him. "Alright Perry, anytime."

He opened the door and turned back. "And if you have any problems with the Lunch Lady, you know where to find me." He walked out and closed the door.

Perry was funny, but he was a good dude. I thought about the advice I gave him and realized I should probably do the same in my relationship with Dawn. I knew she missed that fool, and I knew what I needed to do to make her happy. This wasn't about me, it was about pleasing her. Simple as that.

On the way home from work I looked up Dre's parent's phone number. I figured they would still have a land line and be listed. I called the number.

"Brown residence." It sounded like his Mother.

"Hello, Mrs. Brown?" I asked.

"Yes?"

"This is Macon, Dawn's friend, how are you?" I caught her off guard, she was quiet.

"Umm, oh, hello Macon, I'm fine. It's nice hearing from you, how have you been? Is Dawn okay?"

"Yes Ma'am, Dawn is fine. I was actually calling to speak with Andre."

"Oh... just a moment, let me get him."

I was pretty sure he wasn't far away because I heard her whispering to someone, and two seconds later he was on the phone.

"Yeah?" he said as if he didn't want to be bothered.

"What's up Dre? This is Macon, I wanted to know if I could stop by to talk to you for a minute. It's about Dawn." I hated doing this, but this wasn't about me. I had to keep that in the front of my mind.

"Is something wrong with her?" I had his full attention now.

"Physically she's fine, but there are some other things going on."

"Yeah, cool. Come through, I'll text you the address."

"Thanks, I'm on the way." I ended the call.

About thirty minutes later I was standing on the porch waiting for someone to answer the door. Mr. Brown opened the door and let me in. He reached to shake my hand. "Good seeing you again, Macon. Andre is in the tv room right in there," he pointed.

"Thanks, Mr. Brown, and good seeing you as well." I walked in the direction he pointed, I saw Dre's leg propped up on an ottoman before I walked in the room. He must have heard me coming because he muted the TV.

I walked into the room and gave him some dap. "What's up? How's the leg?"

"Getting better, what's going on with Dawn?" He didn't have an expression, he stared at me like he wanted me gone.

I took a seat across from him. "I know that you and Dawn had an argument or something and haven't been talking lately. I don't know what happened, but I do know it's bothering her." He didn't say anything, so I continued. "Look, she's not doing well, and she needs her friends. I'm asking you to put whatever happened to the side and be there for her."

"So, you need me to help YOU handle YOUR woman?" His eyes were wide.

Maaan.... Whoosah, I paused. "It has nothing to do with me."

"If it doesn't have anything to do with you why are you here?" He cocked his head to the side.

"The only reason I'm here is because I love Dawn and I would do anything for her, including talk to you." Asshole! I wanted to knock his leg off that ottoman. "Listen man, I'm sure you know her Mom's birthday and her birthday are coming up soon. She's crying in her sleep, and she needs everyone that's important to her around."

That seemed to knock a little wind out of his sails. "She's crying at night again?" He scrubbed his face with his hand.

"Yes, but mostly when she's sleeping. I'm not even sure she's aware of it. She's putting up a good front, but she's going through it."

He blew out a breath. "She's been dropping off cookies and stuff over here, but she never comes in to talk to me. I thought she was good since she had you."

"As much as I hate to admit it, I can only do so much. You have her past, and I don't." This was harder than I thought it would be. "She needs her friends, the people that knew her Mom; I hope you can come through for her."

He frowned at me, he didn't like what I said. "I will always be there for Dawn, you ain't ever got to question that!"

I stood. "Good to hear, so I guess that means you'll be talking to her sooner rather than later?"

"I got Dawn, don't you worry." He grabbed the remote and unmuted the tv.

This dude was an asshole, but I sort of felt sorry for him. Dawn was a good woman, and if I were in his shoes, I'd probably be mad too. He had her for over thirty years, and he let her slip through the cracks. Too bad for him, I planned on making her permanent in my life. I turned around and left.

## Chapter 17 ~ Dawn

"Dawn are you sure you're okay?" Tori asked.

"I'm fine, I want to hear about Donald." I was tired of weeping around. We were sitting in a wine bar in downtown Ferguson having a midday drink.

"There's not much to tell, he's nice, but he doesn't have that edge."

I squinted my eyes. "How much more edge do you want? He rides a motorcycle, has a bald head and beard."

She laughed. "Okay well, maybe I'm explaining it wrong. He looks edgy, but he doesn't act the same way, he seems nervous around me."

"Maybe it's because he likes you and he's not sure if you like him. Macon said he was shy at first, but he warms up. I thought he was weird at first, but he's cool. You should give him a chance."

She threw her hand. "I'll pass, I've already friend zoned him. And I've been talking to someone else anyway." She had the biggest smile.

"And how long has this been going on? Who is he? Why don't I know about him?" I took a sip of my wine and folded my arms across my chest.

"Would you relax, I haven't told you because you stay up under Macon, not that I blame you." She giggled, and I blushed. "But I met him a couple of months ago at the shop. He was there getting a haircut, and my car was parked to close to his car, so we ended up talking. His name is Marcus."

"You've kept this for two months? Does Janae know about him?" She nodded. "Am I really with Macon that much?"

Her eyes went wide. "Is fat meat greasy?"

I laughed out loud. "Oh be quiet, you know how it is when it's new. But tell me about him." I was all ears.

"He moved here a few months ago for work. He works out there with Janae, Rob, and Dre, but they don't know him. Well, Rob knows him a little, that's how he found out about the shop. He transferred from Seattle. He's divorced with three children."

I was confused. "You seem to like him based on that Kool-Aid smile you have; so why are you still going out with Donald?" I didn't want her leading him on.

She took a sip of her wine. "I told you I friend zoned Donald and I'm not exclusive with Marcus." I eyed her. "Okay I like him, but it's still early."

"I can't wait to meet him." My phone vibrated on the table, I had a text.

**Dre: Can you come see me?**

"Well I know that's not Macon since you aren't running out the door," Tori said.

I rolled my eyes at her. "Nope, it's Dre."

She scrunched her face up. "What is he up to now? I stopped by to see him last week, and he was pitiful. He looked like he lost his best friend, oh wait, he did." She covered her mouth and laughed out loud.

"Really, Tori?" I shook my head at her.

"Oh, girl please, Dre will be fine. He's spoiled and is used to having you at his beck and call." She tossed her hands up like she was dancing. "But big Macon put a stop to all that! He shut it down! Dre didn't know what hit him."

I decided I'd visit see Dre. I did miss him, and I wasn't mad at him anymore.

**Sure, I'm having a drink with Tori, I'll come by on the way home.**

### Dre: Cool

"You are so mean, Tori. He wants me to come by. I'll go see him, it's time we called a truce anyway. And as for Donald, can you let him down easy?"

"I told you he's a friend, we can hang from time to time."

"Mmm-hmm." I side eyed her. I knew Tori, and she was known for not wearing her feelings on her sleeve. Donald would never know where he stood with her if she didn't tell him something. We talked for another thirty minutes, and then I left to go to the Browns' house. I had been getting updates from Mr. Larry and Mrs. Barbara about Dre's leg. I laughed at myself, how could you be mad at someone and still bake them their favorite desserts?

I pulled in front of the house and walked up the driveway. Mr. Larry was outside raking leaves, it was scary how much Dre looked like him. "Hi, Mr. Larry."

"Hey Dawn, you need to drop off some things for Andre?" He hugged me.

I returned the hug and pulled back. "Not today, I'm going to sit with him for a little while."

He smiled. "Hallelujah! I'm so tired of seeing that boy's sad face I could smack him."

I laughed. "He can't be that bad."

He raised his eyebrows. "It's worse, now you go ahead and fix my boy up like you used to when you were little."

"Yes, Sir." I walked in the garage and went into the house. "Dre?"

"I'm in the tv room!" he yelled.

I walked into the tv room. Dre was sitting on the sofa with his leg on an ottoman. "Hey," I said.

"Hey," he said.

Wow, this was awkward. I sat on the chair across from him. He was different, maybe it was his hair. He usually got his hair cut once a week; I guess he hadn't had it cut in a while.

"Can you come sit next to me?" he asked.

I got up and walked over to the sofa and sat next to him. "How are you feeling?"

His head popped up. "Umm, I'm doing much better, I'm getting the short cast soon."

"That's good." I knew he wanted to say something, I decided I would follow his lead. Dre always took forever when he wanted to apologize. We were quiet for a few minutes.

He grabbed my hand. "Dawn I'm sorry. I handled this all wrong and I feel bad for getting you upset."

"Thanks, Dre, I'm sorry too. I could have done better myself, but you already know I'm a mess."

He let my hand go and looked at the ceiling. "I'm not going to lie and tell you that I don't have feelings for you, because I do, but I'll get over that. But, we go back too far for us not to be talking, that's something I can't get over."

*Why were my eyes getting watery?* I was tired of crying all the time. "We will always be friends, no matter what happens... You know what my biggest fear was over the last couple of weeks?" He shook his head no. "I was worried about losing another person I love." A few tears slipped. He put his arm around me and pulled me to him. The floodgates opened, and I cried like a baby. My emotions were all over the place, my Mom's birthday was a couple of days away and my birthday was after hers. This would be the first year in my life I wouldn't get a call from her singing happy birthday. My family decided that we would release purple balloons on her birthday and I was dreading it. I already knew how I would feel. Empty.

"It's okay." He rubbed my arm. "Dawn I'm so sorry, I can't believe I did this to you."

"I felt so guilty when you first told me how you felt about me." I sat up.

"Why?" His eyes squinted.

"Because you've been there for me and a part of me felt like I owed you."

He pulled my hand until I looked at him. "The last thing I wanted for either of us was a pity relationship. I knew deep down you didn't feel the same way, but you know I'm the man, and I'm used to getting who and what I want." I laughed. "Baby I'm sorry, I didn't mean to cause any more stress in your life, you've been through enough."

He handed me some tissue to wipe my face. "It's okay," I sniffled.

"Big Baby came by."

I jerked my head up. "What!? When?"

"A couple of days ago." He had a smirk on his face.

"He didn't mention it. How did that happen?" I was stunned.

"Well, he called the house phone and asked if he could stop by."

"And?" *Why was he drip-feeding me this story?*

"Basically, he told me I needed to get over whatever problems we had because you needed your friend."

My mouth was wide open. "He did?"

"Yep, I tried to be mad, but he was right. I didn't tell him that though. After he left, I thought about what he said and what he did. I have to be honest, he deserves you." I stared at him, I was in shock. *Was this Dre talking?* "Dude came in here and said he loved you and would do anything for you, which included asking me for help. That's a level of love I can't even begin to understand."

"What do you mean?"

"You said it best. I'm selfish." He shrugged.

I shook my head. "I didn't mean it like that, I shouldn't have said it."

"Naw, it's true. If I was Big Baby there is no way in hell I would have did that, even if I knew it's what you needed. My pride wouldn't have let me do it. I would have tried to fix you up all on my own."

I was so happy and even more in love with Macon. "I'm glad that you see him the way I see him."

He laughed. "I wouldn't say all that, but I get why you like him now."

"I'm glad, because he's going to be around permanently if I have my way." I smiled proudly.

"Oh really? It's like that already?" His eyes were wide.

"Most definitely, I told you this is different with Macon."

"I'm happy for you." I cut my eyes at him. "I'm serious, I mean it. Sitting in this cast and not being able to go anywhere has given me a lot of time to think."

"Okay, what's been on your mind?" I was curious to know if he meant what he said or if he was pretending for my sake.

"For starters, I need to stop leaning on you so much. I didn't realize how much I depended on you until we stopped talking. I've been like a fish out of water for the past couple of weeks. No wonder I don't have a damn girlfriend."

Oh wow, that was the same thing Macon told me. "What do you want to do about it? I want you to meet someone and get married."

He held his hand up. "Alright you're taking it too far, I didn't say anything about a wife."

I laughed at him. "You know what I mean."

"I need to start talking to the women I date and stop calling you so much. I'm sure that will make Big Baby happy anyway."

"No matter what you do, I'll be here to support you. Promise me we'll be friends no matter what happens." I smiled at him.

"Dawn we will always be friends, okay?" I nodded. "And you'll always be my girl."

We sat and talked for another hour. I was happy that we were able to make up, a thirty-four-year friendship was hard to come by. Dre was irreplaceable in my life. I knew our relationship had changed, but I also knew we would always be friends.

~~~~~~~~~~~~~

I pulled up in Macon's driveway, he and Donald were standing in the garage. Macon waved for me to pull in next to his truck. I drove into the garage and turned the car off.

Macon opened my car door and helped me out. He gave me a quick kiss on the lips. "Hey, Sweetheart."

I smiled at him. "Hey Baby. Hi Donald."

"Hi Dawn, how are you?" Donald asked.

I walked over to Donald's bike, it was unseasonably warm for the fall and a good day for a bike ride. "I'm fine, this is a nice bike, but I thought you had one of those cruiser types."

He smiled. "I do have a cruiser, but I have this baby for more speed."

I laughed. "I see. It's very nice." It was a beautiful bike, silver and black, I ran my hand over the front fender.

"You want to go for a ride?"

"Hell no! She does not want to ride with you," Macon said.

I laughed. "Macon, stop it."

Donald laughed. "Baby bro if she wants to go she can speak for herself."

"If she wants to go, I'll take her."

"Man, you don't even ride." Donald could not stop laughing.

"I'll learn before she goes with you." Macon put his arm around my waist.

I shook my head and looked up at him. "Maybe next time, Donald." I winked at Donald.

"Baby do you want me to dismantle Donald's bike?" Donald and I both laughed out loud. "Because that's exactly what's going to happen if you get on it, no way my woman is straddling anybody but me."

Donald laughed harder and put his helmet on. "I'll catch y'all later." He got on the bike and rolled it back out of the driveway. We waved at him, and he took off.

I grabbed Macon's hand. "You are so jealous."

"I sure am, and I make no apologies. Now get in the house and give me a proper greeting." I laughed at him.

After we were in the house and settled, I looked at Macon. I couldn't believe he came into my life at the perfect time. I loved him, and I was happy he loved me. I couldn't have created a better man; he was perfect for me.

"What's on your mind?" he asked.

We were sitting on his sofa. "I went to see Dre today."

His eyebrows went up. "Oh yeah? How did it go?"

"He took your advice." I smiled at him.

He tossed his head back and looked at the ceiling. "So much for that being between the fellas." He looked at me. "Are you upset that I didn't tell you?"

"Of course not. I was surprised but not upset at all. I thought it was the most selfless thing that anyone has ever done for me. Dre thinks so too."

"I doubt that."

"He was impressed, but it warmed my heart. Thank you so much, I'm so happy that you're in my life." I grabbed his face and kissed him. "I love you."

"I love you too, Sweetheart." He brushed my hair back. "I have something for you. I'll be right back."

He went upstairs and came back down a few minutes later with a gift bag. My eyes lit up, I loved surprises. He handed me the bag. "For you, it's an early birthday present."

I sat up and reached into the bag. I pulled out a card and the tiniest swimsuit that I'd ever seen. "Awww, Baby thank you, but I think it's a little small."

"It's supposed to be a clue to the real gift." He side-eyed me.

"Oh...well let me open the card." I opened the envelope and pulled the card out. A folded piece of paper was inside the card. I peeped at him, and he smiled. I read the card out loud, *"Dear Dawn, I love you, I know your birthday is not until the end of the month. Your Mom's birthday is in two days, and I know it will be hard for you."* I covered my mouth to catch my breath, I continued, *"please go away with me this weekend to celebrate your day and honor your Mom's day. Love, The Greedy Savage."* A couple of tears fell, and he wiped them away.

"I hope these are happy tears because this trip is nonrefundable," he said.

I laughed out loud. "Yes, these are happy tears!" I hugged him tightly. "Thank you so much, Macon."

"You don't even know where we're going yet." He tried to pull me from around his neck, and he laughed. "Finish reading."

I pulled back and sat on the sofa. "We could honestly vacation in downtown St. Louis, and I would be just as happy."

His smile dropped. "I wish I would have known that last week."

I laughed at him and opened the piece of paper. I could see the airline itinerary and hotel information. I read a little more, and my eyes went wide. "The Bahamas?"

"I tried to..." I put my finger to his lips to interrupt him.

"I love it." I straddled his lap. "It's perfect, just like you."

*The End*

Thank you for reading! I hope you enjoyed Dawn's story! Please consider leaving a review on Amazon!

Stay tuned for book 2!

**Something About Love Series**
Something Old? Something New? – Dawn's story
'Something Borrowed? Something New?' – Tori's story (Coming Soon!)

Mingle with Marlee!
Facebook: Marlee Rae
Instagram: @marleeraewrites
Email: marleerae45@gmail.com
Website: www.marleeraereadsandwrites.com

49450587R00157

Made in the USA
Columbia, SC
22 January 2019